TOMORROW WILL BE BETTER

VANESSA LAFLEUR

North Carolina

Published in the United States by BQB Publishing
(an imprint of Boutique of Quality Books Publishing Company, Inc.)
www.bqbpublishing.com

978-1-952782-27-5 (p)
978-1-952782-28-2 (e)

Library of Congress Control Number: 2021944171

Book Design by Robin Krauss, www.bookformatters.com
Cover Design by Rebecca Lown, www.rebeccalowndesign.com

First editor: Olivia Swenson
Second editor: Andrea Vande Vorde

For Glenn and Margie Wedekind

PART ONE

LEAVING THE PAST BEHIND

CHAPTER 1

CHARLIE

February 7, 2090

A long, blaring wail ripped me out of my restless sleep. It took my brain a few moments to process where I was in the darkness around me. The clatter of metal wheels on track and the sharp swaying motion were a comfort: they hadn't found me. It had been light when I stowed away, finally escaped from my friends turned torturers, but now, in the dark, I had no sense of how much time had passed or even in which direction I was traveling.

Carefully, I propped myself up and crawled to the open doorway as the train lurched and decreased speed. Dull lights glowed through the thick fog in a little cluster ahead, but before I could get a good look, a gust of icy air drenched me with cold rain, and I slid back a few inches.

Are those lights the next stop? How will I explain if they find me?

I rubbed a hand over my swollen jaw, then tenderly touched the scabbing edges of a rough cut across my left cheek. My breaths were shallow; any deep inhalation sent sharp pains through my ribs that I hoped were just bruised. If I wanted to celebrate my sixteenth birthday free of a home for children and free of The Defiance, I had to stay ahead of trouble.

With a hand on the boxcar wall for balance, I pushed myself to my feet. My vision swam, and I rested there until my head steadied.

Limping forward, I clutched the open doorway and watched bare fields slide by outside. The damp chill sliced right through my long-sleeved t-shirt and jeans. I had to find somewhere to lay low until I knew I hadn't been followed. Taking a deep breath, I leaned forward, stretching one foot toward the conveyor belt of moving ground, and let go.

Finally rolling to a stop, I lay flat on my back in the mud, gulping for air as the train clattered down the tracks. The ache in my ribs burned like a fire beneath my skin, and tears welled in my closed eyes as I waited for the pain to ebb. With the train an ever-fainter rumble, the soft patter of rain filled my ears.

I had just decided I could try to get up when a loud snapping sound shattered the quiet. Sitting bolt upright, ribs searing all over again, I whipped my head around, searching for danger. Did they follow me to the train after all? Are they watching me? Griff would never stop searching for me.

A revving engine sounded, paused, then sounded again. I stumbled to my feet, spinning to survey every dark corner of emptiness. No one stepped out of the monotonous gray around me, though I waited several long moments. When I could no longer tolerate the intense shivering that came with remaining still, I started toward the cluster of lights I had seen from the train, blurred and muted by the fog—my only hope of shelter.

In less than five minutes, my clothes were soaked. My sweatshirt and blankets were back at the Defiance camp in Kansas City, soon to be claimed by some other abandoned kid. What really hurt was losing my notebooks. Pages and pages filled with hundreds of stories I'd imagined from the time I was old enough to write. The notes outlining the details of each day of my life, just in case my own experiences could lend credibility to my writing. They'd be thrown away without a second thought.

Saturated soil tugged at my shoes as I trudged through a field of cornstalks broken and left after harvest, trying to distract myself from my aching injuries, my freezing body. Two beams cut through the haze, closer than the distant lights of what I hoped was a town. The revving engine continued intermittently, sounding closer with each step, but I had more pressing worries. Had I escaped Defiance territory? If so, how long before they made it here in their conquest of the entire country?

The field ended at a gravel road, and from up the road came two voices, the familiar engine rev, and the headlights. I paused outside of the light, debating my next move.

"Try it now. One more time," a male voice shouted. The engine revved again and then returned to a normal idling.

"We're just digging in deeper." The answering voice was female.

I staggered toward the outline of a pickup truck backlit by the headlights that had guided my way. Perhaps they would report me to the authorities for trespassing, but the possibility of shelter and warmth drew me closer. Two figures stood next to a truck with its back tires in a shallow ditch and front end still on the gravel road.

"You can't push it out alone, Max." The female silhouette stood with her hands in her jacket pockets. "If we start walking now, we can be back at my house in a half hour."

"No way." Max rested both hands on the top of his head with his elbows pointing out. "If I come home without this truck, my tio is going to kill me. He thinks I'm at your house right now."

"Well, technically I'm at your house right now, and I was supposed to be home before the streetlights came on." The girl shook her head. "Kinley is going to kill me. We can have a double funeral."

Max laughed. "When you put it that way, why are we in such a hurry to get home again?"

Something about these two kids, laughing about their predicament, was intriguing. It felt so . . . normal. I wanted to be a part of it, and I felt a strange compulsion to help them. Odd. I had learned to avoid people and the trouble they usually brought.

"Do you need some help?" I barely recognized my voice as my feet crunched on the gravel.

"Whoa, didn't I just say we could use a guardian angel?" The girl wiped rain from her forehead and stepped into the light, unfazed by an approaching stranger on a dark, rainy night. She wore jeans and a green coat with a hood pulled up against the rain. Despite being drenched and splashed with mud from head to toe, she smiled. "We're a little stuck."

Max stepped up next to her. His jeans and a gray hoodie were caked with mud from trying to free the truck. Although he wasn't any taller than me, he was built the way I imagined a good basketball player would be. In comparison, the girl was a few inches shorter but lanky. I guessed they were around my age.

"Angel? He looks like a zombie that just escaped his grave." Max tilted his head as if a new vantage point could provide all the answers. "Are you? A zombie?"

The girl elbowed his side. "You can't just say everything that pops into your head. What do you think you look like right now?"

He mumbled something then gently pushed her arm away. "First of all, it would be the best day of my life if I met a real zombie." Nodding in my direction, he smiled. "And to answer your question, I believe I look like a mad scientist with a truckload of thistles to experiment on."

The girl shook her head but smiled. "I'm sorry about my friend." She took another step toward me, getting a better look at me. Her eyes narrowed in concern. "Are you okay? Do you need a ride home?" Her tone was genuine. "Maybe you should sit down for a minute."

I obeyed and stumbled to the truck's bumper. "I'm okay." There wasn't much I could say to explain myself.

"I'm reading a book like this." She studied me curiously. "It's a mystery . . ."

"Don't be ridiculous, Rochelle. Fiction isn't real." Max leaned against the truck. "There's a perfectly reasonable explanation for this guy being here . . . in the middle of nowhere . . ." He frowned.

They both looked at me and I shivered. "I think I'm lost."

He scratched his head. "Hmm . . . How does the book end?"

Rochelle sighed and sat down next to me. "I would know if you hadn't called me to go out in the cold rain and dig up dead thistles."

"They're not dead." Max jumped in front of us, suddenly energized. "They're wintering in a dormant state, but I'm going to turn them into the best renewable fuel to end this fuel shortage once and for all." He waved his arms wildly. "Just think about it. Thistles are a noxious weed. No one likes them. It's about time they do something useful. With my help." He pressed his hand against his chest. "All I have to do is put them in a warm place and trick them into greening up. Then the experimenting can begin."

I nodded as my mind shuffled through hundreds of scenarios for a story. "Good luck. I hope they don't turn on you."

Rochelle laughed. "He has a good point, Max. You'd better be careful."

Wide-eyed, he looked from me to Rochelle. "It would be like that book from English class. Which one do you like better, frankenthistle or thistlestein?"

"Thistlestein for sure." Rochelle laughed so hard she could barely get the words out.

I rubbed the back of my hand over an itchy spot on my cheek then pulled it back from a stinging scrape. "Don't you both want to get out of the rain?" I glanced over at Max. "The two of us can push your truck out." I probably wouldn't be much help in my weakened state, but I needed to get out of the cold.

"We'd appreciate that." He extended his hand. "Maximiliano José Delgado Serano, world's upcoming greatest inventor and scientist. Everyone calls me Max. This is Rochelle Aumont, my best friend and the only person brave enough to be my assistant."

I shook his hand, resisting the urge to smile. They treated me as if we'd been friends for years, but I wanted to keep my distance, keep things impersonal. "I'm Keppler."

"Last name, right?" Max nodded as I did. "It's like we're in a cop movie. Right, Aumont?"

Rochelle gave him a funny look then turned back to me. "Ignore Delgado here. He doesn't take anything seriously."

I led the way to the back bumper, Max following, and we braced ourselves against the slippery ground. Rochelle got into the truck, and Max and I heaved together. I put all of my weight against it until it rolled forward. With nothing to support me, my knees buckled and I collapsed.

"Keppler, are you okay?" Max aimed a flashlight at my face.

I sat up and nodded, focusing on taking shallow breaths.

Max dropped to his haunches and studied me with wide brown eyes. His hood had slipped off, revealing dark hair cut close to his head. "You're a lifesaver. I'll give you a ride anywhere you want to go."

Rochelle came around the side of the truck, eyebrows lifting when she saw me on the ground. She leaned down and smiled, though it was tight with worry. Her eyes, a startling shade of green, reminded me of the first leaves of spring. "We can do even better than that. My cousin is studying to be a doctor, so she can patch you up." She stood and held her hand out to me. "And my little sister is practically a chef. She would love to cook for a guest."

So much for avoiding people and staying out of trouble. Unable to do anything but agree, I let Rochelle take my hand while Max gripped my elbow, and they helped me into the back seat of the truck.

Closed in the warm cab, I felt a little stronger than I had out on the road. Through rivulets of water streaming across the windshield shone the lights I'd noticed from the train.

"What's ahead?" I asked, pointing.

"My hometown, Maibe." Rochelle leaned forward. "Maibe, Nebraska."

A boy with steel-blue eyes and dark hair that fell over his forehead and curled around his ears stared back at me in the steamy mirror. Purple bruises blotched his body and his jaw looked a little swollen. A mess of pink scrapes and angry red gashes crisscrossed his face. I avoided the slightly raised, pink outline of the letter D just below his left shoulder. If I didn't see that mark, maybe this boy was someone else. Someone who hadn't promised his loyalty to The Defiance, a family I could only truly escape in death.

Shivering, I pulled on a loaned sweatshirt and pajama pants, both too big. Upon my arrival to the Aumont house, I had been able to avoid the questions I dreaded. What happened to you? Where are you from? Who's responsible for you? I couldn't answer any of them honestly.

"You look much better." Kat, Rochelle's younger sister, glanced up at me and grinned as she carried a bowl trailing steam to a tray on the table. Her long brown hair, the same color as Rochelle's, hung down to her waist in spiraling curls. She was thin, but not in the same spindly way as her sister.

"Thanks." I rolled up my sleeves as aromas of baking bread and cooked vegetables tortured my empty stomach.

"My dad's clothes are a little big for you." With careful fingers, she arranged a glass of juice and a sandwich on the tray. "Rochelle could fix that. She does sewing and altering for pretty much everyone."

I glanced around, feeling a little uneasy again. "Will your dad mind me borrowing his clothes?"

Kat shook her head. "He passed away last year, but he was a generous guy. He'd be glad someone's getting use out of them."

I cringed. "I'm really sorry. I didn't realize—"

"It's okay." Kat looked down at her neatly arranged tray of food. "How did you get beat up so badly, anyway?"

"I made the wrong people mad." A wave of dizziness left me gripping the back of the nearest chair. "Should have known better."

"Hopefully you've learned your lesson." Kat picked up the tray and balanced it on her arm. "Follow me." She led me through a doorway into a dining room and turned right into a room partially hidden behind half-opened French doors.

A rush of warmth met me at the homey scene. A large bay window with a cushioned seat filled the far wall, with a desk off to the side. To my right was a couch made up with pillows and blankets, a coffee table, and two armchairs. A fireplace, surrounded by floor to ceiling shelves of books, covered the wall to my left.

Kat lowered her tray to the coffee table. "Dinner is chicken and wild rice soup with vegetables, and a ham and cheese sandwich on French bread I baked this morning. If I'd known we were going to have company, I would have made something better. But I promise I'm planning an amazing menu for breakfast."

Too hungry to think straight, I collapsed onto the couch, pulled the tray onto my lap, and swallowed half of the food in a minute.

"You really are pretty bad off, aren't you?" I hadn't even noticed her sit down in the nearest chair. Now her eyebrows furrowed, blue eyes studying me.

I swallowed the rest of my sandwich and winced as I settled back against the pillows propped behind me. "I'm fine, really . . ."

"One of these days, Rochelle, I'm going to ground you for the rest of your life." Rochelle's cousin, Kinley, strode in, stethoscope looped around her shoulders, first aid kit in her hand.

Rochelle followed, shoulder-length brown hair still wet from showering, head hanging. The cousins looked uncannily similar. Kinley stood a few inches taller than Rochelle and wore her hair pulled into a braid that stretched down her back, but in facial features, startling eye color, and lanky build, they were identical.

"I'm sorry, Kinley. I didn't want Max to go alone." Rochelle smiled in my direction. "And I never would have met Keppler if we didn't get stuck. Nothing happens by chance, right?"

Kinley sighed and turned to me, her gaze appraising. Her presence made me feel like a kid who'd just been caught stealing candy from the store. "I should really get you to a doctor."

"No." It came out more severe than I intended. "Please, I really am okay." Doctors asked questions, called the authorities, and sent kids without families to the nearest home for children.

Rochelle put an arm around her cousin. "You're a doctor. Can't you just help him?"

"I'm not a doctor yet." Kinley sighed. "And I never will be if you keep distracting me from my studies." She sat down on the coffee table in front of me. "How old are you, Keppler?"

I was almost sixteen, but I knew I looked younger than that. Confidence would go a long way in convincing these people I was okay. My chin lifted. "Plenty old enough to take care of myself."

She surveyed me with eyes the same hopeful green as Rochelle's but clouded with exhaustion and cynicism. "You're just a kid. There must be someone out there worried sick about you."

I shook my head slowly to acknowledge the sad truth. There

wasn't one person in the world who cared about my well-being. Only my removal.

"If there's something you're hiding, maybe I should let the authorities figure it out."

My courage faded with the threat. "P-please don't call the police." I couldn't go back to a home for children or get sent south to Defiance territory.

"Kinley, please." Rochelle sat down next to her cousin. "He's hurt and we're all tired. Maybe we should save those questions for tomorrow." She rested a hand on my shoulder and I flinched. Human touch was something I had learned to dread. She took the hand away but kept the compassionate look. "Don't worry. We're going to help you."

Kinley nodded and forced a smile. "If you're okay with a student looking at your injuries, I'll see what I can do. I promise it won't hurt much."

I nodded, and she set about cleaning and bandaging the worst of my lacerations, then checked my temperature, heart, and lungs.

"As far as I can tell, nothing's broken." She gently lowered the arm she had been examining. "Get some rest and we'll decide if you need any X-rays in the morning."

"Thank you. I won't be in your way for long." In fact, I wouldn't be there when they woke up. If Kinley intended to involve doctors and the police, the Aumont house wasn't the place for me to hide out.

"You can stay as long as you want." Kat smiled at me and her entire face lit up. Her blue eyes were so spirited and ready to take on the world. "Right, Kinley?"

"He can stay here for the night." Kinley folded her arms in front of her. "Then we'll revisit the question of where he belongs." Her expression was stern, but a gentleness reflected in her eyes. "Let's give Keppler some peace so he can rest."

Rochelle followed her cousin and sister but turned around halfway to the door. "I know today has been rough, but don't worry. Tomorrow will be better."

Closing my eyes, I let my imagination carry me to a familiar world in which I owned a house with a library where I spent dreary winter days writing. Pulling the blanket over my head, I pushed the hopeful thought out of mind. I would be back on the street by sunrise.

CHAPTER 2
ROCHELLE

February 21, 2090

Hands in my pockets, I strolled through a world of glittering snowflakes. I had spent the last two hours sitting next to the heater in Max's garage workshop where Keppler and Max were using all of their mechanical knowledge to fix an old lawn mower. Although I wanted to stay, Kinley would be home for lunch any minute and she wouldn't approve of me spending time with that boy, as she called Keppler. Two weeks had passed since we woke up to find he had vanished from the library, but I still couldn't tell whether she was annoyed he'd disobeyed her or relieved she didn't have to figure out what to do with him.

"Hey . . . Rochelle." I turned, recognizing Todd Tatem's voice, and slowed so he could catch up. We had been best friends since the days when friendship meant sharing juice boxes and saving the nearest swing. He jogged toward me, winter coat flapping open, sandy brown hair fluttering in the wind where it was longer on top. His hazel eyes met mine as he stopped to catch his breath. "What are you doing outside? It's freezing."

"Says the guy with his coat unzipped." I raised my eyebrows, and he fumbled with his zipper. "I was at Max's. He's still trying to fix that lawn mower Mr. Mayhew gave him so it can somehow power his time travel machine."

"So he's told me." Todd flipped my hood over my head. "You just recovered from the fever. We shouldn't take any risks."

In October, most of the people in town had gotten sick, and I was no exception. Unfortunately, I also developed a secondary infection that kept me in bed for months. It had taken until Christmas for me to finally get my strength and energy back.

"Speaking of risks, I'm running late for lunch." I adjusted my hood and started walking. "You know how Kinley is when I'm not home on time."

"In that case, we'd better hurry." Todd linked his arm through mine and propelled me forward.

I laughed and quickened my pace to keep up with his long strides. "Are you going to my house too?"

The Tatems had always been like family. Todd's older sister Emma had been friends with Kinley since kindergarten and his younger sister Lily often tagged along when they came over.

"Emma has my gloves, those really warm ones you made me, at your house. I have to load lumber this afternoon." Todd's dad owned the local hardware store and Todd had joined the family business when he turned sixteen in September.

"I'm glad you're not making her walk all the way to the store in this weather." I stuck out my tongue to catch a snowflake.

"I owe her that and much more." Emma had practically raised him after their mom took off when he was eight. "But I also hoped I would get to talk to you. We live a block apart, but it feels like a hundred miles as much as I see you."

I gave a weak smile. Ever since I had been sick, he looked at me like I would break right in front of him. Everyone worried about me, questioned my decisions, and wanted me to stay inside where I would be safe. It didn't surprise me coming from Kinley, but I needed reassurance from my best friend that I could reclaim my life.

"I'm just getting used to our new schedules. Without school

and you busy at work . . ." I watched my feet skipping over sidewalk cracks. "Life is different now."

"Different? Our lives are falling apart before they even got started. Nothing will ever be the same." The hopelessness in his voice made me wonder if there was something he wasn't telling me.

Of course, it was hard to feel hope in our new normal. The school had closed in October due to the fever and never reopened. In a matter of months, the fever had taken my grandma, aunt, uncle, and half the adults in town. It had taken two months of my life while I recovered and everyone's confidence in my ability to take care of myself. But, despite all that, I couldn't let myself believe there was no hope.

I put one arm around Todd and leaned my head toward his shoulder. "Maybe things won't be exactly the way they were before, but life is on its way to being good again."

We walked in silence until my house came into view through a screen of thick snow. It stood two stories tall with gray siding, a porch swing, and a front path that would be lined with flowers in the summer.

"Rochelle . . ." Todd's voice sounded unsure, cautious even. "Max said you've been spending a lot of time with that guy you found on the road . . ."

"A few hours a day. I'm trying to help him." After he disappeared from my house, Max and I went searching and found him digging through trash cans behind the grocery store. Despite our best efforts to convince him to come back, he assured us he had found shelter and could take care of himself. "I don't think he has anyone to turn to."

"Are you sure he isn't just using you to get free food?" Todd stuffed his hands into his pockets. "People are starting to talk about him being a nuisance. He's always hanging around outside the grocery store like he's casing the place."

Turning to him, I blinked a snowflake off my eyelash. "Don't tell me you believe that hardware store gossip?"

"No . . . I mean, not that he plans to rob the grocery store." He laughed, and I did too, envisioning a masked burglar running with a bunch of overripe bananas. "I mean, why would he?"

"Well, if he planned to rob *me*, he probably would have done it while he was actually inside my house." Keppler had never given me a reason to believe he intended to hurt anyone, and I wouldn't let anyone make me question my instincts.

Todd swallowed and his dimples vanished. "But he could be dangerous. Maybe his family dumped him for a reason."

I stopped in front of the back screen door and turned to face him. "Todd Tatem. That is a terrible thing to say. Just because we haven't known Keppler our entire lives doesn't make him a bad guy."

He reached past me to open the door. "I'm just saying . . . he's a stranger, not a lost kitten."

"I'll keep that in mind." I pushed the heavy wooden door into the laundry room.

"Rochelle Irene Aumont, you're ten minutes late," Kinley's voice scolded as I shed my winter gear and rushed into the kitchen.

"I'm sorry. I was helping Max . . ." My cousin's scowl of disappointment pinned me in place. Even if I had been saving the world from imminent doom, my excuse would have fallen flat in her judgment.

Kat glanced over her shoulder, continuing to stir the pot on the stove. "Lunch isn't even ready yet."

Emma glanced at the clock from where she stood at the table, making sandwiches. "It's just noon now." Even when I was an annoying little kid, Emma had convinced Kinley to let me join their sleepovers. She had taken care of me when I was too sick with the fever to take care of myself and talked me through the anxiety I suffered afterward.

Kinley shook her head at her friend. "The point is, she shouldn't have been out at all. I know she's hanging around *that boy,* even though I told her not to."

"I told her it's not safe." Todd spoke from behind me, and I shot him a glare.

"There's the voice of reason." Kinley pulled plates from the cupboard. "Listen to Todd more and Max less."

"If I don't help Keppler, no one else will." Although he insisted his past wasn't worth talking about, I figured he was just embarrassed about not having a family.

Kinley folded her arms across her chest. "He's not your responsibility. We have enough to deal with taking care of each other."

"At least we have each other." I sank into the nearest chair. "What if I was in Keppler's shoes and no one cared about me?"

"You're not in his shoes." Kinley shook her head, but her stern expression softened. "You're my responsibility and I'll keep my promise to take care of you." That's what she had started to say since she moved back home. Kat and I never heard *I love you* from her anymore, it was always, *you're my responsibility.* "It's sweet that you care about everyone, but if you keep thinking with your heart instead of your head, you'll spend your whole life heartbroken."

"I think we should give Rochelle a break." Emma walked around the table. "Helping someone is never the wrong thing to do." She put a comforting hand on my shoulder. "Plus, she's never late to Saturday lessons, and she always has her homework done. That's more than I can say for the rest of them." When Emma and Kinley found out there were no immediate plans to reopen the high school, they took matters into their own hands. Every

Saturday afternoon starting in December, Kinley taught math and science and Emma taught English and history. I loved their improvised school, Kat attended because Kinley made her, Todd because Emma made him, and Max came so he could stay for dinner.

My sister wiped her hands on a towel. "Speaking of responsibilities, Kinley is sending us to live with the Tatems for two weeks."

"Wait, where are *you* going?" I turned back to my cousin.

Kinley sighed and gave Kat a warning glance. "When I started the program with Doctor Brooks, we knew I would have to go to Omaha a few times a year to take tests. Starting Monday, I'm scheduled for two weeks of testing, and I can't leave you two home alone that long."

Dr. Brooks, one of our local physicians, had started one of the new student doctor programs in the summer. The country had been dealing with a severe shortage of medical professionals for years, which had been exacerbated by the fever. Localized training programs had popped up across the country to provide hands-on training, shave a few years off the traditional medical school trajectory, and allow aspiring doctors to be close to their families. Kinley hadn't been interested in returning to Maibe until the fever changed our lives forever.

"But don't worry." Emma pulled my sister into a one-armed hug. "Time is going to fly because I have a bunch of new recipes for us to try. And, Rochelle, I just read a book you're going to love—"

"Actually, I have a better idea." Kinley's forehead wrinkled as it did when she worried, and she sat down next to me. "One more month and you'll be sixteen . . ."

I waited for Kinley to talk about how irresponsible I was compared to her at my age. She had been accepted early into a medical training college in Omaha when she was sixteen. After she studied there for almost three years, the fever broke out across Nebraska. When she finally made it home after the fever's chaos and found out every adult in our family had been lost, she moved back to Maibe to take care of Kat and me, all before her nineteenth birthday. I knew it had been tough to give up her dream of a prestigious education in the city to return to her little hometown so her cousins wouldn't end up in a home for children. Fortunately, she was able to work out a plan with her college and start studying under Dr. Brooks.

"Why don't you come with me?" She took a deep breath. "You have to start thinking about your future, and I can show you around the college. I'd love to have some company."

I stared at her. "Now, uh, now isn't such a good time." I stumbled over my words. "I have a lot of sewing jobs lined up and . . ." I looked to Todd for some reason I couldn't leave.

Kinley put a hand under my chin and turned my eyes back to her. "Please, Rochelle. I think it'll be good for you to get away, and we can spend time together like we used to."

A year ago, it would have been the greatest adventure of my life to go to college with Kinley. But now . . .

"Please, Rochelle." She looked like she might cry. The last time I'd seen her cry was the day she told Kat and me that life would be different forever. It was unfair for her to have so many worries when she was barely an adult herself. "I promise it'll be fun."

Max would look out for Keppler, but who would look out for Kinley? "Okay. I'll come with you."

"What about me?" Kat's voice held the same resentment as it did when we were kids playing doctor and she had to be the patient while I got to be Kinley's assistant.

My cousin sighed. "I can't take both of you. I'll take you next time, I promise."

"Fine." She blinked hard like she was trying not to cry. "The soup's ready. I'm not hungry anymore." With quick steps, she left the room.

"I'll talk to her." Kinley smoothed my hair with both hands before standing to follow my sister. "You're a mess. Get cleaned up and set the table, please."

I leaned my head back and blinked up at Emma.

"Don't look so worried, sweetie." She cupped my cheek in her hand. "It'll be good for you and Kinley to spend some time together, and I'll take care of Kat." My cousin's shouting followed by a slamming door echoed above us. Emma looked up and cringed. "Todd, your gloves are on the counter. I'll go talk to them and get them down here for lunch."

Since Kinley had become our guardian, she and Kat found something to fight about at least once a day.

Alone with Todd, I shook my head and tried to comb my fingers through wind-knotted hair. "Well, if anyone's going to get dumped off along the road, it'll probably be me. How do I look?"

"Beautiful, like always." Todd slid into the chair next to me. "And if Kinley's afraid to leave you with us for two weeks, she won't leave you alone on the road for a minute."

"Very funny." I smiled and let my hands drop to my lap.

"Don't worry, Shelley." When we were little kids he couldn't pronounce my name, so my dad told him Shelley was short for Rochelle and it stuck. "It'll be good to get Kinley and Kat apart for a while, and you talk about college all the time. It'll be an adventure."

Loud shouting sank through the ceiling and I shook my head. "I suppose you don't have to deal with that at your house." I'd never heard Emma raise her voice.

Todd nodded. "My sisters don't really yell. But Emma does get that disappointed look that slices right through your chest. That's even worse." For the second time that day, Todd looked guilty, like there was more he wanted to say. "At least when Kinley yells it's equal parts scary and entertaining."

I leaned forward until my forehead rested against Todd's shoulder. "As crazy as my family can be, I don't know what I'd do without them. If I were in Keppler's situation . . ."

Todd squeezed my hands in his. "They're not going anywhere, Shelley, and neither am I."

CHAPTER 3

CHARLIE

March 8, 2090

Melting snow dripped into the alley in a constant pitter patter that echoed off trash cans. Cold water seeped into my shoes as I stopped to catch my breath. Clouds slid across the moon and I shivered against a damp chill. It had been an unsuccessful night of scavenging through trash cans, but I wasn't hungry anyway. Just when I thought I was finally recovering from the sore throat that had plagued me for almost two weeks, I developed a cough and a case of the chills.

Ready to catch a few hours of sleep, I trudged through the mud to a lean-to roof. Glancing around to make sure no one watched me, I scaled a stack of old pallets, scrambled over loose shingles, and slid open the second story window. After spending my first night in town at Rochelle's house, I had spent a night huddled against a dumpster in the alley behind the grocery store, where my eyes caught that easy-to-access window. It seemed like a long shot, but I was desperate, and much to my surprise, it slid right open. The second floor of the building seemed to be storage for old dusty boxes and spare furniture, and the heat from below made it somewhat comfortable. Even better, I'd been living there for almost a month and no one had noticed. It seemed that luck was finally on my side.

A stiff wind sent a shiver through my body as I climbed through the window and pulled it shut. My chest ached and, for the third time that night, I couldn't catch my breath. Coughing, I made my way to the front window and looked down over Main Street. It was late enough that the entire town was quiet and dark except for the little streetlights spaced down the sidewalk. A light winking in the window of the vacant pharmacy across the street caught my eye, but by the time I blinked, it had vanished. I pressed a hand to my forehead, hot against my frozen fingers.

Too exhausted to think, I stumbled to the corner where I had assembled a nest of blankets pulled from stored furniture. Kicking off my wet shoes, I burrowed under the blankets. Closing my eyes, I contemplated Max's lawn mower. He didn't know his way around an engine very well, and he was distracted by a million other planned inventions, but we were making progress. My dad had once told me I'd make a decent mechanic, and that was the only nice thing he'd ever said to me. Shivering, I closed my eyes.

A high-pitched siren wailed somewhere outside my head, but it wasn't enough to free me from my dream. Looking around the sparsely furnished room of my childhood, I listened as a gust of wind whistled past my window. In my six-year-old hand, I held a toy car I had found at the park earlier that day. It was a new toy to add to the very few I owned, so I'd spent the evening driving it back and forth across my checkered bedspread.

Mom and Dad had been arguing downstairs for a long time. Sometimes they threw things at each other when Mom felt like fighting back. Often, she stayed in bed all day and Dad yelled at her when he got home. I tuned it out and went back to playing with my car until I heard the loud wailing again. My baby sister, Isabelle, was only three. I thought she had been playing in her room, but the cry was coming from downstairs. Scrambling to my feet, I rushed into the hallway and down to the living room. Isabelle sat in the middle of the floor, sobbing.

Dad stood a few feet away, glaring down at her. He took a

staggering step forward and I knew he was drunk again. "Shut up," he shouted at Isabelle, "or I'll give you something to cry about."

I jumped in front of her and stood up as tall as I could. "I'll take her upstairs." My voice came out small and shaky. "If you hit her she'll only cry more."

"I told you to keep her upstairs in the first place."

A hard smack to the side of my head knocked me to the floor. The ceiling slid one way then the other and I couldn't catch my breath.

A choking, acrid smoke ripped me from a feverish sleep. I really couldn't breathe. My chest burned as I gasped for a few molecules of oxygen. *The building must have caught on fire. Get outside. Hurry.* Scrambling to my feet, I forgot about my shoes and rushed to the back window. Lightheaded, I fumbled with the sliding pane and catapulted myself onto the lean-to roof. I lost my footing and slipped, bouncing once against asphalt shingles before landing on my back in the soggy alley.

After a bout of coughing that left tears in my eyes, I pulled myself to my feet. Voices shouted from the street, barely audible over the sirens. The dark sky accentuated an orange glow flashing shadows on the hardware store behind me. Smoke filled the air and little pieces of ash rained down on the wet ground.

From what I could tell, the grocery store wasn't on fire, but something definitely was. Feet freezing as they tromped through icy mud, I made my way around the building to investigate. On the side street, a fire engine's lights flashed and a gathering crowd gawked at flames shooting through the roof of the pharmacy, wind-driven black smoke plumed around the scene. I made my way to the back of the group to get a better look. Men in firefighting gear sprayed water on neighboring buildings to prevent the gusting wind from setting the entire block on fire.

A blonde girl a few people in front of me turned and scanned the crowd. Our eyes locked. She gripped the arm of the boy next to her, and I watched her mouth form the words "There he is."

I took a step back, then another. My chest ached, but I turned and ran from the fire and flashing lights, the chaotic crowd and stifling smoke. If even one person believed I had something to do with the fire, the rest would be persuaded by morning. I was a stranger, a perfect suspect in a town where everyone knew each other.

Something heavy crashed against me from behind, and my body pitched forward hard onto the concrete sidewalk. I tried to roll over, but a hand pressed my face against the ground as I wheezed.

"It . . . wasn't. I . . . didn't." My attempts came out as inaudible gasps, and coughing wracked my body.

The hand gripped my collar and turned me over. I tried to take a left swing at the tall guy holding me, but I couldn't get enough air into my lungs and my head swam with fuzzy little lights.

"Don't even try it." Angry eyes burned into mine.

"Todd, hey, take it easy." Max sounded out of breath as he approached. "Keppler didn't do anything wrong." He appeared over us and gripped Todd's shoulders as if he could pry him away from me.

"Shut up, Max. You're just as naive as Rochelle." The blonde girl wrapped her arms around herself and shivered. "We should hold you partly responsible for making this alley trash feel welcome in Maibe."

"Todd, tell Molly she's being unreasonable." Max's pleading didn't change anything in the eyes of the guy ready to choke the life out of me. "Give him a chance to explain."

"I have a better idea." Todd let go of my shirt and I fell backward against the sidewalk. "We all respect the mayor's opinion." He gripped my elbow and pulled me to my feet. "Let's go find him."

I shivered, slumped in a stiff wooden chair in the mayor's office. The room consisted of a desk facing the door to the hallway, a shelf of books and knickknacks, a few file cabinets, and most importantly, a window.

"He's clearly the one who burned down my dad's pharmacy." Molly's voice pierced the door to the hallway. "Think about it, Alexander, nothing like this ever happened before he showed up in town. And he reeks of smoke."

With a wad of tissues pressed to my bleeding chin, I eavesdropped on the conversation in the hall. Max had made a big deal about my cut, but that was nothing. It was my shivering and cough that worried me. I was as miserable as I'd ever been.

"I'm sure anyone standing outside smells like smoke, Molly." Alexander's voice remained calm. "That's not real evidence."

"He would never hurt anyone." Max sounded so serious I barely believed he was the same kid building a time machine and experimenting on thistles.

"You just met the guy a few weeks ago." Todd wasn't shouting, but the anger in his voice came through loud and clear. "You didn't even know he was squatting in the grocery store."

I glanced at the window. There were three plants on the sill and a little crank that would roll the glass out into the night.

"Everyone needs shelter." Frustration seeped into Max's voice.

The window was my one chance to escape it all. I stood up, started to cough, and fell back into my chair. What was the point?

"Good thing Rochelle's out of town." Molly again. "Do you really want this guy around the Aumonts, Alexander? We don't know what he's capable of."

"Not starting buildings on fire," Max scoffed.

"Okay. Okay." Alexander's voice, powerful but kind, interrupted. "This conversation is getting us nowhere, and it's late. All of you need to go home."

"You're just going to let him free to keep terrorizing the town?" Molly's voice shook.

"I have to deal with the immediate crisis first. This accusation can wait until morning."

Max trudged into the room amid a muffled muttering in the hallway. He pulled a chair up next to mine and slumped into it. "Don't worry about any of that. Todd misses Rochelle and Molly is just Molly."

Ever since I met Max and Rochelle, my head had been spinning with the names of people I only knew from their conversations. I meant to tell Max I understood I had overstayed my welcome, but an uncontrollable cough burst from somewhere in my lungs and by the time it faded, I felt as if I'd been punched in the chest.

"It sounds like you breathed in too much smoke out there."

I blinked through watery eyes at the mayor. Alexander was a big guy with broad shoulders, the stereotypical football linebacker. He pressed a big hand over his light brown hair and studied me through kind blue eyes. His other arm hugged a bundle of material.

Shaking my head, I held a hand to my tight chest.

Alexander looked at Max, then dropped his armload of stuff onto the desk. He leaned forward to get a better look at me and touched the back of his hand to my forehead. "You're burning up. Maybe we should get you checked out by a doctor."

"No." My voice came out as a weak groan. "I just need some sleep. I'll be fine."

"He doesn't trust doctors." Max leaned forward with his elbows on his knees. "Says they ask too many questions and experiment on you if you can't pay them."

Alexander nodded. "We won't tell Kinley that one." He smiled and patted my arm once then started to rummage through a desk drawer. "But, if she were here, she'd be pretty worried."

I rested my head against the chair and closed my eyes. As much as I wanted to trust Alexander, he reminded me of Griff, and that kept my defenses up. "Why would Kinley care?" Despite my doubts, I'd feel a lot better with her there to treat me.

Max shifted in his seat. "You'd better listen. He knows Kinley better than anyone. They've been a couple since, what? Third grade?"

Alexander laughed. "Minus the days when she's mad at me. Will you at least let me clean up those scrapes?"

My eyes fluttered open to him holding a brown bottle and some cotton balls.

Max patted my shoulder. "He was captain of the football team last year, and now he's the mayor of Maibe. If you can't trust him, you can't trust anybody."

Despite Max's flawed logic, I didn't have the energy to argue, so I just nodded and held still as he applied first aid to my face. "Am I in a lot of trouble?"

"I've had several complaints about you being in town without a guardian." He tilted his head to the left and sighed. "I don't think you had anything to do with the pharmacy, but I will have to address those complaints." He smoothed a butterfly Band-Aid over my chin. "Why don't you tell us your side of the story. Did you see anything suspicious?"

Closing my eyes, I replayed the night's events in my head. "I saw a light in the pharmacy. Only for a second . . . It was a flicker . . ."

"There might have been someone sneaking around in there." Max sat up straight then turned to me. "Or you were delirious."

Alexander gave Max a warning glance. "I'm sure it was some

electrical malfunction." He picked up a roll of material off his desk and shook it into a sleeping bag that he spread on the floor. "Keppler, you look pretty awful. I can make you a doctor's appointment tomorrow. I promise I won't let anyone experiment on you."

A doctor would ask questions about my age and my family. "I won't go. I'd rather die than go back to a home for children." I lowered myself to the sleeping bag and sat with my legs folded under me.

"Maybe we should call Rochelle." Max scratched his head. "He listens to her."

"Kinley and Rochelle need a vacation." He narrowed his eyes at Max. "And Kinley would flip her lid if we got Rochelle involved in all of this. I can handle things." He tossed me a pillow. "Get some rest. I'll find you a place to live."

The last thing I needed was some do-gooder finding me a home in a strange house with cruel replacement parents who just wanted a servant to do chores. "I don't want your help."

"But you need it." Alexander sighed. The lights dimmed, brightened, then dimmed again before shutting off. We waited for them to come back on, but the room remained dark except for moonlight shining through the window.

He flipped the light switch a few times, but nothing changed. "Please tell me it's just this building and not the whole town," he muttered. Pulling his coat from the back of the desk chair, he slid both arms into it at the same time. "Stay here while I deal with this. Don't try to leave, or I'll have to lock you up in a jail cell." He rushed out of the office.

I tried to take a deep breath and broke into a coughing fit instead.

"Easy . . ." Max patted my back. "I'm on your side, but I really think you should see a doctor and let Alexander help you."

I shook my head. How could *he* possibly understand?

For a full minute, Max went uncharacteristically silent. Then he looked at me. "You said you were in a home for children once?"

"Yeah, so what?" I shook the hair out of my eyes and watched the shadow of a tree branch shiver in a patch of moonlight on the floor.

"Well, when I was in the second grade, there was this girl." A big smile spread over his face. "Lareina was staying at the home for children here..."

Despite my misery, I laughed. "Did you have a crush on her or something?"

Max shrugged. "She was really pretty. My point is, we always wondered where she ended up. They didn't send her back, so maybe they found her a good family."

"Maybe." I stretched my legs across the sleeping bag and lay back, letting my head sink into the pillow.

"Can't you give Alexander a chance to do that for you?"

I closed my eyes and tried to recall a story of any orphaned or abandoned kid with a happy ending. None came to mind. "Why would anyone want me? You can't force people to care about someone they never wanted to feed and shelter."

Max leaned back against the desk. "It's not like that around here. When the fever took my parents, my aunt and uncle adopted my sister and me without even thinking about it."

"Because they're your family." I watched Max's smile fade. "What if your choice had been a home for children or random people you've never met?"

He nodded as he pulled a blanket off the desk, unfolded it, and draped it over me. "I'm going to call Rochelle. We're your friends, and the three of us together can solve this."

"Forget it," I said into the blanket I'd pulled over my nose. "And we're not friends."

"*Hermanos* then?"

"What does that mean?"

Max shrugged. "It's a word for someone you talk to occasionally even though you really don't know each other that well." His eyelids and the corners of his lips twitched as if he was trying not to smile. I didn't have the energy to argue with him.

"If you really want to help, could you go to the grocery store and get my shoes and the envelope sitting by them?" As much as I wanted my shoes, I wanted that manila envelope more. It was filled with scraps of paper I'd collected from trash cans and Max's garage. My attempt to start over writing down the stories in my head and my daily notations beginning with my arrival in Maibe. It wasn't the same as the organized notebooks I had lost escaping The Defiance, but it made me feel more myself to be writing.

"No questions asked." He jumped to his feet, eager to help. "That's what *hermanos* are for. And then I'll be your defense attorney and tell off all those people who think you need a guardian."

"Whatever." None of it mattered. I couldn't see any way out of my predicament except to continue the cycle of home for children, escape, and survive on the street—a cold, lonely lifetime of running from my troubles until they finally caught me.

CHAPTER 4
ROCHELLE

March 9, 2090

My feet glided over the sidewalk, hood slid off my head, and a cold mist collected on my face as I ran from the train station to the Maibe City Hall. I imagined Kinley returning to the hotel room and finding my quickly scribbled note. She would be . . . Honestly, I wasn't really sure how she would react except that it wouldn't be good. I had an hour before she got out of class and noticed I was gone. Despite low clouds darkening the sky, it was only early afternoon.

For the moment, my newfound independence and freedom energized me. Never in my life had I been presented with a reason to buy a train ticket and travel one hundred miles on my own, but Max's phone call had made things clear. Keppler needed my help. Leaving without Kinley and especially without even talking to her was absolutely out of the question, but at least with the note, she would worry less.

"My whole family woke up to this loud crackling sound, so my *tio* and I rushed outside to find out what happened, and we could see huge flames a few blocks away. By the time we got to Main Street, half the town was there." Max's description of the fire repeated in my head as I ran along what had been a busy highway cutting through a town of three thousand people. It wasn't so long ago that residents from Maibe commuted to surrounding towns for work in factories and packing plants, and others from those communities drove to Maibe to work at the schools, hospital, and some of our local businesses. That slowed down due to the fuel shortage and ended completely with the fever. At first, I thought people who weren't from Maibe feared some ghost of the virus still lurked on our streets, and then I realized they had all been impacted just as severely by the fever. Many of the adults who used to commute had likely been lost. I tried not to think about it.

I caught the first whiff of smoke as I passed the gas station where Dad used to fill up his truck and let me pick out any candy bar I wanted. It grew stronger as I neared the public library where I would spend summer days with Kat, and it was unbearable by the time I reached the hair salon where I would wait with my grandma while she got her hair done.

At first, I thought it was the mist making everything ahead appear fuzzy, but as I approached, I realized a thick haze of smoke wrapped around the buildings for blocks, held in place by the heavy air. I rushed into the intersection of the highway and Main Street and squinted toward the far end of the block as I stopped to catch my breath. Blackened rubble filled the space where the pharmacy had stood for over two hundred years.

A charred wall maintained the frame for shattered display windows that only revealed the blackened mess of the upper floor collapsed into the business area below. By some miracle the volunteer fire department had saved the surrounding buildings from catching fire and taking out an entire block. An icy pellet of sleet brushed my cheek, pulling my attention away from my brain's struggle to reconcile the photograph in my head with the destruction in front of me.

Pulling my hood up against the sleet, I turned on my heel and walked the remaining two blocks to the city hall.

"Rochelle." Max waved from where he stood under the shelter of an alcove on the front of the building. "You saw it, didn't you?"

He continued talking as I hurried toward him. "My *tia* says she hasn't had a story like this since that tornado almost hit Maibe ten years ago."

Max's aunt was the sole reporter, editor, and distributor of Maibe's weekly paper. In order to continue selling subscriptions to a younger population, Mrs. Delgado reported on local news first and foremost, then other news impacting the country and the world. Not only did she provide the facts, but she posited how those events could change the world and posed questions for readers to discuss. Almost every household had a paper delivered each Thursday morning, and anyone who hadn't read the stories by lunch would be out of the loop.

"It's terrible." I tried to ignore the ache in the pit of my stomach. "How's Keppler?"

"About the same. He's in a meeting with Alexander and the council right now." Max slouched against the wall and rubbed his bloodshot eyes. "Mr. Mayhew is allowed in there to complain about Keppler living in his grocery store, but I'm not allowed to be a character witness."

"They wouldn't even let you wait inside?" I breathed warm air into my cupped hands before shoving them into my pockets.

Max sighed. "Of course they would, but Molly's in there, and we disagree on Keppler's status as the villain of Maibe. I'm pretty sure we could easily tip it in her direction."

I frowned. Molly and I had been elementary school best friends, but by middle school we had drifted apart. After her parents had died during the fever last fall, she had visited me during my illness and recovery. Although she could be stubborn and blunt about her opinions, I could usually have a rational conversation with her. Our dads had been close.

My back found the wall so we were shoulder to shoulder. "Maybe I should talk to her. Where's Todd?"

"His dad and Emma were pretty mad about the way he treated Keppler, so he's grounded." He closed his eyes. "Probably sleeping right now."

"You look like you could use a nap." I wrapped one arm around my friend.

"I'll be okay." Max rubbed a hand over his face. "I promised Keppler I'd see him through, and the meeting can't last much longer."

"How did Molly find out about the fire?" I made my way toward the door. Her house was a few blocks from mine on the other side of town.

"Todd probably called her after his dad got the volunteer fire department alert." He shrugged. "They've been best buddies lately."

That was news to me. It was hard to imagine Molly and Todd having a conversation. When we were younger, she bullied him and he had avoided her. Her treatment of him had been one of the reasons we grew apart.

I pulled the door open, glanced back at Max, who didn't move, and walked into relative warmth. The typically bright lobby, dulled by shadows of winter gloom, reminded me of the other problem Max explained over the phone. The power was out.

"Rochelle, what are you doing here?" Molly sprang to her feet and stared at me as if I were a ghost. "I thought you and Kinley were out of town until Monday."

Growing up in a small town meant people knew more about me than I knew about myself, so I wasn't surprised she knew my travel plans.

"Change of plans." I scraped damp hair off my face. "I was getting homesick and I heard Keppler was in some trouble."

Molly fell back into her chair. "Don't tell me you came all this way to help that criminal." She shook her head. "Todd had just been telling me how Keppler was a nuisance to the town, and a few hours later my dad's pharmacy was on fire. But I spotted the arsonist."

"Todd suspected Keppler?" I sat down in the chair next to her. I had figured Molly instigated the accusation.

She shrugged and stared down at her hands. "Rochelle, that building . . ."

For the first time, I noticed her eyes had become watery with exhaustion, her perfect complexion had paled, and her long hair was knotted. "Molly, I know this is difficult, but Keppler didn't have anything to do with it."

"You don't know that, Rochelle." She brushed her long blonde hair over her shoulder, face rigid, blue eyes scrutinizing me. "You trust people too easily. Even Todd agrees." Molly's tough expression melted into one that indicated she had more to say but wanted to spare my feelings. "We were like sisters once, and I still care about you. I'm worried, Rochelle."

"I have everything under control." I didn't want to be angry with her for clinging to the friendship we used to have. I'd had some rough days since the fever, but I had Kat and Kinley to help me through them while Molly lived in her big house all alone. Her older sister was her guardian, but she lived out of state and, as far as I knew, rarely checked in on Molly.

She shook her head, then seemed to look past me as if seeing something I couldn't. "There's so much you don't know . . . I'm not sure where to start."

It wasn't like her to be anything but absolutely confident at all times. Something was up. "Maybe the beginning would be best."

Molly glanced around the empty lobby then back to me. "I'm just putting all of the pieces together, but when my dad was working in research, he was part of a really important discovery, and he brought your dad into it too. Did your dad ever give you a necklace or mention one?"

This was not the direction I had been expecting her to go. "No, I would definitely remember that." The agents who had questioned us after he died—the TCI, they called themselves—had asked about a necklace too, but I tried not to think about those days.

She took my hands and held them tightly. "I have to figure this out, Rochelle, and you have to help me." Her voice sped up with intensity. "If we get this right, we could save millions of lives." She squeezed my hands so hard they hurt.

Something in her eyes, a darkness, made me pull my arms back. "Of course I'll help you, but . . ." The Molly I knew always had control over her emotions. She was critical, brutal even, but never desperate. "But why would my dad have been involved in your dad's research project? He wasn't a scientist."

Sometime around third grade, Molly's dad began working for a pharmaceutical research company. I remembered she was upset when he started traveling and wasn't home as often. My dad, on the other hand, had a degree in marketing and communication, but after my mom died and we moved in with Grandma, he worked odd jobs and mostly helped my uncle out at his veterinary clinic.

"I know that, Rochelle." She rubbed her forehead the way Kinley did when she had a headache. "I'm trying to piece it all together."

"Have you been sleeping?" I lowered my voice a little for her sake. "Kinley always gets headaches when she stays up too late studying."

Molly smiled and pulled me into an awkward hug. "Rochelle, when I talk to you, I feel like I have a sister." She stood and stretched. "You're right. I'm going to go home and catch up on my sleep. We'll talk again when I can think clearly. Just don't tell anyone else about this conversation."

I nodded and forced a smile.

"I'm so glad you came home early." Molly made her way to the door and turned back. "I feel so much better knowing we can do this together."

"Of course." It was the only phrase that came to mind as Molly slipped outside. *A necklace that could save lives? My dad? Todd and Molly? Molly being so glad I came home early?* My mind skipped over the conversation, unable to settle on any one thought for long, until Max rushed into the room.

"You got rid of her. What did you find out?" He slid into the chair next to me.

I blinked at him, climbing out of my tangled thoughts. "I think she's having some kind of mental breakdown."

"So, nothing new." He laughed. "Had she overheard anything from the meeting?"

"Right, Keppler." I turned toward the closed conference room door.

"Rochelle?" He put his hand on my shoulder. "What did she say to you?"

"I'm not entirely sure."

Max gave me a puzzled look as a door groaned open and low voices approached.

"He needs a guardian and some discipline," Mr. Mayhew argued. "Let the orphan redistribution people deal with him."

"Give me until Monday," Alexander's voice interrupted. "I take responsibility for him until then."

As the men of the town council entered the lobby, Max and I sprang to our feet, but only Alexander seemed to notice us.

Mr. Walters thrust his arms into his coat. "Don't you think you have enough on your plate with this power outage? It's going to get even colder with the storm coming in."

"I have a crew working on that right now." Alexander smiled through the exasperation in his voice.

Mr. Flores shook his head and pushed the door open. "He wanted his chance to run the town. Let him figure it out."

"If you don't report that kid on Monday, I'll do it myself." Mr. Mayhew followed the other three out into the first snowflakes.

Alexander sighed and melted into a chair. "Everyone in this town has lost their minds. Four grown men want to blame a kid, who's too sick to keep his eyes open, for the fire and the power outage, and my council thinks I'm too young to be a competent mayor." He covered his forehead with one hand then let it slide to his chin before dropping to the arm of the chair. "Their terms have all been up for months, but no one will run for their positions."

I had been gone for two weeks and returned to an alternate reality. The Alexander I knew was always patient, calm, and optimistic.

"Forget about them." Max swept his arm toward the door. "You already know it's unfair and cruel to send Keppler to a home for children."

"I wish I had a choice." Alexander sat up and shook his head. "I don't want to send the kid away, but . . . ." Exhaustion dulled his voice and I noticed shadows beneath his eyes.

"But you have until Monday," I interjected. "We can think of something by then. Maybe Kinley or Emma will have an idea."

He smiled and his shoulders relaxed as he transitioned from authoritative mayor to the protective older brother he'd always been to me. "Now there's the positivity and empathy that makes good leaders." He looked from Max to me. "Rochelle, I'm afraid to ask this, but does Kinley know you're here?"

"She's probably reading my note about now." I stepped in front of Max. "I had to come."

Max took a sidestep away from us. "I should probably check on Keppler." He hurried down the hall.

"He called you, didn't he? After I told him not to." He stared after Max then shook his head. "I should have known better. I suppose I should call Kinley and try to explain. At least I'll get to talk to her for a few minutes while she's not distracted studying." His eyebrows furrowed. "She'll worry herself sick until she knows you're safe."

We both knew if Kinley had it her way, I would be locked in the house and cocooned in bubble wrap at all times.

"Do you want me to call her?" I didn't want my choice to come home to become Kinley and Alexander's next fight, but I'd have also preferred to give my cousin time to calm down.

He shook his head and laughed. "We'll accomplish more if you talk to Keppler. He has an appointment with Dr. Brooks in half an hour and he refuses to go."

I didn't know if anyone could convince Keppler of anything, but I had to try. "You've got it." Taking a deep breath, I made my way to the conference room. Keppler sat slumped forward at the end of the long rectangular table, his forehead resting on the top.

Max rested his elbows on the table and looked at me. "He said no doctor, no shower, no help. In fact, he doesn't want to leave this room."

"Just leave me alone." He circled his arms around his head.

"Keppler?" I sat down next to him. "I know you're having a rough day—"

"A rough day?" He lifted his head to face me. Matted hair was plastered to his forehead and two butterfly Band-Aids criss-crossed his chin. "I'm having a rough life." He buried his face in his arms and coughed in a way that made my chest hurt. "I give up."

I didn't understand how Mr. Mayhew and the council could see him and not feel the least bit of sympathy. Even if Kinley never forgave me and Todd doubted every decision I made for the rest of my life, I knew I had made the right decision to come home. It was time to take my life back, and helping Keppler was the first step. Maybe that was the reason we met in the first place.

When I rested my hand on his arm, he flinched but didn't pull away. "If you give up now, you're going to miss all of the good things still coming."

Keppler shivered and coughed into his sleeve. "What good things? I can either wait for them to report me or run away and repeat the process all over again . . . but I'm too tired . . ." His voice trailed off in a whimper that ended in a nasty cough.

"I promise we can come up with hundreds of better options. You just need some of Kat's chicken noodle soup and a good night's sleep. Everything will be better in the morning." *Tomorrow will be better.* My dad used to say that, automatically, any time I was hurt or having a bad day. "Trust me this one time. What do you have to lose?" I stood and held my hand out to him.

"Trusting people is always a bad idea." He sat back in his chair and winced. "But this time things can't get any worse."

To my surprise, he took my hand. I smiled and helped him to his feet. I had no idea how I could keep my promise, but I'd learned if I played the odds, things worked out most of the time. After all, Dad came through on impossible promises for fifteen years.

CHAPTER 5
ROCHELLE

March 10, 2090

Tears streamed down my face, so I could barely see where I was going. Kinley's nine-year-old hand gripped my six-year-old hand as she led me into the kitchen.

"Uncle Auggie?" Kinley wrapped her arm around me.

Footsteps hurried over wooden floors. "What happened?" My dad's voice was gentle as he scooped me up and held me close to him.

"She fell and scraped her knee." Kinley confessed the information as if she had pushed me down.

"It's not your fault, sunflower." Dad rested a gentle hand on top of Kinley's head. "Don't worry, hummingbird. We'll get you fixed up in no time. I promise it won't hurt a bit."

Dad called us by our nicknames more than he called us by our real names. Sunflower for Kinley because of her long, skinny legs and wide green eyes. Hummingbird for me because I never sat still.

Gently, he lowered me onto the bathroom counter so my knee rested over the sink. I held my hands over my eyes while I listened to Dad and Kinley whispering their plans.

"You can look now." My cousin smiled, proud of her work as she watched my eyes travel to the bright pink Band-Aid on my knee.

"Now, I need two volunteers to help me make pizza for dinner." Dad's green eyes sparkled as our arms shot into the air. "Perfect!" He scooped me up and kissed my forehead.

"Rochelle?" A hand touched my forehead. "Time to wake up."

I lifted my head off the table, hoping to see my dad sitting across from me, but the blurry chair was empty. Rubbing my eyes brought Emma and the kitchen into view. I had sat up all night with Keppler, partly because I didn't want him to wake up alone and confused in an unfamiliar place, and partly because I worried he would disappear like last time.

"What happened? Is Keppler okay?"

"Everything is just fine." Emma had come over right after Alexander and I brought Keppler home from the doctor—Kinley must have called her at some point—and decided to stay with us until my cousin got home. "Alexander just left to get Kinley from the train station. They should be here any minute." She sat down in the chair next to me.

Still groggy, I glanced around the room, sure I would see my dad at the counter making pizza. But he had been gone for almost a year. I knew that. My conversation with Molly had sent my memory spiraling back in time, although nothing I remembered included a necklace and world-saving research.

"Do you think I'd be able to work on a secret project without Kat or Kinley finding out?" Snow swirled outside the window. I was glad Keppler had agreed to sleep inside.

Emma looked at me in her usual understanding way, hazel eyes contemplating my hypothetical situation. "Maybe for a little while. I think secrets are easier to keep when you're on a mission for good." She tucked a strand of light brown hair behind her ear and smiled. "Are you planning some covert operations?"

I laughed and stretched my legs under the table. "No, just thinking about everything..."

"Don't look so worried, sweetie." Emma took my hands in hers. "If this has to do with Todd, I promise I'll talk some sense into him. I know he's missed you the past two weeks."

Todd I could handle. But Molly's uncharacteristic behavior

had spooked me. Loneliness was a dangerous thing. Maybe if I just made an effort to talk to her, she wouldn't have to make things up to give us something in common. Whatever she thought she had discovered was probably just part of some game my dad and Eric Bennett played when they were kids.

"I've missed him too." It was true even though I couldn't bring myself to call him. I knew we would argue about Keppler, and I wanted to avoid that fight. "Did Keppler get his medicine?" I glanced up at the clock. Almost five thirty. Dr. Brooks had prescribed an antibiotic for him to take twice a day after diagnosing him with pneumonia.

"About fifteen minutes ago, but I can't get him to eat anything." Emma scooted a little closer so she could pull me into a hug, and I knew she was remembering a few months earlier when I had been even worse off than Keppler. "I'm making all of us some chicken noodle soup."

"Without Kat?" My sister never passed up an opportunity to cook.

"She's been in the library for the past hour." Emma stood and walked over to the stove. "I think she still feels a little left out."

"Maybe I should talk to her before Kinley gets here." I jumped up and hurried to the next room. My sister had hugged me and welcomed me home, but in the hours that followed, we hadn't talked much. The last thing I needed was a fight the minute my cousin got home.

"You should just stay here," I heard Kat suggest as I approached the library.

"Kinley didn't even want me here the first time." Keppler's voice sounded hoarse.

"If you hid during the few hours she's home, she'd probably never notice you. Kinley barely even notices I exist."

"Kat, that isn't true." I walked into the room as Keppler

coughed the deep, chest-rattling hack that made my own chest hurt.

My sister folded her legs under her, her chair pulled close to the couch where Keppler lay propped up slightly by pillows. "When we were sick, she just pretended we didn't exist, so we wouldn't mess up her life."

I sat down on the arm of her chair. "She was sick, too, and stuck in Omaha."

The fever didn't usually kill teenagers, but it still made young people really sick and often resulted in a secondary infection. To make matters worse, when someone came down with the fever, the entire town was put into quarantine for at least a month. No supplies in and, if the local doctors were sick, no one to treat patients.

"And this time, taking a test is more important than we are." Kat crossed her arms in front of her. "You're only defending her because you're her favorite."

Keppler made a face. He looked better after a shower and some medicine to bring his fever down, but still way too pale and exhausted.

"Well, you're *my* favorite." I slid into the chair so Kat and I were shoulder to shoulder.

"Your favorite what?" She squirmed away from me. "I'm your sister and she's your cousin."

I laughed and wrapped my arms around her. "You're my favorite person on the planet."

Although she tried not to, she smiled. "Don't tell Kinley though. If she's in a bad mood, she'll never let Keppler stay here."

"I'm not staying here anyway." Keppler pulled the blanket over his face to stifle a cough. "A home for children is my only option." He sounded a lot braver than twenty-four hours earlier, but I knew he would never stay in a home for children. If he left Maibe, he would end up on the street again, alone, with no one to take care of him.

Before I could say anything, the back door slammed and a murmur of voices rose in the kitchen.

Kinley rushed into the room, still bundled in her winter coat with snowflakes melting in her hair. "Rochelle Irene Aumont. What were you thinking, coming home by yourself? Do you know how dangerous that was?"

"I'm sorry." I stood to face my cousin. The worry wrinkles in her forehead and panic in her eyes made my stomach ache with guilt. "I knew in my heart you would be upset, but my head told me Keppler could be in legal trouble . . . so I listened to my head like you told me to."

Kinley sighed and hugged me so tight it was hard to breathe. "Oh, Rochelle, you're going to give me gray hair by the time I'm twenty-five."

Alexander walked in, hands in his pockets, whistling a tune. "We have some good news." His eyes jumped from Keppler to Kat to me watching him around my cousin's shoulder. He smiled and winked at me. "Kinley, do you want to tell them?"

My cousin released me from her tight embrace but kept one hand on my arm. "We're not done talking about this."

I was too curious about Alexander's news to worry about her threat. "Tell us what?"

Kinley guided me to the coffee table where we sat directly in front of Keppler.

Kat jumped out of her chair and slid next to me, so I was sandwiched between my sister and my cousin. A gust of wind crashed against the windowpane, and I felt fortunate to be warm and safe with my family.

My cousin ignored us and leaned toward Keppler. "Alexander

and I are in agreement that you're not a bad kid, you've just been dealt an unfair hand, and you deserve a second chance." She paused to catch her breath. "As Rochelle recently pointed out, any of us could easily be in your shoes, so I want to give you the option to stay here."

"Kinley and I already signed the paperwork that will make us your guardians." Alexander reached into his pocket and pulled out some papers that he placed in front of Keppler. "All we need is your information."

Keppler shivered as he stared down at the forms, but I couldn't read his expression.

"Did you hear that?" Kat gripped my arm so tightly that I thought I would lose circulation. "You mean forever, right?" She leaned forward to study our cousin's face. "You won't change your mind later?"

"Of course not." Kinley waved a hand at Kat. "This was originally Alexander's idea, and you can choose to live with him once you feel better." She turned her back to Alexander and whispered, "But I recommend staying here where you'll have things like immediate medical care, reliable meals, clean laundry . . ."

"I heard that." Alexander sank into the chair and shook his head. "I know how to do laundry, Kinley." It was a teasing remark; his patience for my cousin was infinite. "Anyway, it's up to you. I promised to find you a home."

I wanted to hug Kinley and Alexander, but Keppler just looked at me with the guardianship form gripped in his hand.

"He wants to stay." Kat leaned forward. "Right?"

He shook his head. "I can't . . ." His eyes locked with mine and they were clouded with uncertainty. "I'd be in the way . . . You don't even know me." The cough he had been trying to fight off burst through and he caved in on himself.

Kinley sprang forward, slid her arm behind him, and propped him up. "Easy . . . Shallow breaths . . . You're okay."

"You wouldn't be in our way," Kat said when Keppler's coughing faded. "Kinley and Rochelle barely eat anything, so I never get to cook what I want to, but if you lived here . . ." She shrugged casually.

I smiled at Kat and then met Keppler's unreadable blue eyes. "If I have someone to help me with yardwork in the summer, it'll go a lot faster."

Kinley, kneeling next to the couch, eased Keppler back against the pillows. "I'm sorry people have been cruel to you, but we want you to be part of this family." She sat back on her heels. "My expectations for you will be the same as for Rochelle and Kat. You'll have some chores, but no more than the rest of us, and we'll talk about rules. I'll want you to participate in Saturday lessons, of course."

"We could set up the basement as an apartment for you." Kat stood. "Then you'll have some privacy."

Alexander moved to the coffee table so he sat next to me. "And I'm here for you when the girls make you crazy and you need someone to talk to."

Kinley smacked Alexander's shoulder with the back of her hand. "What's that supposed to mean?" She looked like a twig next to him, but he recoiled as if it hurt.

"Nothing at all, honey." He laughed and raised his eyebrows at Keppler. "This is your chance to get out of the system once and for all."

Keppler looked at me, eyes tired and shoulders stiff. "I'll stay." His head hung forward so I could barely see his face. "But I'll get a job and pay rent, and . . ."

"We can talk about that when you're feeling better." Alexander nodded at the document. "For now, we have to finish the paper-work."

With a shaky hand, Keppler held out the forms. "Aumont, can you write for me?"

"Sure." I lowered myself to the floor and spread the papers on the coffee table, sitting sideways so I could still see him.

"My first name is Charlie." His voice was faint, but audible. "And my birthday is March twenty-first. I'll be sixteen."

"That's only a week before Rochelle's birthday." Kat clapped her hands together. "That means I get to make two cakes."

I accepted Alexander's pen and jotted down the information, pretending it was normal to learn a person's first name a month after meeting him.

"You're lucky, Charlie." Alexander grinned at Kat. "I didn't even get a cake for my birthday."

"Because you were too busy," Kat said matter-of-factly. "You got one when you were elected mayor."

"Not important right now." Kinley gave Alexander a warning glance and he stuck out his tongue at Kat, which made her laugh. "What was your last address?"

Keppler took a rough breath and shivered. "The Topeka, Kansas Home for Children, but that was a few years ago."

"That's okay." Alexander patted Keppler's arm in an act of camaraderie. "We just have to verify that you were in the system so we know you don't have a family looking for you."

I handed Keppler the paper and pen. "Now it just needs your signature."

He glanced down at the thin, black line and then back up at Kinley and Alexander. "Just our signatures? That's it?"

"Easy as that." Her smile faded. "I agree, it's too simple. Good for us, but not for the other kids caught up in an overwhelmed system." She shook her head. "Hopefully, someday it'll be different, but for now..."

Keppler nodded and scribbled his signature on the line next to Kinley's and Alexander's.

Kat hugged me, almost tumbling off the coffee table in the process. "I have to tell Emma." She jumped up and darted toward the door. "I'll make something to celebrate."

Alexander took the paper, folded it, and slid it into his pocket. "I'll get this turned in for processing right away. Sorry your first month in Maibe was so rough, Charlie. I hope you know you're welcome here." He helped Kinley to her feet and kissed her left temple. "And you should really eat something. I know you skipped lunch."

Kinley nodded and leaned against Alexander in a rare display of affection. She looked like herself, tall and thin, hair pulled back in a neat braid, until you got to her face. Her eyes were dull and face blank as had often been the case since October. I wanted to know what was happening inside her head, but she was so good at hiding her emotions.

"Hang in there, Charlie. You'll feel better in no time." She actually let Alexander take her hand. "I'll bring you something to eat."

"Whatever Emma is making smells really good." He walked toward the door swinging her hand with his. "I can't wait to tell you my new idea for town council..."

I drew my knees up in front of me as Keppler coughed with his hand pressed to his chest. "Are you okay?"

He squirmed in his constant battle to rest comfortably. "I can't be part of your family... I'm not even sure this is real. Maybe I'm delirious right now."

I didn't know anything about Keppler's life, and I didn't

want to say the wrong thing. "I promise it's real, but don't let Kat and Kinley scare you." I rearranged the blankets over his feet, scrambling for the words to make him feel comfortable in my house. "I'll even keep calling you Keppler. And you can call me Aumont until you decide we know each other well enough to be friends. Even if that's ten years from now."

He smiled slightly and closed his eyes. "Thank you, Aumont."

I rested my forehead against my knees. Family could be complicated, but no one deserved to go through life alone. Not Keppler, not Kinley, not even Molly.

CHAPTER 6
CHARLIE

March 13, 2090

Wedged between a shed and a wooden fence, I held my breath, hoping I had eluded the guy following me.

"You're not in trouble, kid." The voice was rough but not accusing. "What you did back there was pretty clever."

Three months after running from the home for children, I found myself on the streets of Kansas City. Hungry to the point of starvation, I posed as a paperboy selling subscriptions to one of the local newspapers and pestered homeowners, exhausted from work or arms full of groceries, as they walked from their cars to their houses. I continued my sales pitch all the way to the door. Although I didn't sell one fake paper, I did memorize a dozen key codes, so when a new workday started, I let myself in to raid the refrigerator and enjoy a warm shower.

"I've been reading stories about the invisible bandit in the paper. It takes a lot of self-control to only take food when you could clean out the valuables."

The food was all I needed to survive. Hoping to end the encounter, and find a warm place to sleep before the sun set, I squirmed back out into a world of gray sky, gray mist frozen on the trees, and gray snow on the ground.

"What do you want?" I curled my hands into fists and tried to look tough. The guy in front of me was four times bigger and stood *at least a head taller. His dark hair was buzzed close to his head, clothes clean, unlike mine.*

He extended his hand. "I'm Griff, leader of a group called The Defiance. It's sort of a club for street kids." He was older than me, I guessed, by four years.

I shook his hand. "I'm Charlie."

"We could use an innovative thinker like you." He looked me up and down. "We all take care of each other, like a family. Even the invisible bandit needs a family."

"That's all right." I turned to walk away. "I'm fine on my own."

"Here's how I see it, kid." Something in his voice stopped me in my tracks. "If I was able to find you, the police can't be far behind. You won't be invisible for much longer without help."

"Right, Keppler?" Max's question scattered my thoughts. I lifted my head off the sun-warmed window and looked to where he sat a few feet away on the window seat.

"What?" Shivering despite the warmth of afternoon sun and the blanket around my shoulders, I rubbed my forehead. Although my fever had dropped and I could breathe more easily, I couldn't shake my cough or inability to focus.

Max laughed. "I was just saying this poster isn't even professional enough to advertise student council."

"I wouldn't know."

Alexander's solution to expired council terms was to lower the running and voting age to sixteen and expedite the election to March thirtieth. Rochelle was disappointed she was only fifteen, and Kinley told her she wouldn't be running even if she were old enough.

"Oh yeah, sorry. You wouldn't have been hanging around school since you were raised by wolves." It was his favorite of the backstories he'd made up to explain the past I didn't want to talk about. If only it were true and I didn't find myself jumping at every little noise, afraid Griff had caught up, sick with dread he would hurt the others because they were with me.

"Max, don't annoy him." The constant whirring of Rochelle's sewing machine in the little room off the library stopped, and she appeared in the doorway.

"We're just talking about the town council thing." Max leaned forward, holding the poster in front of him. "I think Alexander purposely left this loophole because he wants you to run. He just needs a way to get it past Kinley."

It hadn't taken Rochelle long to realize she would be sixteen two days before the election took place, and the rules weren't specific about an age cutoff date.

"What do you think, Keppler?" She sat down on the window seat.

"It sounds like a lot of work." In the natural light I could see the darker flecks of green in her eyes and the freckles across her nose. "What would you get out of it?"

She tipped her head one way then the other. "A once-in-a-lifetime opportunity to do something important . . . something world-changing."

"You guys are supposed to be letting Charlie rest." Kat peeked her head into the room before entering.

"I am resting." Although my basement apartment was warm and more comfortable than I expected, with carpet and walls and everything, I preferred spending my days in the library.

"You also need to eat." She walked toward us, trying to brush a little spot of flour off her shirt. "I made you chicken noodle soup with my grandma's recipe."

In almost sixteen years, no one had ever made me soup when I was sick, but in a matter of days, Emma, Kinley, and Kat had all done their best to coax me into trying their homemade version. I'd only had the appetite to pick at toast.

"I'm not really hungry."

"You have to be starving." Max took a deep breath of soup-scented air. "I guarantee Kat's soup is the best you've ever tasted. I'd stay and have a bowl or four, but I promised my *tia* I'd be home to watch my cousins while she works."

Rochelle glanced up at the mantel clock. "I'll walk with you and stop by City Hall to talk to Alexander. He'll be in his office . . ."

"Maybe you should skip this one." Kat stepped in front of her sister. "You're already on kind of thin ice with Kinley." I hadn't expected that advice from Kat.

"Kinley is the one who's always reminding me of her early admission to medical training." Rochelle's eyes twinkled with excitement. "I could finally live up to her expectations and be the youngest family member on town council, not to mention the first sixteen-year-old on the council ever."

Kat rested her hands on her hips and narrowed her eyes. "Kinley might be an emotionless robot, but she isn't stupid. You really think she won't find out you're doing this?"

"One day at a time." Rochelle took the poster from Max. "The forum is next Thursday. Kinley's scheduled to work at the hospital. Until then, we just have to make sure she doesn't read the paper and hope she's too busy studying to pay any attention to the upcoming election."

"That's reasonable." Max shrugged. "She already told Alexander it's a terrible idea, so she won't be interested."

"If I can just win the vote, she'll be so proud of me that she'll forget I snuck around behind her back."

"It'll be like a secret mission." Max jumped to his feet. "And then Rochelle will be the great leader who brings Maibe back to life. I mean, if you guys haven't noticed, the town is kind of dead."

Kat groaned. "That's the worst plan I've ever heard. First of all, what happens if you don't get elected? Second, when are you going to help me with the garden and canning? Between your homework, your chores, your sewing business, and helping Max with all of his ridiculous inventions . . ."

"Hey, wait a minute." Max did his best to look offended.

"You don't have to worry." Rochelle shook her head at him and pulled her sister into a hug. "I promise I will always find time to help you with anything you need, but this could be my chance to make Maibe better than ever."

Kat looked at her sister and sighed. "Fine. If you can convince Alexander, then I guess it was meant to be." She squeezed her eyes shut. "Just hurry so you're home before Kinley gets out of class."

"You're the best." Rochelle hugged Kat one more time, then put a hand on Max's shoulder and hurried him to the door. "I'll be back in an hour."

Kat shook her head and sat down on the window seat. "I have Kinley, who doesn't care about anything except studying, and Rochelle, who's obsessed with saving the world but not at all worried about what's practical." She leaned forward, elbows on her knees and face in her hands. "The only reason we have food right now is because Grandma kept a garden and put away all of the extra food for the winter. But I've never done those things on my own before, and if the fever keeps popping up across the country, the food rationing is going to get worse and we might not be able to keep our shelves and freezer stocked . . ."

"Rochelle said she would help you." In the month I'd known Rochelle, she'd been the most reliable person I'd ever met. If she said she'd have time for Kat, I believed her.

"That's because she'd rather absorb all of the world's problems than let anyone else be worried or afraid." Kat smiled then cringed. "So, she pretends everything's fine, and all I can do to save her from

herself is make her a grilled cheese sandwich and tomato soup."
She rolled her eyes. "Which is the most boring favorite meal ever,
but at least she eats it."

I nodded, trying to put what she was telling me into a context I
could understand. For a year and a half, Griff was the older brother
I'd always wanted—until he became obsessed with figuring out
how to expand The Defiance's control. He would go days without
sleep or forget to eat. Little did I know, that wouldn't be the worst
of it.

"You can't really save someone from themself." Part of me still
held onto hope that Griff was crazy or, at the least, his plan for
control would fail. What else could I do? Who would believe me if
I told them what he had told me?

"It's different with Rochelle." Kat lifted her head and folded
her legs under her. "When she had the fever back in October . . .
she was sick for such a long time. Kinley and I are worried if she
doesn't take care of herself and gets sick again, so soon, it might be
too much for her."

The fever. Those dreaded two words. The Defiance had required extensive hygiene protocols and created a quarantine
room in the dungeon-like basement for anyone who came down
with the slightest sniffle.

I shivered, imagining myself fighting pneumonia on a dirty
cot, alone in the darkness, instead of the Aumonts' warm house.
"The fever was really bad here then?"

Kat nodded. "It seemed like everyone got sick at the same time
before we even realized we were in danger." She glanced at the
doorway. "Of course, Kinley was away at medical school and she
didn't show up until all of the damage was done."

I couldn't imagine Kinley purposely abandoning her family.
"She's here now."

"Even though she doesn't want to be." Kat folded her arms

and shook her head. "Coming home to raise her poor orphaned cousins was the only *acceptable* thing she could do. Kinley would never sacrifice her perfect reputation."

"It doesn't matter why she came back, just that she did." I couldn't disguise the bitterness in my voice or contain my overflowing cynicism. "At least she didn't sign you over to a home for children and forget about you."

"It matters to me." Her eyebrows furrowed as she tried to reconcile my view of the world with hers. "It's not enough that she's *responsible* for us. I want her to have time to talk to me, you know, notice that I exist . . . I know things can't be the way they used to be, but she doesn't even try to show she cares about me."

Trying to avoid Kat's gloomy expression, I looked down at my blue-and-purple-striped socks. "Either way, you're lucky. You have everything you need." I swept my arm from the window to the bookshelves that carried me back in time seven years to my hometown public library.

Isabelle sat next to me, reading her favorite book while I did my homework. Every weekday we went to school, then my sister accompanied me on my paper route, and then we spent the evening at the library so we didn't have to be at home.

"You got in a fight again, didn't you?" Isabelle stared at the bruises along my jaw. "Charlie, you promised you wouldn't."

"I'm sorry." I looked up from my math assignment and met my sister's disappointed eyes. "I couldn't let some bully walk off with my paper route money. We need that for groceries, so I got it back."

"You didn't have to do it the same way Dad would." Her little hand gripped mine. "Promise this was the last time, Charlie."

"Charlie?" Kat's hand brushed mine. "Are you okay?"

"Yeah, just my head today . . ." Kat's blue eyes seemed to look right into my thoughts. "You should talk to Kinley about everything you just told me and hear her side of things."

If Isabelle thought it was bad to turn out like Dad, I couldn't imagine how she would react to The Defiance brand on my arm. I never meant to push her away, but I was incapable of being the brother she wanted.

"She wouldn't do anything to let you down on purpose."

Kat sighed and let her hands drop to her lap. "How can you be so sure?"

I winced at the burning in my chest that followed my cough. "Because I had a little sister, and letting her down made me feel more rotten than I feel being sick right now."

"You have a sister? What happened to her?" Kat tilted her head, trying to see my face.

"She deserved better and I really hope she found it." As much as I tried to imagine Isabelle in a nice house with people who loved her, it wasn't a likely enough scenario to make me feel better.

I braced myself for more questions, but Kat's expression was more bemused than curious. Without a word, she hurried across the room and selected a thick book from the shelf. "I have to show you something." She carried it over and scooted back so we both rested against the window. "Ready?"

Before I could reply, she opened the book to a family photo. Her finger moved to a tall, lanky man with shaggy brown hair holding a toddler in his arms. "That's my dad and Rochelle, fourteen years ago." Glancing at me, she pointed to a woman with brown hair that hung in tight curls to her shoulders. "This is my Grandma Irene."

Tipping her head to the right, she indicated a man who resembled the first, but with shorter hair and a neater appearance. He had his arm around a woman with long blonde hair. A little girl in a frilly dress and hair curled into perfect spirals stood in front of them. "That's Uncle Arthur, Aunt Grace, and Kinley."

My eyes landed on the woman sitting next to Grandma Irene.

She was young and uncannily familiar. "Is that your mom? She looks just like Rochelle."

"No, that's Aunt Audrie. We don't have time for that story right now." Kat dismissed her with a wave of her hand. "Rochelle's mom died in a car accident a few months before this picture was taken."

I knew Kat was only a year younger than her sister, but no one in the picture was holding a baby. "Where are you, then?"

"In Colorado with my mom and two brothers." She looked down at the picture. "When I was five, the house caught on fire, and they didn't get out. After that, I lived in three homes for children in three months . . . then they sent me here." She looked up, blue eyes lost in thought. "All of the beds were taken, and I thought I would end up on a cot in the hallway like the time before, but Grandma Irene was the director of the home for children. She said she had an extra room at her house and two granddaughters close to my age."

Kat flipped the photo album to a picture of her behind a birthday cake with six candles, Kinley and Rochelle on either side with their arms around her, and her dad off to the side, caught in the middle of singing happy birthday. "I stayed here for a few weeks and then Dad adopted me and life was good again."

I thought of Isabelle with her golden curls and porcelain doll features in comparison to my dark hair and pointed nose and chin. Rochelle and Kat weren't identical, but they looked more like siblings than my sister and I did.

"Dad always said nothing happens by chance. I think he meant the bad things that happen to us eventually lead to something good." She looked lovingly down at the picture then up at me. "I believe your sister found a family just like I did. Maybe someday you'll even find her, but for now, we'll be your family."

Even the invisible bandit needs a family. Griff's words echoed in my head. At the time they had been exactly what I needed. Those words convinced me to join The Defiance—the biggest mistake of my life. I would never be free, always looking over my shoulder, fearing the day Griff would find me. Kat and the others using that word again and again increased my anxiety instead of putting me at ease, like I was sure they intended. Talk of fate or serendipity leading me to Maibe didn't sit right with me either.

"That's not how it works. Our lives don't follow some big, grand plan." I shrugged. "I'm just here because it was too cold to move on and because I got sick and accused of arson in the same week."

"It takes time to see it." Kat gently closed the photo album and rested her head back against the glass. "When I first got here, I wouldn't even talk to Rochelle because I was so afraid I would get sent away in a few weeks."

"But everything turned out okay." Maybe I would never let my guard down enough to have a family, but I did believe the Aumonts would take care of me whether I deserved it or not. Clearly, Griff didn't know where to look for me or he would have found me already. And what would tip him off to look in some little Nebraska town? If the past was truly behind me, I didn't have to worry about putting the Aumonts in any danger. I could embrace having a *family*.

"Eventually." Kat laughed and pointed to the next room. "I used to spend the entire day hiding under the dining room table. When Rochelle came home from school, she would get her coloring book and crayons and we would sit under there and color. She didn't know it, but coloring was my favorite thing to do. It made me feel safe here."

"So you think I should start coloring?" I laughed, hoping to keep the mood light.

"No." Kat grinned. "I'm wondering if there's something you like to do that would make you feel more comfortable. Maybe drawing or playing a musical instrument or building things?"

My daydream of writing in the library returned to me.

"Promise not to tell anyone?" I'd always been secretive about my writing since my dad considered it a waste of time and The Defiance prohibited reading and writing.

Kat nodded.

"I like to write. Short stories, mostly." I watched her face, expecting judgment, but she only smiled.

"Why is that a secret?" She slid forward and stood. "When you're well enough to take Saturday lessons with us, you'll love Emma's class. She always has us writing stuff." She made her way over to the desk and opened groaning drawers before holding up a notebook and a pen, which she carried over and placed on the cushion beside me. "Kinley and Rochelle might be a little distracted, but we all want you to feel safe and comfortable here."

For the first time, I saw my opportunity to live a normal life stretching out before me. I smiled. I couldn't help it. "Thank you."

"Now you just need some chicken noodle soup. Then you can write all afternoon." She held out her hand to me. "I promise it's really good."

I nodded and took her hand. Griff's threat felt a million miles away and his plan to take over the country, ridiculous. Finally, the invisible bandit found himself the family he needed, plus a warm place to sleep and chicken noodle soup.

CHAPTER 7
ROCHELLE

March 13, 2090

"The poster says I have to be sixteen to be on the council, not sixteen to run for the council." I leaned forward in my chair across from Alexander's desk. "If it's written that way in the rule book..."

"Rochelle, does Kinley know you're here?" Alexander looked up from the envelope he had been addressing through my argument.

"Not exactly." I had been caught in the one fact I couldn't get out of. "But..."

"But nothing," he interrupted. "You and Kinley and I already talked about this. Remember when we agreed that your health is first priority and..."

Tuning out the lecture I'd heard a hundred times, I glanced around the familiar office. Papers and books stood in stacks on one side of the desk and a nearby chair. The three plants on the windowsill had grown larger, and I wasn't surprised. Alexander had inherited his mom's talent for growing any kind of plant, and I wondered if he would keep the family business going. I had been to the Brewster plant nursery at Alexander's house a hundred times with my dad or grandma. They lived a few miles outside of town, and I always looked forward to exploring their greenhouse. Alexander had lost his entire family—his mom and two older sisters—to the fever.

"Rochelle, are you listening to me?" He waved his hand in front of my face.

"My health is important. I agree completely." If I could just get him to see my side. "But why can't being involved in something important be good for my health?"

Alexander pressed a hand to his forehead and let it slide down his face slowly. "Kinley is the expert and your cousin. We have to believe she knows what's best for you." He stood, crossed the room to a shelf of binders, and picked up a thick one.

I leaned back in my chair, toes and fingers finally warm after the chilly walk. "Are you afraid of breaking the rules, or are you afraid of Kinley?"

"Here's the thing." He dropped the binder on his desk and flopped into his chair. "Between you and me, there are no rules, at least not anymore. Since the fever, our state has no governor and no organized leadership for me to answer to. At the federal level, we lost three-fourths of the chain of command. This country is being held together by duct tape and bale wire." He slumped forward with his elbows on the desk. "And as terrifying as that is, Kinley is ten times more intimidating."

"I promise I'll talk to her again when she's not busy."

Alexander's eyebrows slid up. "When is Kinley not busy? I can't even get her to have dinner with me." He shook his head. "She'll kill me if I let you run for the council."

"Please." I made the saddest face I could muster. "Remember when I was so excited about being elected to the student council at school?"

"The day before they closed for the fever. I remember." He pressed one hand to the back of his neck. "Reopening the high school is one of my top priorities right now." His other hand patted the thick binder. "But I have a lot of those at the moment."

"I could help you if I were on the council. Kinley thinks education is important too."

Alexander stood and walked over to the window. He slid each plant an inch to the left. "She thinks your well-being is more important, and I agree with her."

"You and Kinley were both sick a few months ago too, but neither of you stay at home to rest all day." Melting snow dripped against the window, making me dream of spring and hope for a future within my reach. Unable to sit any longer, I crossed the room and stood next to Alexander. "I'm tired of watching from my window as my town dies. I want to fix it."

He sighed and turned to me. "That's not as easy as you might think." His words came out flat and he knew it. "But everyone deserves a chance to try." Alexander smiled and shook his head. "Almost sixteen? When did you get so old?"

"Is that a yes?"

"I reserve the right to change my mind if you aren't getting enough sleep or doing all of your homework."

"Thank you." If Alexander weren't five times bigger than me, I would have tackled him with my hug.

He hugged me back and I felt him sigh. "How am I going to explain this to Kinley?"

"Maybe we shouldn't tell her unless I get elected." I stepped back and gave Alexander an innocent smile. "Why give her more to worry about unless I'm actually one of the three council members?"

"That's tempting." He walked back to his desk. "But not responsible. I'll talk it over with her when the time is right."

He pulled out a sheet of paper and wrote something on it. "It's incredible and impressive so many kids your age have come forward to run for this position when I couldn't convince one adult to take it on. Maybe this will be the fresh start our town needs."

"I can't wait for the forum." I smiled as someone knocked at the door. "I have so many ideas."

"For now, you need to get home in time for dinner." He put a hand on my shoulder and guided me to the door. "I'll come check on Charlie tomorrow afternoon, and we can talk more about the forum and election."

He pulled the door open to reveal Molly and Todd standing in the hallway. "Hey, guys. What can I do for you today?"

Molly looked at Todd and he nodded. "We want to run for the town council. Is that why you're here, Rochelle?"

"She's considering it." Alexander spoke before I could. "I'll have to do a quick interview with each of you, individually."

"Go ahead, Todd." Molly stepped back into the hallway. "I need a minute with Rochelle."

I pulled the door shut behind me and followed Molly to the lobby where we had talked during Keppler's hearing. She sat down in one of the chairs, crossing one leg over the other.

"I can understand why you and Todd drifted apart." When she leaned forward her bangs slid over one eye. "He whines all the time about how you don't talk to him anymore, and he thinks the fever changed you or messed with your head somehow. It's really annoying."

I sank into the chair next to her. "He's telling people I'm crazy?"

"Who cares what Todd says." She brushed her hair behind her ear. "I've known you and Todd my entire life, and as sweet as it was for him to save you in October, he wasn't actually sick. He doesn't know what you've been through."

The fever had hit Kat and my grandma first. Although I felt the symptoms come on the next day, I fought through two more because I was the only one left to take care of them. When I got too sick to get to the phone, Todd came with his dad and took us to his house. Miraculously, Mr. Tatem and Emma didn't get sick at all while Todd and his little sister Lily only ran slight fevers for a few days.

"If he had gotten sick . . ." I cleared my throat and looked down at my hands. "But how can he expect me to be the same?"

Molly put a comforting hand on my shoulder. "He can't. None of us will be quite the same now that we understand how dark and cruel of a place the world can be."

I nodded, not sure I understood. "Why is Todd telling you all of this?"

"I'm not really sure." She looked both ways down the hall, but there was no one there. "I'm just helping him with a project and he jabbers a lot."

"What project?" Todd always told me everything, but suddenly he had a secret partnership with Molly?

"He doesn't want me to talk about it." She took my hands in hers. "But don't let his opinions bother you. Here's how I see it. He put himself and his family at risk to help you, so how can he judge you for doing the same thing for that Charlie kid?"

Is that what I had done by bringing Keppler home? Put my family in danger? "I thought you didn't want me to help Keppler."

"It's your life. You can help anyone you want. I just said you shouldn't trust him."

She was all over the place. "Molly, about what you said here last week . . ."

"Did you remember something?" She glanced toward the hallway.

"The only jewelry Dad gave me was a bracelet with a hummingbird charm." After fighting a mysterious illness for months, he seemed to understand he wouldn't be surviving it. A few days before he passed, he gave Kinley, Kat, and me each a charm bracelet.

Molly shook her head. "No, that's not it." She reached into her coat pocket and pulled out a chain with what looked like a thin piece of plastic shaped like a tear drop. It was small, only covering the very center of her palm, and the black glaze glinted when it caught the light. I studied the little pendant. White lettering spelled out *Tomorrow* across the rounded edge. "It looks just like this. He must have hidden it away somewhere safe."

The urgency in her voice got my attention. "I can look around the house for it. Maybe it's packed away with his things." We had been too heartbroken to sort through Dad's stuff, so we packed it in boxes and put it in the attic to deal with when we were done grieving. They remained untouched. "You know, Molly, we can talk any time, even if our dads weren't involved in some kind of secret mission."

Molly took a breath for the first time since she mentioned the pendant. "I know you probably think I'm crazy for making such a big deal about this, but I promise it's important. Just give me a little more time to figure out the details and then I'll explain it all." Her eyes darted down the hall as Alexander's office door groaned open. "Just don't tell anyone else until we know more."

Todd entered the area and stuffed his hands into his coat pockets.

Molly stood. "I should go. I have a lot of suggestions for Alexander. Rochelle, I look forward to serving on the council with you."

Todd watched her disappear into Alexander's office, then turned back to me, eyebrows raised in a question. "Hey, Rochelle. How was your trip with Kinley?" He sat down next to me as if his conflict with Keppler had never happened, as if he hadn't stopped just short of telling Molly I was insane.

"It was good, but I'm still trying to sort out everything that happened here while I was gone." I hoped he could hear the annoyance in my voice and understood why it was there.

"Whatever Keppler tells you, I didn't hit him." He ran a hand through his hair, his gentle hazel eyes surveying my every emotion like only he could. "I know you and Max both think I'm rotten, but I had to do something before he hurt someone."

"What makes you so sure he did anything wrong?" I swung around to face him. "Alexander thinks he's okay, Kinley is letting him stay at our house, and even your sister said he's a polite kid."

"Maybe he's just a really good actor." He took a breath to stay calm. "What is it about him that makes you trust him over me?"

Todd had never been anything but patient and kind to everyone he met, so I couldn't understand his sudden issue with Keppler. "Is that what you've been discussing with Molly?"

"This has nothing to do with Molly." He glanced down the hall as if he expected to see her there, listening in on our conversation. "I'm worried about you."

"Don't be." I stood and took a step away from him. "Contrary to your beliefs, I'm not a bad judge of character, and I'm not crazy."

"I would never . . ." Todd slumped back in his chair. "I'm trying to protect you."

"Protect me from what? I'm not jumping out of a plane or swimming with sharks."

Todd recoiled from my sharp tone. "It's only been a few months since I found you so delirious you didn't know who I was or where you were." His wide eyes betrayed his stern expression with guilt and sadness. "I sat with you for days, trying to get you to swallow a few spoonfuls of broth. I was really scared, and I never want you sick or hurt again."

The last thing I remembered before waking up at Todd's house was getting Kat a glass of water and then lying down to rest for just a minute before checking on my grandma again. Then I woke up with Emma at my bedside. I had been at the Tatems' for six days, Kat's fever had broken, Grandma was gone, and Kinley was figuring out how to get home. For the weeks that followed, I was too weak to do anything without help from Todd or Emma.

"I should have come right away." He ran a hand back and forth over his hair.

Blinking hard to stop my tears, I shivered with the memory of being alone, sick, and unequipped to help Grandma and Kat, the misery of Kinley's weak voice on the phone telling me to just keep them hydrated and everything would be okay, and my own words, shaky from my illness, telling Todd I could manage even though I wanted him there to comfort me.

"I never could have forgiven myself if you got sick." Swallowing over a lump in my throat, I sank back into my chair, feeling as if the air had been knocked out of me.

Todd's expression softened as he watched a tear slide down my cheek. "I'm sorry, Shelley . . ." He pinched his eyebrows between two fingers and scrunched his face as if trying to get some other person in his head under control. "You know I would have traded places with you in a minute."

I nodded, knowing I would do the same for him even in the middle of a fight. Taking his hand, I tried to read the conflicting emotions in his eyes, sure he was holding something back. "I'm sorry I didn't call you when I got home, but Emma said you were grounded..."

Todd shook his head. "It's not your fault." For a minute, I thought he would spill everything he'd been hiding, but instead he pulled a folded square of paper from his pocket and slipped it into my hand. "It's an early birthday present." He smiled, but his eyes were sad. "Rochelle, no matter what happens, remember, I care about you."

"I care about you too." The folded square in my hand was a familiar comfort. From the time we were little kids, Todd had been a natural artist, sketching everything he saw around him, although his favorite subjects were the detailed buildings and bridges we found on old postcards and calendar pages.

I unfolded the paper to reveal a shaded drawing of a bridge, meticulously sketched with every support beam and suspension cable drawn to scale, stretched across a river with a city skyline in the background. Many others like it already adorned the walls of my room, but that didn't make it any less impressive.

"Thank you. It's your best one yet." I refolded it and slipped it into my pocket. "Todd, do you want to come over for dinner? I'm pretty sure Kat is making spaghetti and her fancy garlic bread."

"That sounds really good right now, but I can't." He glanced outside. "I have to get back to the store and help Dad close, then we have a leaky roof to fix at the Osdens'." Todd wasn't the kind of person to just sit around, so without school, football, and basketball to keep him busy, it didn't surprise me he would work as much as possible. "Maybe another day?"

"You're always invited." I stood and pressed my hands over his ears. "It'll be really cold out when we lose the sun. Make sure you wear a hat and gloves."

He smiled and for that moment, we were the kids we used to be before we knew risk and fear. It was a rare moment of calm to carry us through the turbulence yet to come.

CHAPTER 8
CHARLIE

March 23, 2090

"These people talk too much," Max whispered. He dropped his notebook and pen to his lap and shook his hand.

I had already been at the town auditorium for hours because Alexander had enlisted me to help set up folding chairs on the basketball court before the forum began. By the time we finished, Rochelle and Kat arrived, and we helped Rochelle practice presenting her ideas on stage until the other candidates got there.

"Here." I held out my hands. "I'll take over." Even before the forum started, Max had been complaining about having to take notes for his aunt's newspaper.

"You can barely see." He turned to me, eyebrows raised. "Every time you read something, you hold it an inch away from your face."

"I won't be reading, just writing." My vision had always been a little blurry, but I'd survived sixteen years that way, so it didn't seem like the big deal Max made of it.

"Whatever you say." He practically tossed his notebook and pen at me.

The first half hour of the forum had been pretty boring with Alexander asking questions while Rochelle, Molly, Todd, and the other three kids on stage gave unimaginative answers. Thanks to Max's running commentary, I knew all about Kiara Fernandez, the most organized person in their class; Trevor Herbolshimer, his teammate in football and basketball; and Neil Olsten, the class clown.

I squirmed a little, thanks to both the hard folding chair and the room packed with strangers. Other than Kat, Emma, and Max, I didn't know a single person seated in the chairs around me.

Alexander, with one elbow on the podium, picked up a note card from the pile he had been drawing from. "You're all old enough to remember a time before the fever and economic disaster, when we lived in a united country. Now, many cities are governing themselves as if they are their own country. Should we, here in Maibe, proceed as our own little island or try to connect with a larger network of government in the state?"

"We should definitely proceed on our own." Molly looked out at the audience, confident and professional in her navy-blue dress. "The last thing we need are strangers and outsiders deciding what we can and can't do in our own town."

Rochelle leaned toward the nearest microphone, smoothing back her frizzy hair. "I respect your opinion, Molly, but I think working with nearby towns would make us stronger, and I don't believe we would lose control over our own community."

"I love your optimism, Rochelle, but we can't make decisions based on hope." Molly nudged Todd with her elbow. "We need certainty."

Everyone on the stage turned to Rochelle. She looked out at the crowd, and I wondered if she could see us. "Well, no one up here can guarantee anything—"

"That's not true." Todd cleared his throat. "As long as we choose to govern ourselves, we know that we're in control of our own future."

"And we'll know that we don't have any dangerous outsiders coming to town." Trevor shuffled his notecards absentmindedly.

"I've read that sometimes when towns join forces, they choose one location to send all of the criminals."

I pretended to focus on writing out the forum transcript that looked like a play in Max's notebook, avoiding the eyes I felt on me.

Kat's hand rested on my arm for a second, and she glared at a boy down the row from us until he looked away.

"It's a little premature to jump to conclusions that bringing back a state government would result in Maibe becoming some kind of prison town." Rochelle sounded so calm and confident despite a lack of support from fellow candidates. If Todd was really such a good friend, why would he shoot down her argument?

"We have to be prepared for all of the possibilities." Kiara played with the bracelet on her arm. "Right now, we're relatively safe."

Rochelle shook her head. "We can't isolate ourselves and never let anyone new into Maibe. What happens when we all get old? What kind of future does Maibe have then?"

"A great one, Rochelle." Molly ran a hand over her blond hair pulled back in a tight bun. "Some of us are eventually going to have children, and we'll pass our leadership roles down to the next generation—"

"Perfect," Neil interrupted. He leaned back in his chair, but his voice was loud enough that he didn't need a microphone. "Then we'll all be related. One big, happy family." Pockets of laughter rose amongst the audience. "I'm with Rochelle. We shouldn't have to figure everything out on our own. We could share that responsibility and enjoy our lives a little."

Obnoxious applause rose from one corner of the bleachers. Neil stood and took a bow for the friends who found him entertaining.

"Safety and security should be our number one concern."

Molly's voice sliced through the commotion and the room quieted. "We've all been through enough trauma without putting ourselves at risk for another unforeseen threat."

Rochelle pressed her hands flat against the table as if she might stand up, but she remained seated. "We're not safe right now. We barely have the things we need to live comfortably. Our hospital doesn't have enough medicine or supplies, and it's understaffed. But there are medical students, many of them from surrounding communities, training there right now. That's the kind of collaborative solution we need."

Kiara laughed. "Did your cousin ask you to pitch an advertisement for her program? Is she going to save us all?"

"We have the only hospital in a hundred-mile radius." Rochelle ignored the comment. "We can't turn people away. Think of all the good we can do. If we could get businesses back up and running, people would come here to shop and eat. Our town would be alive again and even better than before."

"It's a huge risk," Todd protested. He was definitely opposing her on purpose.

"It's a huge opportunity," Rochelle shot back.

Neil rolled up the sleeves of his plaid shirt. "Don't worry, Todd, reopening the bakery and the flower shop won't take business away from your hardware store."

More obnoxious laughter. Alexander's eyes pinned Neil to his seat so he didn't dare take a second bow.

"I think we've heard enough on that." Alexander shuffled through his notecards. "This is a time of immense fear. The fever persists in our country, and an estimated two-thirds of the adult population has been lost. In neighboring states, The Defiance is becoming a radical political group that is pushing some regions to the brink of war. What is your primary concern at this time and what is your solution to combat it?"

Kiara leaned in toward her microphone. "We've already dealt with the fever, and The Defiance is far away. Our most immediate problems are hunger in our own community and children without families."

"And that's exactly why The Defiance is gaining ground." Rochelle looked up as if she'd just recognized her own voice speaking. "They're targeting children who have nowhere to go, no education, no family . . ."

"So they're filling the void that Kiara just identified in our society." Molly glanced at her fellow candidates. "Maybe we could take some pointers."

A low hum of discussion erupted in the crowd. Everyone at the table remained silent.

"How can she say that? The Defiance isn't a substitute for family." Max and Kat turned to me, surprised by the anger in my voice. "I mean, I've heard they brainwash kids and stuff."

Kat nodded and leaned toward me. "She'll say anything to get attention. No one will take her seriously."

Trying to extinguish the anger burning in my chest, I lifted the notebook closer to my face to read where I left off with my transcript.

Alexander held a hand over his microphone and said something to Molly before he looked at Rochelle as if begging her to change the subject.

Smiling, she took a breath and leaned toward her microphone. "It's great that we have an elementary school, but it's not enough. We need a middle and high school. My cousin and Todd's sister would never stand for us," Rochelle swept her arm toward Todd and back to herself, "not getting a complete education, but not everyone in this community is that lucky."

"Writing papers and solving math problems makes you lucky?" Neil shook his head dramatically. "I don't know about the rest of you, but I don't have time for school. Helping my family keep our farm running is a full-time job for me."

"Same here," Trevor added. "We need more workers in this town, not students."

Rochelle took a deep breath and retained her smile. "We need educated workers and future leaders. The only way we can achieve that is with a complete education system."

"Where is that funding going to come from?" Todd's voice sliced through the thick air. "We can barely keep the elementary school going. My little sister is a sixth grader, and she's always talking about leaky sinks and books missing pages and the places they have to put buckets when it rains." His words sounded rehearsed.

"That's something that should have been addressed a long time ago." Rochelle's voice came out flat and for the first time, she appeared to share my annoyance with Todd. "What kind of leaders are we if we can't even keep a school roof from leaking?"

"I'm for keeping up infrastructure." Neil leaned back in his chair with his hands behind his head. "No use letting everything fall apart just to rebuild it again. Todd, don't you shingle houses with your dad?"

Everyone on stage turned to Todd. Alexander leaned forward against the podium with one hand on the back of his neck.

"So I'm supposed to single handedly keep up every building in town?" Todd forced a laugh, but he stared down at the back of his hands. "I can't even find time to keep my own house from leaking."

"Todd, what are you doing?" Emma covered her face with her hands, but I could still see her cheeks turning pink as Kat whispered something to her.

"Does anyone else out there know anything about roofing?" Neil pointed into the crowd on the basketball court. "How about you?"

"All right," Alexander interrupted. "I promised to get everyone home in time for dinner, so we'll wrap this up. Let's hear a brief sentence or two summarizing your priority for Maibe." He took a breath and closed his eyes. "Go ahead, Molly."

She smiled and seemed to look right at me. "I promise to protect Maibe from dangerous outsiders."

I continued my writing, hoping to avoid another round of unwanted attention and braced myself for Todd's comment.

He looked at Rochelle and then back to Molly as if he had forgotten what he wanted to say. "I'll make sure we don't take any unnecessary risks." From what I could tell, it didn't have any obvious connection to me, but Rochelle turned away from Todd and shook her head.

Kiara said something about revitalizing the town, Trevor wanted to look into funding, and Neil just wanted to keep up the infrastructure already in place.

Rochelle smoothed the sleeve of her green dress. "I'll find a way to reopen a middle school and high school for the future generations of Maibe."

Alexander nodded and let his notecards fall to the podium. "Thank you everyone for attending our town council forum. I'm sure it's one we'll remember." He gave the details about the upcoming voting and everyone applauded as I finished up Max's notes.

"These are really detailed notes, *hermano*." He flipped through the pages before closing the notebook. "My *tia* should hire you as a reporter or something."

"She'd have to fire you first."

"That was interesting." Emma stood and looked around a little nervously. "Maybe I should have helped Alexander plan a little better . . ."

Kat shrugged. "He's the one who recruited a bunch of high school kids."

Max patted my shoulder. "Let's go congratulate Rochelle and Alexander." He pushed me past Kat and Emma. "We'll get Todd and Rochelle and meet you guys around front."

We squeezed through the crowd on the basketball court and pushed through a door that led us to a side stage area. Max jogged up the steps where Alexander, Neil, and Trevor still talked behind the closed curtain. I was about to follow him when I felt a cool breeze from a partially opened door to my right and heard the murmur of arguing outside.

"Well, now you have it. My full attention." Rochelle's voice carried on the wind. "What is going on with you, Todd?"

I pushed the door open slowly and stepped outside. Todd and Rochelle stood a few feet away, so wrapped up in their argument they didn't notice me.

Todd ran his hand back and forth over his hair. "Are you upset because I disagreed with you or because I agreed with Molly?"

"I'm upset because the Todd I know would never say any of those things. You didn't even believe any of that stuff."

Todd shook his head, face growing red. "What do you want me to say?"

Rochelle took a step back. "I want to know why you're acting weird and what you're not telling me."

He stepped toward her, and for a second I was watching my dad, face red, clutching mom's arm too tight. If I didn't get in the way he would hit her.

"What are *you* doing here?" He turned before I even realized I yelled.

"Just looking for Aumont." I took a few steps toward them. "Kat's ready to go home."

"I'll bet Kat sent you." Todd's voice dripped with annoyance. "Her name's Rochelle, by the way."

Rochelle put out her arm, catching Todd across his chest, so he couldn't get any closer to me. "That's enough."

My fists clenched, but I made myself remember the cake Kat had made for me. For the first time in sixteen years, my birthday had been celebrated. If I gave in to my temper, Rochelle and the others would give up on me. Like Isabelle did.

I took a breath and shook my head. "You're not worth it."

"Unbelievable . . ." He stepped around Rochelle and shoved me. "What's your problem, anyway?"

I stumbled back but kept my arms at my sides. "I'm not looking for a fight." In the background, I heard Rochelle yelling, but my attention was on Todd.

Todd's eyebrows slid together and he shoved me again. "Why? Are you afraid I'll beat you up again?"

It's not a real fight when one guy has pneumonia. "The opposite, actually."

He lunged, fist slamming into my jaw. My logical thinking switched off and survival instincts kicked in. Twisting out of his grasp, I started swinging, ignoring the shouting around us even as we toppled to the ground.

Two hands gripped my arms and pulled me to my feet. "That's enough." Alexander held me in place, pinning my arms behind my back. Todd stood in front of me, Rochelle and Max each holding one of his arms. Trying to catch my breath, I surveyed Todd's bloodied face, already swelling eye, and Rochelle's wide eyes. For a moment, I thought they were Isabelle's—disappointed and withdrawn.

I had thrown away the last chance I would ever get.

CHAPTER 9
CHARLIE

March 23, 2090

harlie, that temper. I couldn't get my mom's voice out of my head. *Just like your dad's.*

I stared at my reflection in the bathroom mirror, just as I had done the first night I'd arrived in Maibe. It had been as clear then as it was now: I didn't deserve a family. The hands that had a mind of their own had betrayed me, and they shook now as they had when I was eleven and read my sister's last words to me.

Dear Charlie,

Grandpa and Grandma want me and Mom to come live with them. She said we can't take you along because you get in too many fights and have a bad temper. She said you'll grow up to be just like Dad, and Grandpa and Grandma never liked him. I'm sorry I have to leave you here, and I'll miss you.

Love, Isabelle

I didn't even know I had grandparents or where they lived. If my own mom thought I was rotten, how could people I barely knew ever forgive me? Alexander had yelled at Todd and me as he drove us from the auditorium to the Aumonts, but four blocks into the eight-block trip, he had started talking to himself about how we were just kids. When she got home, Kinley showed me how to pinch the bridge of my nose to stop the bleeding, then told me to get cleaned up.

Knowing I couldn't hide in the bathroom forever, I splashed water on my face. My nose had stopped bleeding ten minutes earlier, and that was my only injury. I had never walked away from a fight without so much as a bruise, but there was a first time for everything.

I slicked my hair back, trying to look as presentable as possible and less like my dad. No matter what Alexander told Kinley, she would never believe the fight wasn't my fault. Even I didn't believe it wasn't my fault. Living at the Aumonts had been my only chance for a good life, and I had tossed it in the trash. Who wanted a violent teenager living in their house? Wanting to kick myself, I dried my face and walked into the kitchen.

"What kind of mayor are you anyway? I tell you it's a ridiculous idea to let sixteen-year-olds run for town council, so you plot with my cousin and help her run behind my back?" Kinley's voice shouted from the dining room where Emma and Alexander were trying to explain what had happened.

"Keppler, are you okay?" Rochelle sat at the table next to Todd, but I tried not to look at the bruising on his face becoming more obvious by the minute. "You're kind of pale. Maybe you should sit down."

"I'm fine." It had taken far too long to get my breathing under control. Kinley initially thought I was having some kind of relapse into pneumonia until Emma suggested a panic attack. Emma diagnosed it right. "Are they still . . ."

"I signed the guardianship papers too." Alexander argued far more calmly than Kinley. "I get a say in the kid's life."

"I don't care if you signed the Declaration of Independence," Kinley shouted back. "You're irresponsible and you shouldn't be raising any kids."

Kat tipped her head back to look up at me from where she sat across from Todd and Rochelle. "They're fighting over you like a divorced couple, so you have a fifty percent chance of living with one or the other."

"Keppler isn't going anywhere." Rochelle dabbed a washcloth against the scrapes on Todd's face. "None of this is his fault."

Todd flinched and leaned back in his chair. "Ouch."

"That'll teach you to start fights." Kat folded her arms across her chest.

I sank into the chair next to her, looking down at my hands, trying to ignore the catch in my chest from the argument in the other room.

"It'll be okay, Keppler." Rochelle dropped her washcloth to the table. "Todd is going to explain exactly what happened. Right?"

"Of course." Todd took her hand and she didn't pull it away. "Shelley, I'm sorry . . ."

"I'm sorry I didn't tell you. That was a mistake." Alexander managed to keep his voice calm even while being yelled at. "But Rochelle deserved a chance."

Rochelle shook her head slowly. "And now they're back to me."

"I told you it was a bad idea to hide something from Kinley when the rest of the town knew about it." Kat leaned forward so she didn't have to raise her voice. "If you would have just listened to me then you wouldn't be in trouble and these two wouldn't have gotten into a fight, and—"

"Kat, give her a break." A pained expression spread over Todd's face as he watched Rochelle's chin sink toward her chest. "She's the only qualified candidate running for the council."

"She's just a kid. What does she know about running a town?" Kinley still sounded upset but her voice was quieter.

"What do I know about being a mayor? What did you know

about being a doctor before you went off to school at sixteen? Sometimes we have to learn from experience."

"My mom was a doctor and my dad was a veterinarian. I spent a year studying to get into that school. I didn't just walk in blind or I would have been humiliated."

"Rochelle was very professional at the forum." Emma's voice projected a much-needed calm. "You would have been proud of her."

"Maybe under different circumstances." Kinley's volume rose with each word. "Like if this traitor here didn't help her lie to me."

"Have you ever considered . . ." Alexander paused long enough that I thought he wouldn't finish the sentence. "You're not always right about everything."

"Get out, Alexander." I imagined Kinley standing in the next room with her hands on her hips, bony elbows pointing out at sharp angles. "I don't need you here to undermine my authority."

"Fine." Footsteps approached and Alexander didn't look at us as he passed through the kitchen. At the door he paused but didn't turn around. "I'll call Emma later and find out what you've decided about our kid."

"Kinley, don't be mad at Alexander." Rochelle stood to face her cousin in the doorway as the door slammed. "He was trying to help me. I just thought . . ."

"No, you weren't thinking. You couldn't have possibly been thinking." Kinley approached her cousin. "When I tell you you're not allowed to do something, that does not mean to sneak behind my back and do it anyway. I expected better from you, and I have never been so disappointed in my life."

"Kinley, don't be so hard on her." Emma looked like she wanted to step between them, but she didn't move.

"You can decide Todd's consequences. The rest are my responsibility." She turned back to Rochelle, and for a second I thought they would both cry, but Kinley's anger won. "I can't believe you would humiliate me by participating in that forum. Go to your room and stay there."

Rochelle took a step back like someone had punched her in the stomach, but she didn't argue and she didn't fight back. Instead, she locked eyes with Todd for a second, then turned and left the room.

"Come on, let's just catch our breath." Emma took Kinley's arm and walked her to the chair next to Todd. "Sit down here and we can sort this all out, calmly."

Todd, who had been watching the empty doorway Rochelle disappeared through, snapped to attention when Kinley sat down. "Please don't be mad at Rochelle. She's just trying to be more like you, so you'll be proud of her."

"She sure has a questionable way of showing it." Kinley rubbed her forehead and cringed when she got a good look at his face. "Wow, Todd, you're a mess."

He looked up at his sister standing next to Kinley, then down at his hands on the table. "Don't blame Charlie. I started the fight."

Kinley turned to me with eyebrows raised. "This isn't one of those situations when you can say, *you should see the other guy,* I suppose."

Every fight I'd been in had either been fair or tipped in the other guy's favor. Pounding Todd out of anger was just as bad as my dad smacking around a kid who wasn't equipped to defend himself. I couldn't find the strength to lift my head. "I messed up."

Emma's hands rested warm and comforting on my shoulders. "Kinley, they're just kids and it sounds like they've both learned their lesson."

"Charlie, look at me." Kinley's voice wasn't as cold as I expected.

Slowly, I lifted my head until I met her stern green eyes, not at all like Rochelle's hopeful, forgiving ones.

"I want to make it absolutely clear there will be no fighting." She sighed and glanced at Todd. "With each other or with anyone. Am I clear?"

We both nodded.

"Todd, I've known you your entire life and I've never even heard you raise your voice. What's going on with you?"

His head bowed forward, giving me the impression he had as much respect for Rochelle's cousin as his own sister. "It'll never happen again, Kinley. I swear."

"I'll hold you to that." She slid her hand under Todd's chin and turned his face one way then the other to examine his split lip and swollen eye. "You don't need stitches, but you should ice that eye in fifteen-minute increments for the next day."

"We'll do that the minute we get home." Emma's voice was so calm and reassuring I wished she had signed my guardianship paper. "Come on, Todd."

He stood and extended his hand to me. "I'm sorry about everything I've said in the past few weeks and especially tonight. I know you were only looking out for Rochelle, and I respect that."

I shook his hand. "I'm sorry too." It was impossible to hate him when he was the one with the black eye and still apologizing to me.

"Can I talk to Rochelle for one minute?" He was just short of begging Kinley's permission. "She was really upset and—"

"Nope." Emma wrapped an arm around her brother before Kinley had a chance to answer. "You're grounded, and that means we're going straight home. No talking to Rochelle." She guided him to the door and waved to us with her free hand. "We'll let Dad decide how long."

"Do we have to tell him?"

"I think he'll notice—" The door slammed, cutting off the rest of Emma's sentence.

Kinley shook her head and looked at me. I waited, holding my breath, for her to pronounce her decision about my future.

"Charlie, I know it's going to take some time for you to adjust to living here, but we're going to figure it out." She sighed and rubbed her face. "For now, you're grounded, which means you're not leaving this house until I change my mind. Am I clear?"

"Absolutely." The weight on my chest evaporated as I realized she wasn't throwing me out but locking me up *in* the house. I wouldn't be spending that night, or any night, in a cold alley. Was it really that easy? "I'll stay out of trouble from now on."

"Good. And, Kat, if you lie for your sister again, there will be consequences." Kinley stood and zipped the coat she hadn't bothered to remove. "Now, I have to get back to work. When I get home, I expect the kitchen to be clean and both of you in your rooms."

"You're leaving?" Kat stood. "What about Rochelle?"

"I'll deal with her when I get home. After she's had plenty of time to think about her questionable decisions." Kinley stuffed her hands in her pockets. "Don't look at me like that. It's my responsibility to take care of you guys, but I also have my studies and my responsibilities at the hospital." She pulled Kat toward her and kissed the top of her head. "I'll be home by ten thirty."

Kat walked over to the sink and watched through the window as Kinley walked away. I stared down at my hands, feeling uncertain about my future. Did I deserve the forgiveness I'd been offered? How many times had people forgiven my dad before they couldn't anymore?

"We're better off without her anyway." Kat walked over to the table and slumped into the chair next to me. "What's wrong?"

"I just want to get this right." My breath caught in my chest. "I've never had people really give me a second chance."

"It was just one misunderstanding, Charlie." Kat's blue eyes studied me with an intensity that made me worry she could read my thoughts. "Kinley's mad at all of us, but she'll get over it."

"She shouldn't have to. Not with me." I leaned back in my chair and pretended to study the painting of *The Last Supper* hanging on the wall so I could avoid Kat's eyes. "I'm going to get a job or three and do all of that homework she gave me so I don't even have a spare minute to get in trouble."

Kat leaned forward and hugged me so quickly I didn't even have time to protest. "It would be the end of the world if Kinley didn't fulfill all of her responsibilities, so rest assured she'll never throw you out."

The last person who hugged me had been my sister, almost five years ago. Rochelle had tried a few times, but I always squirmed away. My brain associated any human touch with a punch to the stomach or a back hand to the face, and I wasn't ready to let my guard down. But this quick hug felt . . . comforting.

"Do you think Rochelle is okay?" I felt responsible for Kinley finding out about the forum, and I didn't like the way she just sent Rochelle upstairs.

"I'll check on her in a little while. Right now all I want to say is *I told you so*, and that's not what she needs to hear." Kat stood and pushed in her chair. "Are you hungry?"

It was already eight o'clock and we hadn't eaten since lunch. I should have been starving, but I really just wanted to stop thinking about everything that had happened. "I'm not sure."

Kat smiled and reached for her favorite binder of recipes on the counter. "Do you want to learn how to make homemade macaroni and cheese? I'll teach you."

It was an invitation I couldn't refuse. Kat rarely approved of Kinley or Rochelle cooking in her kitchen, and in the weeks I had been there, I had never heard her request their assistance.

"Okay. What can I do?"

I felt as if I had passed my first test. My new family hadn't even come close to giving up on me after I made a huge mistake. Living in Maibe truly was the second chance I had been waiting for.

CHAPTER 10
ROCHELLE

March 23, 2090

A soft knocking bounced around inside of my head. I opened my eyes to my bedroom light still on and a blanket covering me. When I had curled up on my bed, overwhelmed and alone after Kinley's judgment, I wasn't thinking about blankets, so someone had been in my room. Rubbing my eyes, still blurry from falling asleep crying, I noticed a folded piece of paper in front of my face. I sat up and opened it.

> *Don't worry about us. Charlie is just grounded, and Kinley ignored me like usual. We still think you were the best candidate at the forum. If you're hungry, there are cookies in your sock drawer.*
>
> *Love you. Kat.*

The same soft knocking that had woken me up came from my double window that overlooked the front yard. Sliding the note under my pillow, I slid off my bed, crossed the room, and pushed the curtain aside. Todd, face a little contorted from his injuries, waved at me from the other side of the glass.

The big oak tree in front of my house had perfectly spaced branches to get us up to the roof of the porch right outside my second story bedroom window. It wasn't the safest or easiest climb, so we reserved it for emergency situations.

I unlatched the window and slid it open. "What are you doing?"

"We never got to finish our conversation." Thunder rumbled in the distance.

"You mean our argument." A streak of lightning exploded across the western horizon. "It couldn't wait until morning?"

Todd sighed. "We're both grounded. If I didn't come while everyone was asleep, I wouldn't see you until Saturday and then we would be at lessons and . . ." Thunder overpowered Todd's words. "I think it might rain."

I reached my hand through the open window. "Get in here before you get struck by lightning. I can't handle this day getting any worse."

"And it would be worse if I died?" Todd took my hand and climbed over the windowsill. "That's a good sign." He shrugged his shoulder and let the bag slung over it drop to the floor.

Slowly, I slid the window shut so it wouldn't slam and alert Kinley, who was probably still up studying. Fortunately, my room shared a wall with the stairwell on one side and the empty room that once belonged to my dad on the other. Kat's room was across the hall from mine and Kinley's next to hers at the top of the stairs, so as long as we spoke quietly, they'd never hear.

"Emma wouldn't let me talk to you before we left." He looked at me closely, and I rubbed my puffy eyes. "I knew you were upset."

"Really?" I laughed so I wouldn't cry. "What led you to that conclusion?"

"You're still wearing your dress and you hate dresses." He swallowed hard and ran a hand back and forth over his hair. "You would have changed by now except you were crying and . . . fell asleep—"

"Great detective work," I interrupted, struggling to keep my voice under control. "So it's okay for you to point out when I'm not acting like myself, but when I do that to you it blows up into a fight. It's so awful for me to go out in the cold or talk to strangers or run for the council, but you can climb trees in the lightning and get yourself beaten up beyond recognition."

"Rochelle . . . I'm sorry." He studied the carpet as if it were a priceless painting. "Were you crying because of what I said or what Kinley said?"

"Both . . . neither . . ." I sank to the edge of my bed, wishing I had changed out of the dress that failed to warm my legs from the knees down. "I just miss my dad, I miss my grandma, I miss the life I had before I got sick and everyone started treating me like I'm five years old." As much as I didn't want to cry, a few tears escaped, tickling my cheek on the way down. "All I want is to pick up whatever pieces are left of my life and move forward, but no one will let me."

"Rochelle, I get it, but—"

"No, you don't." I couldn't stop until I had finally said everything I'd been holding in since December. "I know I was really sick, the world is scary, bad things happen, and everyone's worried about me, but I can't just hide in my room. I have to do something with my life or I might as well have just died."

"Don't say that." Todd's voice was soft as he sat down and wrapped his arms around me. "We can fix this. What can I do?"

"Promise you'll leave the worrying to Kinley and we'll just live." I rested my forehead against his shoulder so I wouldn't see his eye and imagine how much it hurt. "Like when we were kids and you had no problem with me climbing under that fence to rescue your frisbee from Mr. Grosen's lawn even though everyone said there were landmines, or when we thought it was exciting to go shoe skating on the pond even though Emma said the ice was thin."

Todd smiled. "There were no landmines, and the water would have only been chest-deep if we fell through."

"We didn't know that back then." I sat up and wiped away a stubborn tear.

"We didn't know one of us could die either . . . I didn't know I could lose you, at least not until we got old, and then I figured I'd die first anyway." Thunder rattled the windowpane and the first round of raindrops splattered the glass.

"You didn't lose me." The sinking sadness on my friend's face made my chest ache. "We're here, together."

"That's not what I mean." He scratched the area above a scrape on his cheek. "It's impossible to imagine anyone meeting you and not falling in love with you . . . so what happens to our friendship if you fall in love with one of them?"

What happens to our friendship if we fall in love with each other? That was the real problem in the room, but the only time we came close to talking about that was September when Todd asked me to the homecoming dance that was cancelled in October. "Keppler isn't in love with me. We don't even call each other by our first names."

Todd's expression collapsed into that mixture of guilt and sadness that made me sure he was keeping something from me, but instead of explaining, he picked up his bag from the floor. "You didn't eat anything, right? I brought your favorite." He unzipped his bag and pulled out something wrapped in tin foil and a thermos.

"Tomato soup and grilled cheese?" I smiled. "Weren't you afraid your dad or Emma would catch you cooking in the middle of the night?"

"I was careful, but Lily caught me anyway. I promised that if she didn't tell, I'd buy her the velvet material she wants for the dress she's designing." He held one tin foil package out to me. "She'll probably be talking to you about making it."

I hadn't eaten since lunch and I was starting to feel hungry, so I took the sandwich. "I love Lily's dress designs."

"Why are you looking at me like that?" Todd poured some of the tomato soup into the cap of his thermos.

"Because I know there's something you're not telling me, and you're stalling again."

"It's kind of a long story. We should finish eating."

Folding my legs under me, I took the cup of soup. "I can eat and listen."

He set his thermos on the nightstand and rubbed his hand back and forth over his hair. "Okay, but before I start, I wish I would have talked to you about all of this a long time ago. I know I can't protect you from the world, and trying to is only making life harder for both of us." He took a breath and I waited patiently.

"In December, my sisters and I got a letter from my mom. It said she had been thinking about us because she read about the fever hitting Maibe and she hoped we were all well. She wrote that she loved us, but her choice to leave was the best thing she could have done for all of us."

Todd's mom had left without warning when he was in second grade. We hadn't talked about her in years.

"I had so many questions. Why would she send a letter now? Does she have another family? Does she miss us? How was her decision a good one? Emma had to be our mom when she was eleven, and Lily never even remembers having a mom at all." He looked out the window, his eyes were distant.

When he didn't speak for a full minute, I prompted, "Did you write her back?"

He started, then looked at me and shook his head. "There was no return address and Emma threw it away. She said it would upset Dad, and we weren't going to let Mom disrupt our lives again." His gaze dropped to the carpet. "Last month, when Molly came into the hardware store, we just started talking for some reason. I told her the envelope was postmarked Arizona, and she said her dad had a friend who was some kind of cop or something. That she'd mention it to him and maybe he could find out more about my mom."

"Has she found anything?"

"I don't think so." Todd studied his half-eaten sandwich. "She's been manipulating me, making me believe Keppler would hurt you, that you were replacing me with him . . ." He shook his head. "She started coming up with conditions I had to meet in exchange for her help. Like running for the council and saying all of those things at the forum. She said people who talk the most get elected to office, and she wanted you and her to end up on the council." His eyebrows slid closer together and he frowned. "I'm beginning to think she was never looking for my mom at all, just using me to get to you."

"Don't read too much into it." I rolled my tinfoil into a ball between my hands. "She's been weird lately."

"Either way, I'm done working with her. I've survived the past eight years without Mom in my life, but I'm lost without you."

I put my hand over his clasped ones and for several minutes, we sat in silence, listening to the rain hammering on the roof outside. Molly had been manipulating both of us. But why?

"Todd, when I was talking to Molly, she said you implied I was crazy. That the fever did something to my head?"

"Absolutely not. Rochelle, she's making things up. I would never say anything like that."

"I believe you." My dad, in his final months, imagined people sneaking around the house and trying to hurt him when he was home alone. Hallucinating for reasons the doctors couldn't explain. "She's been saying a lot of things."

Todd pressed his hands to the top of his head. "If she's harassing you, we should tell Kinley or Alexander."

"Actually, I'm kind of worried about her." Molly had warned

me to keep her story about my dad and the pendant to myself, but she would never know if I told Todd. The last thing I wanted was to upset Kinley or Kat with old memories, but Todd could help me sort it all out. "What I'm about to tell you has to stay between us until we know more."

He nodded, brow furrowed.

As a torrent of rain slammed against my window, I recounted Molly's story about my dad and hers working on important research and how there was a little pendant that my dad should have.

"What are you going to do?" That was the Todd I knew, asking about my plans instead of making them for me.

"I want to play along." I sighed and scanned Todd's sketches hanging on the wall in front of me. "Maybe she really does know something about my dad that I don't. Or, more likely, she's reaching out to us because she needs someone to talk to."

"I don't know. I still think she has a plan. She's hiding something."

"That's why we should investigate." I jumped up and made my way to the dresser. "What do you say? We'll work together to find out if there's any truth to Molly's theories. I'll pretend I didn't tell you, and you'll pretend you don't know but you'll be working undercover while I subliminally interrogate her." Just as Kat's note promised, I found a bag of six chocolate chip cookies in the top drawer. "It'll be like something out of Sherlock Holmes."

"Why are there cookies in your dresser?" He bit into the one I offered him.

"Because Kinley considers them clutter if I leave them out in the open."

He smirked. "Do you think your dad used that kind of logic to hide a top-secret pendant?"

"He didn't really have an obvious place to store valuables like a safe or a secret room." I nibbled at my cookie, glad Kat had remembered me and a little disappointed Kinley hadn't bothered to talk to me even if it meant waking me up. "It must have gotten packed away with his stuff in the attic or maybe the garage. It could be in the pocket of a coat he never wore, or maybe he cut out the inside of a book . . ."

"Do you remember when he would take us to the park to play basketball or fly a kite, and then he would almost forget the basketball or kite?" Todd laughed. "That one time we actually forgot the baseball glove." It had become one of Dad's famous rainy-day stories, and he made up a hundred adventures for that baseball glove. It traveled across the country in the back of a truck, made it onstage for a famous singer's concert, and even went to the moon with astronauts.

"You don't think he lost the pendant? If it really exists, I mean." The more I thought about it, the more I wanted it to be real. Proving to the world my dad was a hero instead of just a beloved member of the Maibe community who died tragically young, and the excitement of investigating the mystery all appealed to my need for adventure.

"Well, he never forgot *us* at the park." He smiled. "Auggie was a good guy. He knew his priorities and he took care of what was important." Todd wrapped his arms around me and rested his cheek against the top of my head. "I'll help you solve this pendant thing, but remember, I'm grounded and you probably are too."

"Don't worry, I have everything under control." I hugged him tight. "We can pass notes at Saturday lessons."

"And after church on Sunday." He held me in front of him, eyebrows raised. "Do you still have your walkie-talkie?"

"Under my pillow. Set to channel three. I'll check in every night at eleven."

Todd grinned. "We're all set for Operation Baseball Glove."

"I like that code name." I examined his left eye, half swollen shut, and the dark bruises that looked worse by the minute. "We'll start tomorrow, but for now you'd better get home to rest." Gently, I pressed my hand to the side of his face. "Are you ready for Operation Sneak Down the Stairs? Because I'm not letting you climb down that tree in the storm."

"So you're not mad at me anymore?"

"I was never mad." How could I be when our conflict had come from each of us dealing with our losses from the past? "But from now on, let's not keep things from each other."

"Agreed." Todd leaned forward and kissed my forehead. "I've learned my lesson."

CHAPTER 11
CHARLIE

March 25, 2090

"What is the answer to number twenty-nine, Max?" Kinley asked for the second time.

Max held the paper up to his face. "Um, well, it could be a twenty-six, but on the other hand, it kind of looks like a seventy-eight."

Kinley paced from one end of the dining room to the other, carrying a math textbook. Max, Rochelle, and Todd sat in a cluster on one end of the table, going over the geometry lesson Kinley had assigned the week before. I sat at the opposite end of the table beside Kat, writing my history report.

"You can't tell the difference between a twenty-six and a seventy-eight?" Kat glanced up from her half-finished algebra assignment.

I coughed into my sleeve as I studied the photograph in my history book of eight kids my age all holding what the caption called smartphones. The history report Emma had assigned involved comparing technology use from the first half of the century to the last.

"I got Rochelle's paper," Max complained. "I've never been able to read her math scribbles."

"Here." Todd reached for the paper. "I can read her math scribbles."

Rochelle played with the pages of her textbook. "Would you guys quit saying scribbles."

Kinley shook her head. "You know this wouldn't happen if you would use one of the many pencils I bought you instead of scratching out your mistakes in pen." Their conversations had been strained in the aftermath of the forum. Although Rochelle had been on her best behavior and apologized to Kinley multiple times, Kinley remained distant.

Rochelle shrugged. "I'm trying to be confident in my abilities. A pencil screams unsure."

Max laughed. "If you were confident you wouldn't have to scribble out your answer four times."

Thunder rumbled outside and the radio in the kitchen droned on, alternating between sad music and flash flood alerts we all ignored. My first experience with being grounded had been pretty manageable. Since we'd had a relentless heavy rain since Thursday night, I didn't want to go outside anyway, and between the thunder and my cough making a comeback, I'd only gotten a few hours of sleep. All I wanted was to go to bed.

I tried to ignore Kinley's geometry lesson, however entertaining. Listening to Rochelle, Max, and Todd banter so comfortably only reminded me I was an outsider. How could I ever be part of friendships formed from the time they were little kids? Even Molly fit into it all somehow. She would probably understand their inside jokes about Max's class clown antics and stories about a lost baseball glove. It felt even more unobtainable when I realized the people I grew up with probably didn't even notice when I stopped showing up to school five years earlier. Trying not to think about it, I rubbed my blurry eyes and read the last paragraph of my report.

Only allowing Internet access to libraries and places where

it is necessary for business has not restricted freedom of speech or availability of information. Eliminating social media has prevented false information and "trolling," or anonymous harassment. People are still able to conduct accurate and reliable research at their local library or, if they are a student, in their school's computer lab. People are still able to openly express their opinions in newspapers and books. Humanity's move to use technology and the Internet as a force for good instead of a hodgepodge of distractions, scams, and misleading information has, in fact, changed the world for the better. In conclusion, no one's opinions have been suppressed, information is more reliable, and the best uses of online resources have been maintained while their negative impacts have been eliminated.

"That's definitely a fifty-six." Todd smoothed Rochelle's paper in front of him and scratched the eyebrow above his black eye. The bruising on his face was far more pronounced than it had been two days earlier, but he didn't complain about it and everyone else avoided the topic.

Kinley sighed. "The answer should be thirty-two."

Todd pointed to the paper. "Aw man. You were right the third time."

Rochelle laid her head on the table. "Geometry is so hard."

"You'll have plenty of time on your hands to study." Kinley had grounded Rochelle and me both for the next two weeks and given us plenty of extra homework and chores to fill the time.

Todd shifted back to the other paper. "You know, Kinley, I could help Rochelle study if you'd make a stipulation in our punishment. What if I only come over when you're here so you can make sure we're studying every minute?"

"Nice try. We have a test next week and you'll all have to study on your own." Kinley went on to explain the upcoming assignment, and I was thankful she had decided I wasn't ready for geometry. I was learning algebra with Kat instead.

I needed a better word than *hodgepodge*, but I was so tired I couldn't believe my writing was even coherent. Kat had already elbowed me twice so Kinley wouldn't catch me dozing. Fortunately, Emma was up next with English and her lessons involved more discussion and acting out scenes and hilarious writing prompts.

"Before we finish, can we backtrack to science?" Max closed his math book. "I was at the library reading studies on the fever, and one paper proposed that some people who never experience symptoms may be the carriers sparking the new, unpredictable outbreaks."

Kinley sighed and rubbed her forehead. "Max, I think—"

"Sorry, I should explain since Keppler wasn't here for our earlier discussions." He turned to me, eyes bright and animated. "According to my research, the fever is actually an old virus, an ancient ancestor of the flu. The first known outbreak occurred in Asia after a team of researchers returned from the Arctic. They unknowingly encountered the virus that probably thawed out of the permafrost. Eight out of the ten got really sick and infected a few hundred people before the outbreak was brought under control. A few months later there was another outbreak of about a hundred people in Texas, and it turns out one of the two researchers who never showed symptoms had traveled there. Six months later there was one more small outbreak in Europe of unknown origin."

Max glanced around the table at each of us. "And it's been hopscotching around the world ever since, more like a bunch of different epidemics than a pandemic because it only affects a dozen or so locations at once instead of spreading everywhere."

"What is your question exactly?" Kinley suddenly looked tired and a little pale.

"Well, my original hypothesis was that anyone who didn't get sick with the fever would be a lifelong carrier and if we could identify those people, we could stop the spread, but..." Max raised his eyebrows at Todd. "We all know someone didn't get sick, and he should have because he was with Rochelle most of the time she was sick. But he's been around Keppler who's never had the fever and Keppler didn't get sick..."

"I did technically get a little bit sick." Todd closed his math book. "Wait, you've been experimenting on me?"

Kat continued writing out an equation. "No, he's been experimenting on Charlie." She shook her head. "It's not okay to experiment on your friends, Max."

"I wasn't experimenting on anyone, only observing them."

"Well, Emma really didn't get sick. No symptoms." Rochelle slid her math book away.

"What about me?" Emma glided into the room with an armload of books.

Max shook his head. "You've been around Keppler, so you're not a virus carrier either."

Emma made a face at Kinley. "Well, that's a relief. Was that something to worry about?"

"No." Kinley shook her head at Max. "We're all safe now and there's no reason to dredge up bad memories."

Emma's sister, Lily, strolled in holding a notebook that she put on the table between Rochelle and Kat. "Do you think you could make this dress, Rochelle? If I could get the material for it?"

I lowered my head, trying to ignore them and finish my report, but I couldn't stifle the tickle in my throat.

"That sounds worse every time I hear it." Kinley's hand pressed against my forehead. "Does your chest hurt?"

"No." It did a little, but I didn't want to end up back at the doctor again. "It's just a scratchy throat."

"Grandma used to make chamomile tea with honey and lemon when we had coughs." Kat glanced up at Kinley. "Maybe we should try that."

"It couldn't hurt." Her hand slid from my forehead to my cheek. "You feel a little warm. I'll find the thermometer."

Kat nodded. "And he looks really tired."

"I'm fine. I've been far worse." I tipped my head sideways until Kinley's hand fell away. I didn't know how to react to so many people wanting to take my temperature, make me soup, and tuck me into bed.

"And I'm not going to let you get worse off than you already are. We'll start with some tea and see what happens." Kinley's hand rested on my head for a second before she made her way to the kitchen. "They're all yours, Emma."

"What did you guys say to her?" Emma whispered when Kinley left the room.

Todd narrowed his eyes at Max. "Fever theories again."

"Max." If Emma meant to scold him, she didn't sound very intimidating. "We've talked about this. That's a bad topic for Kinley. It brings up trauma that she hasn't dealt with."

"But I did what you said." Max raised his eyebrows. "I went to the library and I read peer-reviewed journals, but the experts don't have solutions."

"Not yet." Emma rested her hands on Max's shoulders and glanced from Rochelle to Kat. "I know it's an awful thing to experience and hard to watch people you love fighting it. But I'm sure scientists are looking for cures and treatments right now."

"They'd better hurry or I'll beat them to it." Max shook his head. "I wonder if thistles could be the answer."

Kat sighed. "Maybe if you'd put as much effort into reading

Hamlet as you do experimenting on thistles, we'd be done with the play by now."

"It's not his fault he gets distracted." Todd clapped Max's shoulder. "When it gets this late he starts daydreaming about what we're having for dinner."

Thunder roared over the house as a gust of wind seemed to come from all directions and splatter rain against every window at the same time.

Max brushed Todd's hand away. "We all know who you're daydreaming about all day." He nodded toward Rochelle.

Rochelle and Todd each hit one of Max's shoulders with their books.

"Hey." He scooted his chair back from the table. "Emma, did you see that?"

Emma smiled and shook her head. "Be nice, you're all friends, and open your books to act two, scene one."

Kat scooted closer to Rochelle to see the book they shared. She had lent me her copy.

Max leaned back in his chair and flipped through the pages of his book. "Keppler, do you want my part? I'm not feeling like Hamlet today."

"After you experimented on me?" I pulled the book closer to my face, wanting to read a big part but not wanting to volunteer. "No way."

Todd looked at Max and laughed.

Rochelle smiled. "Come on, Max, you talk a lot in real life like Hamlet. You're perfect for the part."

"Fine. At least Rochelle says it in a nice way."

"Perfect. Same parts as last time. Let's get started."

I noticed Emma watching me squint at the words on the page in front of me. She didn't say anything, but I'd had plenty of experience with teachers showing concern about my vision in elementary school. My dad, though, wouldn't have a son with glasses. Holding books a little closer to my face hadn't killed me.

Before we could even begin reading, a loud knock pounded on the back door.

"Alexander, what are you doing here?" Kinley's voice indicated she wasn't happy to see him.

"I'm not here to argue." He sounded like he had run all the way to the door. "We have a town emergency. Where is everyone?"

"The dining room, but—"

Alexander was in the room, coat dripping on the floor before Kinley could finish. "We're about to experience a five-hundred-year flood. We have to evacuate everyone from first to fourth street—"

"Wait." Max stood, grin vanishing from his face. "I live on second street. Is my family okay?"

"Nothing's flooded right now." Alexander looked grim despite the positive news. "I'm hoping it'll stay that way, but we have to prepare for the worst-case scenario."

Kinley rubbed her forehead. "And what do you want with the kids exactly?"

"I could really use help from my future leaders. I drove through more water than I should have to get into town, so Trevor and Neil won't have a chance. But Rochelle, could you call Molly and Kiara? If the three of you could go door to door in the evacuation zone..."

"I'm on it." Rochelle rushed past Kinley into the kitchen.

Alexander looked at Todd. "Your dad is already organizing a sand bagging effort, but I need as many hands as possible to finish in time."

Todd tossed his book aside. "I'm there."

"Me too." Max pulled his jacket from the back of the chair. "I just have to evacuate my family to ... to where exactly?"

"The high school. I'll give you a ride home in just a minute."

Alexander turned back to Kinley and Emma, who stood shoulder to shoulder. "A few of the ladies from church are setting up the shelter, but you two are the most organized people I know. I'd feel so much better if you were there to help."

"We're on our way." Emma wrapped one arm around her little sister at her side and glanced at Kat still sitting next to me. "I think we should get a bunch of hot chocolate going and round up some snacks."

Kat jumped up, gripping my shoulder to keep her balance. "I have a bunch of cookies in the freezer."

There was a moment of chaos and excited talking as everyone rushed around to find coats, shoes, and keys. I remained at the table, looking at the homework spread out in front of me, part of me wanting to crawl into bed and sleep through the disaster, but the other part determined to help the community that I wanted to be a part of.

"Keppler, you want to come with us?" Todd slid into the chair beside me. "We can fill sandbags as a team." It wasn't a challenge but an invitation.

I nodded, surprised he wanted anything to do with me, but grateful to be included. "Sure, I'm in." Standing, I coughed into my elbow before turning to face Kinley.

She shook her head and I thought she would tell me I couldn't go. "I want you dressed warm. Wear a sweatshirt under your coat and keep your hood up. If that cough gets worse, I want you inside immediately. Okay?"

"Okay." I side-shuffled past her and walked to the library to retrieve a hoodie from a basket of newly folded laundry.

"Alexander, I know this is an emergency, but if you're going to take these kids out there, you have to promise me they'll be safe." Kinley's voice shook as I pulled the hoodie, still warm from the dryer, over my head.

"Kinley." He reached out like he would take her hand but changed his mind. "You know I love them too." In the time I'd lived with the Aumonts, Kinley had never actually said she loved either of her cousins. I had no doubts that she did, but I'd never heard her verbalize it.

I watched sheets of rain blowing against the bay window as Todd put on his shoes. I wasn't looking forward to going out there, but I felt a need to prove to the others I could be a part of their group. To prove to the town I wasn't some delinquent looking for trouble. And, most of all, to prove to myself I was completely different from people like my dad and Griff. If I could walk out into the cold rain when I really wanted to be in my warm bed, I couldn't possibly be capable of the same selfish cruelty as they were.

CHAPTER 12

ROCHELLE

March 25, 2090

Cold rain pelted my face as I held two little hands and ran from the front porch of the Garzanias' house to the car parked on the half-flooded street. Moving one hand to clutch my coat, I opened the car door and lifted the two little girls inside. I knew them as the kids who sat in the pew in front of me at church every Sunday morning since November. They had lost their parents to the fever and had come to live with their aunt and cousin, Lucy, a classmate of Kinley's. And after that loss and being uprooted, they were facing the terrible possibility of having nothing to return to but a flooded house.

Thunder crashed overhead and the little girls huddled together in the back seat.

"It's okay." I ducked into the car and sat with one foot inside and one still on the curb. "The storm won't last much longer, and when we get to the high school you can have cookies and hot chocolate."

"What if the flood washes us away?" The older girl hugged her little sister and watched a waterfall flow down the windshield. I wasn't sure how fast the water would come up. I knew the tsunami wave I kept picturing wasn't accurate, but I couldn't get it out of my head.

"You'll be safe. I promise." What else could I say? How could I save my town if the rain wouldn't stop?

Loud voices and yelling came from the house as the rest of the family—two little boys, Lucy, and her mom—ran through the rain carrying sleeping bags and duffel bags. I got out of the car and helped them load everything in the trunk. After three hours of going door to door and helping families evacuate, I was soaked through, but I knew what needed to be done to move people as fast as possible to safety.

"Thank you, Rochelle." Lucy closed the door to the back seat and hugged me. "I was so impressed with what you said at the forum, by the way. You have my vote."

"I appreciate that." I wasn't sure how to explain that I'd have to suspend my campaign due to being grounded. "Kinley and Emma are at the school with refreshments and snacks and probably other good things I don't know about."

Lucy smiled and got in the car. "Stay safe and get inside soon."

I waved as the car pulled away, leaving me alone in the rain. A torrent of water ran down the abandoned street as if looking for a place to send a second creek cascading through town. The houses, so far, had remained untouched.

"Rochelle. Hey." Molly shouted over the storm as she approached. "Are you done?"

"The whole street's clear." I held a hand to my head so the wind wouldn't sweep my hood off again, not that my hair wasn't soaked anyway.

"Kiara and I finished too. She went home to change. I'm on my way down to check on things at the shelter." Even dressed in a bulky raincoat and knee-high boots, Molly looked fashionable and composed. "Rochelle, are you all right?"

I looked at the row of houses, dark and frozen in time, awaiting disaster. "It's just so awful. How many disasters can we have in a year? What are all of these people going to do when..." Looking in the direction of the creek, I shivered.

"It's a good thing we live on high ground." She adjusted her hood. "That gives us the advantage to swoop in and save the day. Perfect timing before the election."

"That's not what I meant."

"I know. I know." Molly linked her arm through mine and propelled me away from the potential destruction zone. "While we have a minute . . ." She looked up and down the street, but no one else braved the wind-driven rain. "Have you found it yet? The pendant?"

"Uh, so far it hasn't turned up." I hadn't even started to search. I needed to, though, if I wanted to learn what she knew. "But I have a lot of stuff to sort through."

"Oh." She took a deep breath, and when she spoke again, the disappointment was replaced by cheeriness. "I'll give you a break this one time, since you've had a lot to deal with. I saw Todd's face. Him and Charlie really got into it, I guess?"

"Molly." I stopped, forgetting how much I wanted to get inside. "Don't give Todd a hard time about that letter from his mom. It's all tough enough for him already."

"He told you about that?" Her shoulders slumped. "I thought he wanted to take care of that one without you."

"It's not that he doesn't appreciate your help. We're just used to telling each other everything."

"You didn't tell him about the pendant?" Her eyes flashed with panic.

I shook my head, hoping she wouldn't see through my lie. "Of course not. You told me not to tell anyone."

"Good." Molly finally took a breath. "I'm trusting you with this, Rochelle, and you have to believe it's important. Once we're both elected to the council, I'll explain everything."

Before I could ask any questions, familiar voices shouted my name from down the block. We both turned to Todd, Max, and

Keppler trudging toward us, holding their hoods up against the rain.

Todd trotted ahead, splashing through the water flowing down the street between us. "Are you done with the evacuations?" He stayed close to me, avoiding eye contact with Molly.

"We just finished." Molly answered before I could and made a big deal of cringing at Todd's face, his eye still black and blue, the scrapes raised and angry. "I'm going to the high school to do a little campaigning. Rochelle, you should do the same. I'll see you there." Without acknowledging the boys, she turned and started the uphill walk through the rain.

"You should see the creek, Rochelle." Max stepped up beside me. "It's up to the bottom of the bridge. It's like we have a river now."

Keppler dropped his head into his coat and coughed in a way that reminded me too much of when he was sick a few weeks earlier. I tilted my head to see his face and extended my hand toward his forehead.

He took a step back. "I'm fine, Aumont. The cold air just makes the coughing worse."

"We're on our way to the shelter so Max can check on his family and we can all warm up." Todd glanced at Keppler. "The sandbags are all full. The rest of the team is just finishing up with placing them."

Max looked over his shoulder in the direction of his house. "I hope my lab doesn't flood. Those thistles are finally starting to come around."

"Remember, Alexander said we're planning for the worst-case scenario. That means it's just as likely things won't be as bad as we're preparing for." I hoped everyone's house would still be on dry land in the morning, that the shelter would be empty by lunch, that everyone would be home after one scary night.

"His basement is already under water." Keppler looked grim, with his face bowed forward to avoid the rain.

Max shrugged. "I don't need my clothes or my bed as long as I have my lab. Although I could use some new socks. I can feel sand between my toes, and pretending I'm walking on the beach isn't cheering me up."

I wrapped an arm around my friend. "We'll make sure you have whatever you need. No matter what happens. You can even stay at my house."

Max laughed. "I'm glad I have that option in case my family ever kicks me out. But for now, I'd better stick with them and keep their spirits up. If we don't get to the shelter, they might worry I'm buried in a pile of sand or something."

Keppler and Todd fell into step beside us and we made our way in silence, heads bowed to avoid the drenching rain on our walk to the high school.

It was a relief to walk through the doors. I didn't care if I was soaked as long as I wasn't being pelted in the face by cold rain. The building was busy with families setting up sleeping bags in the gym and little kids sitting on the floor playing board games. Some sat at tables in the cafeteria enjoying a meal.

"Rochelle, there you are." Kinley's familiar voice was a warm comfort, despite our recent disagreements. "Look at you, you're soaked." She took my face in her hands and brushed my wet hair back from my forehead. "Are you okay?"

"Kinley, what if all of these people lose their homes? What happens next?" It had been the weight collecting on my shoulders, compressing my chest since I'd started the evacuation.

"We'll figure that out one day at a time." She wrapped her arms around me even though my clothes were dripping a puddle onto the floor. "That's what we do here, right? Take care of each other."

I nodded against her shoulder, enjoying the warmth of her

arms around me. "I'm really sorry I lied to you last week. I know you're just looking out for me."

"Rochelle, about that . . ." Kinley held me in front of her. "I've realized I overreacted. In the past few hours, all I've heard people talk about is how impressed they were with your professionalism at the forum. I'm sorry I ever doubted you. I just need you to know you can talk to me about anything. Okay?"

"I'll never keep anything from you ever again." I made cautious eye contact with my cousin. "Does that mean I can still run for the council?"

"If I said no, who would I vote for?" A smile spread across her face.

I threw my arms around her. "Thank you, Kinley. You're the best."

She hugged me back, but I could feel one hand trying to work a tangle out of my hair. "As soon as Alexander checks in, I'll have him drive you and Charlie home where it's warm to get dried off and get some rest."

"What about everyone here?"

"We have a lot of help right now." She looked around at the orderly scene. "But that might not be the case in the morning, so we need you to be rested and ready to help with whatever the next step is."

"Okay." I nodded. "You're right."

"Very good." Kinley kissed the top of my head. "Now go take a break." She helped me out of my sopping coat and handed it to me. "It looks like Kat's passing out hot chocolate again. I'm going to check on things in the kitchen."

I parted ways with Kinley and trudged to the table where Todd sat and talked with Kat, who held a tray of paper cups. On the other side of the room, I spotted Molly talking with a group of people. She still wore her damp clothes but appeared to have dried her hair and smiled as she spoke animatedly to those around her. Campaigning for votes, no doubt.

As I approached, Todd jumped up and pulled out a chair for me and then draped his blanket over my shoulders when I sat down.

"You look exhausted and cold." Kat slid a steaming cup in front of me. "Did Kinley tell you the good news? Everyone's been saying such nice things about you, she doesn't think you're an embarrassment to the family anymore."

I laughed, knowing I could always count on my sister to say exactly what was on her mind. "She didn't even tell me I'm a mess."

"How could she? You're beautiful." Todd leaned forward with his hands flat on the table and smiled at me.

Kat shook her head, but her eyes were bright with hope. "Do you say that to other girls or just to Rochelle?" She had been as excited as I was when Todd asked me to homecoming and equally disappointed that we never got to go, and Todd never said anything more about it.

He grinned. "It's always true about Rochelle."

"Aww, that's cute." Kat nudged my shoulder, but I ignored her and sipped my hot chocolate. "Just think, we should have had homecoming right over there in the gym . . ."

"Hey guys, guess what?" Max jogged toward us with a football in one hand as Keppler trudged behind, and I was glad he interrupted before Kat could make Todd uncomfortable. "My *tia* gave Keppler a job! He'll be delivering the paper starting Thursday and taking notes at upcoming council meetings because the ones he took at the forum were so impressive."

Keppler sank into the chair between where I sat and where Kat stood. "She actually wants me to write the meeting minutes for her to publish in the paper." I think he was excited, but he was so exhausted his words came out a little slurred.

Kat pressed the back of her hand to his forehead. "You need to get home and go to bed or you're not going to be well enough to do any of that." She rubbed her hand on the bottom of her shirt. "And take a shower—you're covered in sand."

"Shower, bed, got it." He folded his arms on the table and laid his head on them. "That's the best plan I've heard all day."

I patted Keppler's damp shoulder. "Good news. We're going home as soon as Alexander can give us a ride."

"Back up a little farther."

I turned, confused, to find Max poised to throw his football across the room to Todd.

Emma swooped around Max before I saw her coming and snatched the ball out of his hands. "Does that count as an interception?"

"Come on, Emma." Max reached for the football, but she stepped back and cradled it in her arms. "Rochelle's going to win the election and start the school back up. And then I'll be on the football team, so I need the practice."

"You'll have time for that when the weather cooperates." She wrapped her arm around him. "For now, you should be more concerned about changing into dry clothes."

"I don't have any dry clothes." Max put a really sad look on his face. "My room is underwater. That football is all I own now."

"It's true." Todd approached, arms at his side as if he expected Emma to scold him.

"Todd has a whole pile of clean laundry on his dresser. He'll lend you whatever you need." She used her free hand to fish keys out of her pocket and tossed them to her brother. "Get everyone home for a change of clothes and something to eat. Grab the sleeping bags from our house and get my car back here in an hour." She took a few steps away.

"What about my football?"

Emma glanced back over her shoulder. "I'll take care of it until we find you two a better place to practice."

"See you guys at home." Kat picked up her tray and followed Emma toward the kitchen.

Max slumped into my chair, so I had to scoot over to make room. "What are the chances we'll hydroplane if Todd is the one driving?" He whispered it loud enough for all of us to hear.

"What is that supposed to mean?" Todd folded his arms across his chest.

Max grinned. "The last time we rode with you, in perfect weather, you almost ran us into a pole."

Todd shook his head. "That's a huge exaggeration."

I turned to Max and laughed. "The last time I rode with you, you got stuck in a ditch. I'm pretty sure we'll make it a few blocks with Todd."

"Keppler, you want to weigh in on this?"

Keppler lifted his head and gave Max a skeptical look. "I'm just as tired now as when I pushed you out of the ditch. I really just want to go home."

Max stood and shrugged. "Let's hit the road then. What could possibly go wrong?"

Keppler shook his head and followed Max toward the door.

Todd picked up my coat and unfolded it. "Are you and Max really scared of my driving?"

I stood. "Of course not, just surprised by it." He gave me a funny look, so I explained, "You're always really cautious about everything you do. You know, if Max drives us into the ditch or I take us out on thin ice, no one is surprised, but if you take a corner too fast, it seems really reckless in comparison to everything else you do."

Todd flipped my hood onto my head. "You think I'm too cautious?"

"No." I zipped my coat. "I think you're cautious enough to keep the rest of us alive and well."

He shoved his arms into his coat. "Right now, I'm just cold."

"Drop Keppler and me off at home and I'll make something warm for all of us to eat when you and Max get there."

"Since when do you know how to cook?" We drifted toward the door.

I laughed. "Since Kat made soup and all I have to do is heat it up."

"Works for me." He smiled as we made our way toward Keppler and Max. "Did I tell you Emma is teaching me how to cook? When we're not grounded anymore, I'll make you scrambled eggs and pudding. It's a terrible combination, but that's all I know how to make besides grilled cheese and tomato soup."

"I'm in." I glanced at the gym as we passed and imagined it decorated with streamers and white lights. The dance would have been fun, but not the defining moment of my life. Everything good was still to come.

CHAPTER 13

CHARLIE

March 31, 2090

The old pickup truck in front of me was all rusted bumpers and chipped paint coated in a layer of thick dust. Clearly no one had driven it in a long time, and I suspected it didn't run. I was mesmerized. The thrill of fixing it up, making something old work like new, consumed me. For a minute, I forgot why I was in the garage in the first place.

"There's a tool bench in the garage," Kat had told me when I volunteered to work on the broken dryer. "You'll find whatever you need out there."

I was looking forward to working on something mechanical that would challenge my brain after a long week of helping people carry wet carpet and drywall out of their basements. Fortunately, the flooding hadn't destroyed any homes, and after two tense nights in the shelter, the creek receded enough for everyone to go home. Although there was cleanup to be done, we had averted the worst-case disaster.

Pulling myself away from the truck, I made my way to the tool bench in the corner, noticing but less interested in a car parked in the second stall. I flipped open an old metal toolbox and found the contents more than adequate for the job at hand.

Taking one last look at the truck, I picked up the toolbox and lugged it out of the garage, across the patio, and into the laundry room. I left it next to the dryer and walked into the kitchen where

Rochelle sat at the table, mail scattered in front of her, reading what appeared to be a letter.

"I thought you were going to study with Todd?"

"Check this out, Keppler," she said without looking up. "My Aunt Audrie hasn't had contact with my family since I was three and this is a letter from her."

"What does it say?" I leaned forward.

"Dear nieces," she read. "I hope this letter finds all of you well. I know I haven't been a part of your lives as I wish I could have been, but if you'll give me a chance I can explain, and I hope things can be different in the future. I would like nothing more than to have a real conversation with you."

Rochelle glanced up at me. "She even left a phone number where we can contact her. Why would she reach out now?"

"Are you sure that's really your aunt?" I didn't know the full story about Aunt Audrie, but I'd heard enough to understand she had abandoned her family and cut off contact with all of them about twelve years earlier. Rochelle's grandma and uncle had taken it pretty hard. Her dad held on to the hope that his little sister would come home and the family could reconcile whatever went wrong. "Don't people send letters like that to trick you into giving them money?"

"I'm not going to send anyone money." She smoothed the letter on the table in front of her. "What if it really is her?"

The screen door creaked open and then slammed shut as Kinley made her way into the kitchen wearing green scrubs and carrying her bag of books. "Hey guys, what's going on?"

"We got a letter from Aunt Audrie." Rochelle held it out to her cousin.

Kinley took it and sighed. "Yeah, we've been getting these once a month since we lost your dad. Grandma figured it was some kind of scam." She refolded the letter and dropped it in the trash. "I thought you'd be at the Tatems' by now."

Rochelle stood. "I'm on my way right now." She gathered up her geometry book and a notebook from the chair next to her, probably afraid Kinley would change her mind after finally giving in and granting her permission to visit Todd. "I'll pass that test tomorrow if I have to study all night."

"Sleep is important too." Kinley pulled Rochelle closer and kissed the side of her head. "Be home by nine." She continued into the next room, on her way upstairs to change.

"Are you sure you don't want to come?" Rochelle fished the letter out of the trash. "We can help you with your algebra too."

"I'm going to start on the dryer." What Rochelle did with her aunt's letter was none of my business, but it gave me a bad feeling. "Do you really need to keep that?"

She laughed and shifted her books to her other arm. "I just want to compare handwriting when the next one comes. I won't actually call." She slid the folded paper into her notebook. "Good luck with the dryer. I'll see you later."

Once she left, the kitchen seemed too dark and quiet. Kat had already left to volunteer at the home for children, making a special birthday meal for some of the kids. Every day since I had lived there, Kat was in the kitchen cooking by four thirty. Feeling an old loneliness creep around me, I flipped on the light switch, opened the refrigerator, and let my mind drift back to the truck in the garage. It would give me something productive to do, and if I got it started, we would all have a ride when the weather wasn't good for walking.

"I guess without Kat we'll have to fend for ourselves." The sudden sound of Kinley's voice made me jump. "Sorry. I didn't mean to scare you."

Not sure how long I'd been staring into the refrigerator, I closed it and turned. "It's okay. Hey, did you know there's a truck in the garage?"

Kinley laughed and stuffed her hands into the pocket of her sweatshirt. "And a car too, although I haven't been out there for a while."

Suddenly my method to steer the conversation felt clumsy. "I just needed tools to fix the dryer, and Kat said I'd find them out there . . ."

"You know how to fix the dryer?" She pulled a chair out and sat down, cringing at the mail Rochelle left behind.

I shrugged. "I know enough not to make it worse."

"Fair enough." She nodded at the chair across from her. "What did you want to know about the truck?"

"If it doesn't run, I could work on it so no one would have to walk in the rain anymore." I slid into the chair, bracing myself for disapproval.

"Is that something you've done before?"

"A few times. My dad was a mechanic." Any enthusiasm faded from my voice with the memory of my dad's hand on my shoulder, for once commending instead of hurting. "He wanted me to be one too."

Kinley's face scrunched into a puzzled expression. "But you didn't want to be?"

Although my plan was always to be a writer, there was nothing stopping me from becoming a mechanic too. I liked the work, but if I had something in common with my dad . . ." I didn't want to be anything like him."

"I've thought the same thing, I suppose, about going into the medical field like my parents." She looked unsure about her own words but continued. "They were good people, but they were perfectionists and because they wanted me to have a bright future, they could be really hard on me at times. They were tough to face when I didn't live up to their standards. I guess that extreme is what I don't want to emulate, not the profession."

I felt my shoulders slump. As much as I hated talking about my past, Kinley wouldn't understand without more information. And something was pushing me to open up. Maybe I trusted her.

"Dad was . . . he . . ." My fumbling for words didn't seem to bother her. "He was an alcoholic. He was neglectful at his best and abusive the rest of the time."

"I'm sorry to hear that." I couldn't read the emotion in her eyes, but I hoped she wasn't studying me for the terrible traits my mom feared would surface in me. "What about your mom?"

She didn't put it into words, but I knew she was asking if my mom was a decent parent. "Mom ignored my sister and me during her bad weeks when she was too tired and sad to get out of bed and then yelled at me about folding the towels wrong or putting the silverware in the wrong drawer on the days she was too agitated to sit still. But I don't think it was all her fault. I read some psychology books, and I think she was bipolar."

Kinley shook her head and watched me through sad eyes, but she didn't interrupt.

"My mom took my sister and left when I was eleven. They didn't say goodbye, just left a note saying they were afraid I'd turn out like my dad and . . ." What else could I say? That I'd taken a big step in that direction by joining The Defiance? No.

"You don't sound anything like him to me." She reached across the table and patted my arm. "We don't automatically turn out one way or another just because of the family we're born into."

"What about all of that nature and nurture stuff? I had both." Reading books on psychology had only stoked my fears instead of calming them as I'd hoped.

Kinley smiled so big her eyes glittered like her cousin's.

"My dad and Rochelle's dad were brothers who grew up here in the same house with the same parents, but they were complete opposites. My dad was a perfectionist, reserved, always too busy, while Uncle Auggie was carefree, made friends with everyone he met, and always had time for Rochelle, Kat, and me. My grandpa died before I was born, so I'm not sure if one of them turned out more like him than the other, but I would think if there were more truth to your theory, they would have been more alike."

"Rochelle sounds a lot like her dad though."

"In a lot of ways, absolutely." Kinley brushed a loose hair behind her ear. "But that has nothing to do with DNA and everything to do with the amount of time she spent with him. That also explains how Kat turned out so much like Grandma." She grinned. "I'm guessing you probably weren't spending much time with either of your parents."

My mind drifted back to me glancing out my bedroom window, watching my dad in the backyard fixing up the latest junky vehicle he planned to sell while I wrote. As long as he was outside, he wouldn't catch me. "No, not very much."

"Well, based on that and what I know about you from the past months, I don't think you have anything to worry about."

It was an unexpected relief to hear that Kinley didn't see any darkness in me. Earning her respect felt like passing an important test, although I knew better than to push my luck by mentioning the brand on my arm.

"As far as that truck goes, it broke down on Uncle Auggie once a week, but he refused to give it up. Even when my dad got a new car and offered my uncle his old one." She brushed her braid over her shoulder. "I'm sure it needs a lot of work. He's been gone almost a year now."

I didn't know exactly what had happened to Rochelle's dad, but I'd heard enough to understand he was gone before the fever.

"Was he in an accident?" The truck didn't appear damaged, but I hadn't looked closely.

"No, he got sick. None of the doctors, not even the specialists, ever really figured it out." Kinley rubbed her forehead. "Last February, Rochelle and Kat came home from school to find him huddled in a corner. He was talking nonsense about someone breaking into the house. He was dizzy, disoriented, couldn't even make it to the couch without their help. By the time I came home from school to visit that weekend, everything was back to normal, but the same thing happened again a few weeks later and then even more often after that." She shook her head. "The doctors couldn't find anything wrong until his liver and kidneys started failing." She suddenly looked too sad to ever smile again, too tired to even blink. "I wish he were here now. You would have liked him. He gave great advice."

"Like tomorrow will be better?" I'd heard the phrase tossed around several times by all three Aumonts.

"If you learn the lessons from today." Kinley forced a smile and stood. "We tend to cut that second part off. I suppose people find it less comforting when they realize they'll have to put the work in to get to those better days."

I smiled. It felt more comforting to believe that life was in my control as long as I made the right choices, which, in that moment, seemed easier than it had ever been since I had shelter and enough to eat. "I like it better with the second part."

"The truck is yours to work on." She took a few steps forward and rested her hand on my head for a second. "If you want to become a mechanic, don't let bad memories make your decisions. And try new things! You have plenty of time to figure out what's right for you."

I nodded and my hair flopped over my face before I quickly pushed it back.

"By the way, Emma noticed you're having trouble seeing your book, so I'm making you an appointment with the optometrist when she comes to town next month. And maybe we could look into a haircut? What do you think?"

"I'll save the money from my paper route and pay you back." I didn't have a clue what all of that would cost, but I didn't even have a dollar in my pocket.

Kinley shook her head and rested her hands on her hips. "You'd better save your money for the truck. There's a salvage yard outside of town, about a mile from Alexander's house. When you figure out what you need, ask him to take you there."

"Are you sure?"

"I'll make sure you have the things you need. You be a kid while you still can." She pulled the refrigerator open. "Now, what sounds good for dinner?"

Before I could answer, a soft knock came at the door and Alexander walked into the kitchen carrying a paper grocery bag.

"Hey guys. I brought everything we need to make a pizza." He lowered his bag to the table.

"You should have called and let me know you were coming." Kinley's hands returned to her hips. Her tone softened slightly. "You look exhausted."

Alexander sank into the chair next to me. "Between the flood and all the rest of the problems this town already had, I've slept in my office three nights this week. But I guess that's better than when I'm home and I don't sleep at all because the plants have to be ready in a few weeks if the Brewster Nursery is going to stay afloat."

Kinley sighed. "Why aren't you at home sleeping right now?"

"Because I haven't seen you all week and I heard Kat wouldn't be home, so I was worried you'd skip dinner."

"Fine." She didn't sound as annoyed as I expected. "We'll make some pizza and then you're going to lie down and rest. It isn't good for you to lose that much sleep."

Alexander and I exchanged a look because we both knew Kinley never took her own advice, but neither one of us wanted to spark a fight when she was in a good mood.

"Perfect." He clapped my shoulder with one hand. "Charlie, decide what toppings we're putting on the pizza. Everything I bought isn't going to fit."

"You have pepperoni, right?" I stood and started digging through the bag as Kinley and Alexander laughed.

"Pepperoni it is." Kinley put one hand on my shoulder and one on Alexander's. "But we definitely need some vegetables too."

How could I argue? I had everything I needed plus a truck and a family that wanted to take care of me without asking anything in return. My life had never been so good.

CHAPTER 14

ROCHELLE

April 5, 2090

I sipped hot chocolate from the cup Molly had refilled twice. The room was bright and warm compared to the cold mist collecting on the window that overlooked a gloomy, gray backyard. It had been years since I'd been in Molly's big house with its spiral staircase in the foyer, chandeliers, and perfectly decorated rooms, but I'd accepted her invitation for hot chocolate and cookies. We'd spent two hours in her sitting room laughing about the times we would dress up and perform skits, sneak into her sister's room to use her makeup, or spend winter afternoons in the backyard building elaborate snow forts. Those days suddenly seemed so close that it was hard to believe it had all just stopped. Then I remembered middle school, when Molly's comments got a little too critical and she would make passing comments at Max and Todd to humiliate them, then say she was just joking.

"The best was the time Dad came sledding with us." It was normal for my dad to participate in sledding, swimming, piling leaves, or whatever activity came with the season, but Molly's dad rarely played with us. "We must have raced down the hill a hundred times, you and your dad versus me and my dad."

Dad and Eric Bennett had probably been sledding on that hill thousands of times when they were kids. They played football and basketball together in high school and went to the same college so they could be roommates. Even after my dad lost my mom, Eric and Lena Bennett invited him over for dinner once a week. In the years that followed, my dad and Mr. Bennett went to baseball games and football games. He visited my dad often during the months when he was sick. They were more like brothers than my dad and Uncle Arthur.

"That's what we have to talk about though, right? How your dad and mine ended up working on a project together?"

Molly smiled and fiddled with her hands. "Are you sure I can't get you more hot chocolate first? Or another cookie?"

"No, thank you." I glanced up at the clock. "I have to be home for dinner in an hour and Kinley will worry if I don't eat everything on my plate." Taking another sip of my hot chocolate to be polite, I contemplated why Molly, usually composed and in charge, appeared so uncharacteristically nervous.

"Did you find your pendant yet?" She leaned forward, eager.

I shook my head. "I spent an entire day searching the attic and an afternoon in the garage, but there's nothing there."

"I'm sure he hid it away carefully. Keep looking." She sighed and leaned back again. "For now, you just have to promise to believe me, even if this all sounds crazy."

"Okay." The intensity in her eyes compelled me to agree with her as a low rumble of thunder reverberated around the house.

"For most of the time we were in elementary school, my dad was working with a team to develop a vaccine that would be universal for all viruses." Molly's eyes went wide with wonder. "Imagine, one vaccine and you're covered for any current or future virus, even the fever."

"What happened?"

"It was promising in the lab trials, but never made it to human trials." Her wonder collapsed into disappointment. "It wasn't a sure enough thing to hold onto funding in this rotten economy. When the group ran out of money, they shelved their research, but they wanted a way to be able to pick up where they left off if things changed in the future. That's where the pendants come in."

I frowned, intrigued in spite of my reservations about Molly. "How many are there?" I wished I had been more attentive when she showed me her dad's. "What do they do? Yours looked plastic."

"Eight pendants for six research scientists: Mr. Welch, Mr. Iverson, Mr. Davis, Mr. Spencer, Mr. Zimmer, and my dad. When they're pieced together correctly, they become the key that unlocks whatever safe the research is stored in."

"And how did my dad get involved? He wasn't a scientist."

"That happened later. When the fever popped up a second time, my dad and the others thought they would have an argument for funding." Molly leaned forward, lacing her fingers together. "But they also had to consider the potential negative repercussions of their work."

"Wait, how could a vaccine possibly be a bad thing?"

Molly shrugged. "Imagine if one country had this opportunity for a healthy population but chose to keep it to themselves. There's suddenly this incentive to create diseases that competitor countries aren't immune to, but your people are."

I nodded slowly. "Diseases have decided wars in the past. It just seems too crazy to think any one country or group of people would keep something so good all to themselves."

"Not necessarily my belief." She shrugged. "But that's what your dad thought."

"My dad?" I laughed. "No way."

"My dad brought your dad in as the ethical advisor, an outside perspective. By then the fever was already under control, so I guess

Auggie decided the vaccine wasn't worth the risk, and he earned himself a pendant to be part of any decisions going forward."

"But he was gone before he could see how severe the fever would get." My thoughts raced. "That can't be right. How could he . . . do that?" My grandma, Kinley's parents, millions of others—they'd still be alive.

"He made the best choice he could with the information he had at the time." Molly sighed. "Remember what happened after your dad died?"

I frowned. Two weeks after my dad's funeral, I came home from school to find the house torn apart from federal agents searching for evidence of fraud and Grandma crying. I swallowed a lump forming in my throat. "Did the TCI agents come here too?"

Molly nodded. "As soon as the threat of the fever had passed."

"What do they want?" My chest felt tight, and as much as I wanted to hear the answer, I also didn't want to know.

"Our pendants, what else?" She noticed my confusion and continued. "The Threat Collection Initiative is a government agency who investigates and eliminates threats to the country's safety. You know, things like radioactive materials, chemical weapons, anything that puts human existence at risk. Either they agree with Auggie's assessment about this potential vaccine or they want to use it the way he feared they would." Molly shook her head. "Your dad was never involved in fraud—that was just a way for them to search your house without tipping you off."

She squirmed a little and fidgeted with a button on her sweater. Why was she so antsy? "Maybe they even . . ." She squeezed her eyes shut. "My dad said the way Auggie died . . . it was like he'd been exposed to some kind of toxin, but it never showed up in any of the screenings."

My head ached as my divided thoughts went to war over

whether to accept Molly's revelations. Everything she had said was impossible to believe but impossible to make up at the same time. "What if they already have Dad's pendant from when they searched the house?" My throat went dry with panic. "Do you think he knew they were after him?"

Molly scooted forward and covered my hand with hers. "Your dad was smart. He would have hidden it somewhere they'd never look." She studied me. "I know this is all really hard to hear."

I shivered. "What are we going to do?"

"We're going to finish what our dads and the other scientists started."

"Even if we do find the research, it's not like we can just follow it like a recipe and mix it up in the kitchen." I rubbed my forehead the way Kinley did when she was stressed, but it didn't make me feel any better.

"Hey, one step at a time." She squeezed my hand. "I'm in touch with some of the others my dad worked with. One of their sons, Griff Spencer, is on board with helping us. I met him a few times when we were little kids."

Large raindrops slammed against the windowpane with a gust of wind, and I jumped. "Molly, I . . . I want to help, but . . ."

"I know, it's a lot to process. From the time my dad mentioned the pendant in his delirium to now . . . well, I know what you're feeling." She sighed and glanced at the gloom out the window. "But remember, you can't tell anyone about this. Not Kinley, not Todd, not anyone."

"Why not?" Suddenly I wanted to run home and spill it all to Kinley. She would know what to do. She always fixed any problem I brought to her.

"Rochelle." She stood. "Remember those TCI agents? They're

dangerous and they'll be back. The more people know, the more likely they are to get hurt. Keeping this to yourself protects the people you love."

I stood, nodding. It seemed unlikely the TCI would suddenly come back to investigate, but Molly had all the facts while I was just trying to piece together memories.

"Don't worry. You're not alone." She pulled me into an awkward hug. "We're going to figure this out together and make sure the world is a better place in the future."

As much as I wanted to tell Kinley and Kat everything Molly had told me, I would never want them to feel the same weight I felt on my chest or the same sinking in the pit of my stomach. It was my problem to face—mine and Todd's.

I nodded again, too overwhelmed for words.

Molly gripped my shoulders. "Very good. But you have to keep looking for that pendant and any other information your dad left behind." Her eyes scrutinized my face as if searching for clues there. "You really didn't know about any of this until I told you?"

I shook my head. "But if there's anything to be found at my house, I will find it."

"Okay." Molly looked suspicious and relieved at the same time. "I know you probably need some time to think about this and you have to get home soon, but let me know what you find and I'll do the same."

Molly walked me to the door, not saying another word as I put on my coat and shoes. An involuntary shiver ran through my body. Was there more to what she wasn't saying than what she was? Stuffing my hands in my pockets, I hurried down the front walk. Cold rain snapped me out of the trance I felt overtaking me.

Could my dad have really kept all of that a secret? When did he have time to hide a pendant, deal with threat collection agents, and still help us with our homework? Did his choice to keep the research locked up leave the world vulnerable to the devastation of the fever? I had to know why he made that decision. There had to be something he'd left that could explain why he chose the safe option when a little risk could save the world.

CHAPTER 15

CHARLIE

April 14, 2090

"We all had pretty different ideas at the forum. No matter which three of us are elected, we're going to have some conflict to deal with." Kiara sat across the conference room table from Rochelle and me. We had been the first to arrive since Alexander picked us up, and Kiara arrived soon after.

"That can be a good thing though." Rochelle leaned back comfortably in her chair. "Maybe we'll have a better chance at finding the best solution instead of just a quick fix that doesn't work in the long term."

The two of them had been chatting for the past few minutes while I scribbled in my notebook, pretending to be busy so I wouldn't have to weigh in with my opinion. Alexander had been pretty cryptic when he called in the morning and told Rochelle he would pick her up for a meeting to go over voting results at five o'clock. The election had taken place a day earlier, postponed by a week due to the flood and its aftermath. Although we didn't know what to expect, I had been allowed to tag along with my notebook and pen to practice taking notes so I'd be ready to report on the upcoming council meetings.

"I'm not late?" Todd rushed into the room and slid into the open chair next to Rochelle, still trying to catch his breath. "I had to finish a project at the store and . . ."

Rochelle smiled and flung her arm around him despite something gray blotched all over his face and hands. "You're just in time."

"Did Alexander call all three of you? That can't be right." Molly stood in the doorway, face scrunched in confusion as she observed Rochelle, Todd, and Kiara all seated at the table. "There should only be three of us. And what are you doing here?" She glared in my direction.

"Take a breath, Molly." Kiara rolled her eyes. "I'm sure he called all of us. That's the courteous thing to do."

"I guess." Molly looked annoyed as she sat down next to Todd. "What happened to you? Is your dad so poor now he can't afford soap?"

He rubbed his chin with the back of his hand. "I was . . ." He looked at Rochelle then back to Molly. "I was painting and I was in a hurry . . ."

"Now I know where that disgusting smell is coming from." She fanned the air in front of her as Todd pulled his arm down and pressed it to his side. "Switch seats with Rochelle before I throw up."

"Be nice, Molly." Rochelle stood and nudged Todd's shoulder until he slid over to her seat next to me. "Don't listen to her, you smell fine," she whispered as she sat down.

Molly gripped Rochelle's arm and pulled her closer. She whispered something that sounded like *did you find it yet?*

Rochelle just shook her head as Trevor and Neil came into the room followed by Alexander. Todd had been helping Rochelle look for a baseball glove in the attic earlier; I wondered if Molly was somehow involved with that, but I doubted it. A clamor of conversation filled the room while everyone got settled.

Alexander sat down at the head of the table, opening a binder in front of him. "Thank you for coming, everyone. I wanted to let you know in person that things didn't exactly go according to my plan." He made eye contact with everyone sitting around the table as they anxiously awaited the news in silence. He leaned forward, arms spread in an all-encompassing gesture. "I know the election was supposed to result in three of you being elected, but the vote was really close. Since I value all of your ideas and believe Maibe needs as much help as we can provide, all six of you are in."

Neil leaned back in his chair and laughed. "But I had the most votes, right?" He waited for someone to laugh, but everyone else was already talking.

"That can't be right." Molly glared across the table at Neil. "Now would be a good time for you to forfeit. You have to be the least qualified person in this room."

"Not a chance." Neil leaned back in his chair with his hands behind his head. "The people of Maibe voted for me to represent them. I won this title."

Kiara shook her head. "None of us won. We just didn't lose."

A loud whistle sliced through the room and everyone turned to Alexander. He dropped his hand back down to the table. "Let's not fall into chaos. We have a lot to organize, so I need all of you to listen. First of all, the structure we've set up for Maibe's government sounds traditional, but there is no way we'll be operating in the same way as past councils, so I want you to throw out everything you know about how a town council operates."

"Aren't we just supposed to argue with each other? We're already good at that." Neil grinned, but no one laughed.

"What's wrong with you?" Molly leaned forward with her elbows on the table. "If you don't have any good ideas, go home."

Neil rolled his eyes. "I have one. Let's not follow The Defiance model like you proposed at the forum."

Everyone turned to Molly, who sat stiff, blue eyes fierce. "At least they have some leadership and structure."

"Enforced by fear and violence." I didn't realize I was the one muttering the words until they were out of my mouth.

"It sounds like Charlie knows plenty about The Defiance..."

Rochelle nudged Molly's arm before she could finish her sentence.

"That stuff is in the papers all the time." I wasn't afraid of Molly and I wasn't about to back down.

"What are you writing over there, anyway? Your plans to torch all of Main Street?" Molly spat the words at me.

"I'm taking down the minutes of this meeting for the paper." I lowered my pen and met her eyes. "But don't worry, I'll do you a favor and leave those last few comments off the record."

Neil made eye contact with me from across the table and failed at stifling a laugh. Rochelle pressed a hand to her mouth so no one would see her smile. The other's waited anxiously for Molly's response.

"Alexander, you can't let him do that." Her jaw trembled. "If we feel uncomfortable speaking freely, we're not going to accomplish anything."

Alexander's nose twitched, a habit I'd noticed him use with Kinley to prevent himself from smiling at the wrong moment. "Our meetings are open to the public and the press. If you're worried about having your words published, you probably shouldn't be saying them."

Molly sat back in her chair knowing she'd lost as Alexander looked at each of the new council members in turn. "Does anyone else have a problem with anyone sitting in this room?"

Based on what I'd witnessed at the forum and the current meeting, that was a dangerous question, but fortunately everyone remained silent.

Alexander flipped through his binder before looking up. "Our inexperience will be a challenge but also an opportunity for a fresh start. We're not going to sit here and attack each other. Instead, I have a problem of interest for each of you to think about and come up with a solution for, to discuss at our next meeting. And I don't want to just hear your solution, I want a detailed, step-by-step explanation for how we can make it work. At our first official meeting, next Thursday at five, you'll each have a turn to present your case and then we'll discuss it calmly."

"So we have homework?" Trevor leaned forward until his forehead rested on the table.

"It's not homework." Molly brushed her bangs aside. "This is about fixing our hometown's problems. When you ran for the council, what did you think we would do? Just get together and eat cake?"

Neil laughed. "That's a great idea, can we do that?"

Kiara sighed. "I can bring cake, but I'll only give it to those who are actually working. So, probably not you."

Todd looked at me. "Do you think any of us are qualified to be on this council?"

"Me, Rochelle, and Kiara are qualified," Molly shouted over the clamor. "My dad was mayor for three years, Kiara's mom was on the council once, and Rochelle's uncle was a business owner and her aunt was a doctor."

Neil scratched his head. "Wasn't Rochelle's dad some kind of con man or something?"

The room went silent. Molly's face contorted in horror. Rochelle looked like she wanted to say something but couldn't find the words. I remembered what Kinley had told me about Auggie Aumont's strange demise as I watched Todd's hand find Rochelle's under the table.

"You'd better not have written that down." Molly narrowed her eyes at me.

I slid my notebook in front of Todd and Rochelle so she could read it. *Neil made an idiotic comment. Again.*

Molly laughed as Rochelle shook her head at me, although she smiled. "You can't publish that either."

The table shook beneath us with a loud boom. "Enough." Alexander sounded angry and all conversation ended. "If you're not going to take your obligation as part of this council seriously, then get out now."

I stared down at my notes, watching the others from my peripheral vision. None of them moved.

"All right then." Alexander stood and snatched a piece of paper from the table. "Your assignments. Kiara, I want you to look into revitalization of the town, from appearance to morale. Trevor, what can we do about economic growth? Neil, how can we fix our current infrastructure and improve it for the future? Todd, you're in charge of security. How can we make Maibe the safest place to live? Molly, I want a plan for disasters and emergencies. Lastly, and probably most important, Rochelle, I want a plan for education in Maibe." Alexander took a breath and tossed his paper onto the table. "The six of you can do amazing things for this town, but we're going to have to work together if we're going to accomplish anything." He sighed and shook his head. "You're all dismissed. I'll see you next week."

"That's it?" Molly stood abruptly. "This has been a complete waste of time. You could have told me that over the phone." She pulled her jacket from the back of her chair and stormed out of the room.

"Wow." Kiara slid her arms into her coat. "I know Molly can be mean, but she's really on a roll today."

"We should give her a break." Rochelle looked at the empty chair beside her. "She's alone all the time since she lost her parents. She's having a hard time with it."

"We've all been through some hard stuff, Rochelle." Kiara wasn't harsh but matter of fact. "None of our hearts became a block of ice, although Molly was well on her way years ago."

Trevor stood and shook his head. "The meetings aren't always going to be like this, right?"

"Depends on how well we learn to work together." Alexander sounded very tired.

Neil watched Kiara and Trevor as they disappeared into the hall. "Do some hand exercises for next time, Charlie. Molly can fight me on every word, but I have some great ideas that you'll want to get in the paper."

I just nodded as he made his way out of the room, causing another loud eruption of conversation in the hallway. Alexander sighed and let his hand slide from his forehead to his chin.

"I don't know how your teachers dealt with all of you in the same room, but I feel like bringing you all together just set the doomsday clock a whole minute closer to midnight." He tried to force a chuckle, but his eyes landed on Rochelle, who rubbed her forehead in a way that reminded me of Kinley. "Are you okay, Rochelle? Neil's comment was completely inappropriate and totally wrong."

She nodded but exchanged a strange look with Todd. "He didn't mean any harm. I'll do a better job of helping Molly stay on track at the next meeting."

On the night of the fire, I thought Molly and Todd were friends. On the night of the forum, I thought Rochelle and Molly were enemies. Suddenly I wasn't sure where one alliance existed and another had never formed, but I figured it was none of my business.

Alexander smiled. "I'm glad I have you three to give me hope for your generation." He stood and gathered up his binder. "I'll drive you all home, just give me a minute to put a few things away in my office."

Todd slumped in his chair as Alexander left, so I could see Rochelle, arms folded on the table, green eyes staring ahead as if lost in thought.

"Did I make things worse by arguing with Molly?" The last thing I wanted was to cause more conflict when there seemed to be plenty already, but I couldn't back down from a challenge.

"No, she needs someone to stand up to her once in a while." Todd rubbed the side of his face with the heel of his hand. "It's something I've never been able to do, but then again, I can't even wash my face right. My reflection looked fine in the grocery store display window."

"Let me see you." Rochelle took his face between her hands. She rubbed his forehead with her thumb and giggled. "That's definitely paint."

He nodded. "The sign on the front of the store was chipping really badly, but it doesn't look much better now . . . No wonder no one wants to sit by me."

"I think you just work too hard and you're having a rough day." Rochelle leaned forward and kissed his forehead. "I still want to sit next to you."

Todd smiled and looked at Rochelle in his usual way—as if she was the only spot of color in a world of gray.

If I could be sure of any alliance, it was the one between Rochelle and Todd. A magnetic force seemed to pull them together despite any disagreements or misunderstandings. It would be nice to trust someone so completely. I could make any mistake or share any secret, knowing they wouldn't think less of me because of it. Then again, for me to share my history with The Defiance with anyone would be dangerous for both of us.

"You should take a break from work and come over for dinner," Rochelle told Todd. "Keppler, do you know what Kat is making?"

I closed my notebook. "She said something about baked chicken, and she always makes enough for a family of twelve." He probably knew that already, but I wanted to make him feel better, or welcome at least.

A real smile spread over Todd's face. "That sounds good. After I shower though."

"Come on, guys." Alexander peeked his head around the door frame. "Let's get out of here."

CHAPTER 16
ROCHELLE

April 20, 2090

I slid a round slice of carrot back and forth across my plate, carefully circumventing the baked fish I hadn't touched. The conversation around the dinner table barely even registered as I ran through the details of the first official council meeting in my head.

Kiara had plans to spruce up Main Street and put on a festival later in the year to boost morale, which we all voted to proceed with. Molly had a binder full of detailed notes in slip covers with color coded tabs. She knew how many people had been affected by the flood and the stage of repair for each damaged residence, and she was working on plans to deal with anything from a future flood to a meteor strike. Trevor had been working with Alexander to find grants from the federal government that could help get local businesses up and running again. Only Molly opposed drawing people from outside communities to Maibe, so the vote to proceed passed five to one. Todd presented an idea about consulting with Max to create a sort of camera surveillance system for the train station, so in an emergency, we would know who came and went. That was also popular with everyone except Molly. Neil had practical plans to update worn electrical lines and rusty transformers so we could avoid another major power outage and repave Main Street in the summer. Since both projects fit within the budget sheet Alexander had handed out at the beginning of the meeting, it passed.

It was when I presented my plan to reopen the school for seventh through twelfth grade in September that everyone, except Todd, raised protest. Neil and Trevor said they had plenty of farm work without school getting in the way. Kiara said something like an apprentice program would be more useful. Molly said the elementary teachers were already stretched thin, teaching multiple grades, so she doubted we'd be able to find enough to support a high school system. Todd had been the only one to join me in the vote to move forward with my plan, so I had a lot of hypothetical problems to solve before the next meeting.

"Rochelle, are you listening to me?" Kinley's voice crashed through my thoughts.

I glanced around the table. Keppler's plate was empty. Kat and Kinley were almost finished eating. "Sorry. What?"

My cousin sighed. "Are you feeling okay? You've barely eaten anything."

"I'm just not very hungry, I guess." I lowered my fork to my plate.

Kinley turned to Keppler with her eyebrows raised. It had become her custom to immediately check with him or my sister anytime I gave her a vague answer, and they usually complied by explaining what I hadn't put into words.

"Her ideas didn't get voted through at the meeting." Keppler picked up his glass of water. "For the record, I would have voted in favor if I had any voting power."

"Thanks." I slid my plate away from me. "I still would have been one vote short."

I waited for Kinley to lecture me about taking care of myself or being more prepared for my meetings, but instead she squeezed my shoulder. "Rochelle, it's okay if things don't work out on your first try. Sometimes you just have to be persistent. Okay?"

"Okay." On some level I knew she was right, but it didn't make me feel any better. "I'm really tired. May I be excused?"

"Isn't it your turn to clean up the kitchen?" Kat wasn't about to give me any slack.

"I'll switch with her." Keppler piled his silverware on his plate. "It's not a problem."

"Thank you." I stood and gave him my most appreciative smile. "Good night, everyone."

Before Kinley or Kat could stop me and try to talk me into eating something, I hurried through the dining room, swung a sharp left in the living room, took the stairs two at a time, and made my way to the bathroom at the end of the hallway. After brushing my teeth and washing my face, I trudged back to my room, flipped on the light, and fell back onto my bed. For a few seconds, everything was silent and then I heard three distinct knocks.

Groaning, I stood, walked to the window, and slid the curtain aside to reveal Todd out on the roof. "You know Kinley would have let you in the door, right?" I asked after opening the window. "I wouldn't have been up here for another hour if I had kitchen duty."

He smiled so big his dimples appeared and extended his hand to me. "Come out here, the weather is beautiful."

"Is everything okay?" It wasn't like Todd to ignore my questions or to show up outside my window in the absence of an emergency. I took his hand and settled in with my back against the cold siding and my legs stretched across the shingles. "Did something bad happen?"

Stars glittered across the dark sky and the newly budding tree branches swayed in an unseasonably warm breeze.

"Something good, actually." He sounded more nervous than

enthusiastic. "I've been picking up the mail so I could intercept her letter, just in case she wrote again, and she did."

I didn't have to ask. I knew he was talking about his mom. "What did she say this time?"

He reached into his pocket and pulled out a trifold piece of paper that I took in a shaking hand.

My dearest Todd,

I miss you so much, and I don't even have the words to describe how much I regret leaving you and your sisters behind. Please don't be angry with me. I've been ill through the winter and all I really want is to see my family again.

I should have come home a long time ago, but I'm not well enough to travel by myself. I'm writing to you because you always had such a gentle, understanding heart and all I want is to hug you and see my little boy all grown up.

I'm currently between homes, but I've included the address of the hotel where I'm staying and a train ticket to get you here. I hope you'll give me the chance to talk to you in person because it's so difficult to write it out on this paper. I miss you.

Love, Mom

The letter itself was printed on a thin piece of paper in shaky writing. On the back, its writer had scrawled the address to a hotel in Phoenix, Arizona. The details weren't any comfort because I kept up with the news in the papers, and I knew traveling by train could be dangerous if the route ran through Defiance territory, which seemed to expand every day.

"Are you sure it's really from her?" Even the illumination of bright moonlight couldn't reveal a trace of a clue to confirm the writer's identity. "Kinley said these can be scams." I couldn't ignore the uneasy feeling in my chest, and I needed Todd to consider all of the possibilities, not just the one he wanted to believe.

"It looks like her writing." He took the letter carefully as if it might crumble to dust and held it in both hands. "At least what I remember of it. And I know she didn't like to write very much, just like me, so it makes sense that she would rather explain in person. Plus, if it were some kind of scam, what would they get out of sending me a train ticket?"

"Todd . . ." I sighed and squeezed my eyes shut. "It just seems too good to be true."

"It's all in the letter, Shelley." His voice was patient and gentle as usual. "She's sick and she's alone at a hotel. She needs me to come and bring her home."

"You actually plan on going?" I opened my eyes to see Todd's face drawn tight with worry. "When?"

"Tonight. I'm a little nervous about it, but I'm trying to see it as an adventure, like you would." He refolded the letter and slid it into his pocket before turning back to me. "I wanted to say good-bye and make sure you'll be okay."

Was he asking for my permission or looking for an excuse to cancel the trip? What kind of friend would I be if I let him go? Would it be selfish to ask him to stay? "It's too dangerous," I blurted. "You need time to investigate and make a plan so you know what you're getting yourself into. That's what you always tell me. That's what you always do."

He took my hand and squeezed it gently. "Shelley, I'm already scared, please don't make this harder. I know you think I'm always cautious, but some things are worth the risk, right? If I'm going to do one brave thing, I need to help my mom. To get answers to my questions."

"I never meant you weren't brave. You came and saved Kat and me from the fever. Nothing could be braver than that." I drew my knees up in front of me and blinked hard so I wouldn't cry. Todd's hand felt warm around my icy one. I held it tightly and wished we could sit on the roof forever. Just the two of us in a place where our worries couldn't reach us. There had to be a reason he couldn't leave for even a day. "And I need your help with Operation Baseball Glove."

"Don't worry. We're going to get to the bottom of everything Molly told you. But I'm pretty sure, for whatever reason, she's making things up. We've been through every box in the attic and the garage. If your dad really had one of those pendants, we would have found it by now." He clicked his fingernail against the zipper on his jacket. "Just avoid her while I'm gone and then when I get back in a week, we'll figure out what she's up to."

Soft moonlight shimmered on newly budding tree branches. Todd needed closure with his mom. He wouldn't be at peace until he had answers, and I didn't want to take that from him. But I had a heart-sinking, irrational fear that letting him walk away would mean never seeing him again. I didn't want to say goodbye to one more person, especially not Todd.

"What did Emma and your dad say about this?" I knew he hadn't told them or he wouldn't be sneaking around to explain it to me.

Todd took a long breath in and let it out. "I left them a note explaining, and they can ground me forever when I get home. But I don't want to fight with them before I go."

I linked my arm through his and laid my head on his shoulder. "We should at least get advice from someone. Kinley is downstairs right now, and—"

"Rochelle, if I talk to anyone else, I'll lose my nerve to do this. I just have to find my mom, and we'll be on the next train home in less than a week."

He'd never had his mind so made up about anything that I

couldn't sway him. Usually, I was the one looking for an adventure while Todd was the voice of reason.

I shook my head. "I'll miss you."

He sighed and rested his head against mine. "I'll miss you too."

"Did you pack everything you'll need? Enough clothes, snacks, water, your sketch pad?" I loved Todd for wanting to rescue his mom even though she abandoned him, and I understood his past would haunt him without the closure her answers could provide. Since my meeting with Molly, I had found myself wishing I could have just one more conversation with my dad. While I would never be able to talk to him again, Todd had a chance to escape the weight he'd been carrying around since we were second graders.

"Are you kidding, that's the first thing I packed. I can live three weeks without food, but only a few hours if I can't draw."

I tried to fight it, but a smile spread across my face. "I'm trying to be serious."

"I packed everything I need."

"Maybe I should come with you." Nothing bad could happen to him if we were together. I glanced through the open window into my room and started to pack a bag in my mind.

Todd shook his head. "Kinley would panic, and I need you to look out for my sisters while I'm away. Emma will need someone calm to talk to and, just a heads up, we got the velvet Lily wants for her birthday, so you'll probably be making a dress."

I tried to smile but the ticking of Todd's watch reminded me our precious time was slipping away. "How am I supposed to tell them I let you go?"

"Don't even tell them I came here." He sat up and turned to me. "Promise you'll take care of yourself too. None of that scary not-eating stuff like when you were sick."

"I promise I'll take care of everyone until you get back."

Todd wrapped me in a tight hug, and we stayed like that until a train whistle sliced through the night. He gradually loosened his grip until he held me in front of him. "Everything will be okay. I love you, Rochelle." He leaned forward and kissed my forehead.

"I love you too." I gripped his hand in mine. "Be careful and call me when you get there."

I felt like I had swallowed an entire jar of peanut butter as I watched Todd climb down the tree, pick up his bag, and jog down the front walk. He stopped when he got to the street and waved at me. I waved back and watched until he vanished into the darkness. A cold wind swept my hair over my face and sent a shiver through my body. I slipped back through my window, huddled under the blankets on my bed, and willed the time to pass quickly so Todd would be back.

PART TWO

THE PAST CATCHES UP

CHAPTER 17

CHARLIE

July 16, 2090

A single tear slipped down her cheek, caught the sunlight, and projected an entire spectrum of colors. It was a glimmer of hope from a manifestation of despair . . . This story will be continued on your next birthday.

I carefully tore the pages of Kat's birthday story out of my notebook and folded it to fit in the envelope sitting on the seat of the truck beside me. At first, I had planned to buy her something new for the kitchen, but I had spent all of my paper route money on parts for the truck. Then I decided to take her for a drive, but I still couldn't get the truck started. So I finally decided to write her a story, which I had finished with minutes to spare. It was almost ten o'clock on a Sunday morning, and the Aumonts would be home from church any minute. Kinley always invited me to go with them but never forced it.

Taking a breath, I propped the envelope between the dash and the windshield as Rochelle had instructed, so the location would match the clue she wrote for Kat's gift scavenger hunt. My stomach growled. In my rush to finish writing, I hadn't eaten breakfast—or cleared my books off the dining room table like Kinley had asked. She wanted the house to be extra clean and orderly since Emma, Lily, and Alexander were coming over for Kat's birthday meal.

Leaning back in the driver's seat, I adjusted my new glasses that had finally come in after two months of waiting. The summer brought my life a stable routine of chores, homework, delivering the paper one day a week, writing my council reports, helping Rochelle with yard work and Max with experiments, and working for Alexander when he had a big landscaping job. Of course, Kinley prioritized everything above working on the truck, which meant I wasn't making as much progress as I had hoped, but I didn't mind.

Pushing the door all the way open created a draft, and the envelope flopped over. Sighing, I leaned forward to adjust it, bracing my other hand behind me. Feeling squishy foam instead of rough material, I pulled the blanket covering the seat aside to reveal several holes in the upholstery. Rochelle could probably be persuaded to make a seat cover. Reaching into the cushion to push the foam back into place, my knuckle brushed something cool and smooth.

Twisting my fingers around the small object, I worked it loose and pulled it free. A familiar chill ran through my body. A teardrop pendant with a smooth black surface dangled from a chain. White lettering spelled *P-E-S-S-I-M-U-S* around the curved section. I squeezed my eyes shut and I was back at The Defiance camp sitting across the table from Griff.

"It's hard to believe that's the most valuable thing my dad owned, isn't it, kid?" Griff never took his eyes off the pendant I held up in front of me. "Now jus' need the other seven."

After not seeing him for three days, I went looking. After all, he referred to me as his brother. The others were just there to follow orders in exchange for food and shelter. Knocking twice, I had opened his door and found him sitting at the table, empty bottles lined up in front of him, notebook pages scattered across the floor around him.

"What is it?" It reminded me of the cheap plastic jewelry my

sister sometimes picked out as a prize at the school carnival. The letters I-N-S-T-R-U-O followed the curved side.

"Something the world doesn't want us to have." He took a long drink from one of the bottles on the table, and I made a mental note to dump it out the minute he wasn't looking. "They killed my dad for it, but he was one step ahead of 'em." He had told me about the strained relationship he had with his father. They had barely talked since Griff ran away from home at sixteen. "He might not have been there when I was a kid, but he came looking for me to make sure I knew about this. Said if anything happened to 'im, I had to get to that safe deposit box."

"So it's some kind of heirloom?" I sat down and slid the bottle away from him. He wasn't making sense, and he wouldn't be in any condition to answer coherently until morning.

Griff laughed. "No. My dad and his research team spent years trying to prevent all viruses with one vaccine, but instead they found a way to do the opposite. With their research, any virus becomes ten times more severe."

"You don't want that." I dumped the pendant back into his hand. "You're terrified of the fever."

"Exactly. Look how people react when it infects a few hundred people. Imagine if we had the cure and the virus. People would hand over whatever we wanted in exchange for their health."

I nodded. Who knew how much Griff had drunk to get like this? He'd talk sense after sleeping it off. I helped him to bed.

"Lock it up in the file cabinet over there." He held the pendant out to me. "We can't take any chances."

Its cold surface touched my hand and I shivered, finding myself back in the truck staring down at the pendant's twin, a year later, in Maibe. My breath caught in my chest as I tried to reconcile how the evil little object could show up just when life was finally good.

Did Rochelle know it was there? Did she know it existed at all? It was none of my business, but whose business was it? If it belonged to Rochelle's dad, was it hers, Kinley's, Kat's? I didn't want Griff to come poking around asking them questions. I didn't want him anywhere near them.

"Charlie?" Kat's voice drifted through the open garage door. "Charlie, are you out here?"

I shoved the pendant into my shorts pocket, jumped out of the truck, and hurried out onto the patio.

"Kinley was looking for you." She held a paper up in front of her. "Tell her I'd rather make my own birthday lunch than spend the morning searching for my presents." The whole point of the traditional scavenger hunt was to keep Kat out of the kitchen for an hour.

"Check the garage for the first one." The pendant felt heavy in my pocket, though it didn't actually weigh enough that I would feel it. "Happy birthday, by the way." I remembered to smile, but Kat made a funny face and I knew I wasn't acting like myself. "I should find out what Kinley needs." How could I ruin her birthday by trying to explain my own fears?

She just shook her head and made her way into the garage as I crossed the patio and pulled the back door open.

"I don't know if I should send it." Emma's voice came from the kitchen as I kicked off my shoes in the laundry room. "Lily has been more anxious without Todd around, and I want to have enough time to take care of her and Dad."

"Of course you should send it." Kinley hugged her friend as I walked to the refrigerator. "You always planned to be a teacher. If it weren't for the fever you would have been in college already."

Alexander turned to me as I poured a glass of milk. "Charlie would agree. Emma is a great teacher, right?"

"The best I've ever had in my life." I smiled as I grabbed a cookie from the jar on the counter. I knew they were talking about Emma's application to an accelerated program for aspiring teachers.

Rochelle had finally found the right compromise to get the votes she needed to make her school reopening a reality. She would begin by adding seventh and eighth grade, and they wouldn't start classes until January. That provided enough time to prepare and would serve as an experiment to indicate whether upper grades could be added the next year.

To help with the teacher shortage issue, Alexander found out about an accelerated teaching program, which would allow future teachers, like Emma, to start classes in August and complete the basics by Christmas so she could get a student teaching license that would allow her to teach in her own classroom by January while continuing her coursework. It was similar to Kinley's program in that Emma would complete her assignments at home, submit them using a computer at the library, and only travel to the college occasionally to take tests.

Kinley took the application from her. "There's nothing to be nervous about. I'll even go with you the first time you have a test and help you find your way around, and Lily can hang out here with us anytime." She exchanged a glance with Alexander. They both knew it would also be a good distraction so she didn't dwell so much on why her brother hadn't come home.

"Thanks guys. Won't Todd be surprised when he gets back and finds out I started college?" She smiled but blinked away a tear.

"He'll be so proud." Alexander wrapped his arm around her. In the letter he'd left for his family, Todd had promised to be home in a week, but no one had heard from him in almost three months. Emma and Rochelle still believed he'd come home, but the rest of us knew that chance dropped every day, and there was nothing we could do about it.

Kinley shook her head at me. "Is that supposed to be your breakfast?"

"I didn't eat anything yet," I said through a mouthful of chocolate chips.

"Kinley, it's a special occasion. One cookie won't hurt him." Emma smiled at me and her eyes brightened. "Charlie, I haven't seen you since you got your glasses. They look good with your haircut." She pulled me into a one-armed hug. "If you see Lily, tell her we're almost ready to frost the cake."

"And clean your stuff off the table." Kinley raised her eyebrows at me. "We need it in an hour."

"You got it." Part of me wanted to tell her about the pendant. She would know what to do, and it wouldn't be my responsibility. Instead, I gulped the rest of my milk and set my glass in the sink before making my way to the next room. In the library, Rochelle and Lily sat on the floor with a roll of red material and several sheets of thin paper with various shapes sketched on them.

"Todd promised he would teach me to play checkers and take me for ice cream when the diner reopened and go running with me so I can be on the track team when you reopen the school." Lily carefully marked an adjustment on her plan. "He never should have left."

Rochelle smoothed a section of the material. "He'll be back soon, and I'll do all of those things with you until then." For the past three months, Rochelle had been obsessed with doing anything and everything Todd would have done—chatting with Emma, hanging out with Lily, and even helping his dad do some inventory at the hardware store. Kinley thought maybe it helped her cope with losing him, but we both agreed she was exhausted.

Lily picked up the sketch and examined it carefully. "When Emma is busy with all of her teacher classes, I can still hang out with you, right?"

"Absolutely." Rochelle enveloped her with one arm and nodded at the sketches. "We'll need plenty of time together to make this dress and do all of those other things."

I cleared my throat and took a few steps into the room. "Hey, guys. Emma and Kinley said they need some help frosting the cake."

"Finally." Lily was on her feet in a second. "Charlie, will you help me hang the balloons and streamers a little later?"

I nodded. She reminded me of my little sister. Isabelle would only be a year older than her. "Of course."

"Thank you." She hugged me quick then disappeared into the next room.

"Are you sure you should promise all of those things?" I took a few steps toward Rochelle, trying to decide what to reveal about the pendant. "That's a lot to keep up with."

She sighed and stood. "I can handle it." She looked sad, but I knew she wouldn't divulge what was on her mind. All she ever said concerning Todd was, *he'll be home soon.* "Are you okay? You don't look well."

"Fine. I just hid Kat's present. Did you know the seat in the truck is all ripped up?"

Rochelle laughed. "Yeah, Dad had a story to explain that. Something about his friend's hunting dog."

"Is that the only story... about the seats, I mean?" If she didn't know about the pendant already, I wasn't going to add another worry to her pile of problems.

"Come here." She took my hands and walked me over to the couch. "You're shaking. What's wrong?"

I sank into the cushions. "Nothing."

Rochelle's forehead wrinkled like Kinley's. "You know you can talk to me. I'm never too busy for that."

Nodding, I forced a smile. She saw good in everyone and hope in every tough situation. How could I ever describe to her the world I had escaped? How could I expose her to the darkness that came with knowledge of that pendant?

I dabbed sweat from my face with the sleeve of my shirt. "I'm just anxious about Kat reading my story." I had to pull myself together, but it was hard to calm down with the pendant in my pocket.

"Don't worry. She'll love it." Rochelle pinched the cuff of my long-sleeved t-shirt between her fingers. "You know, it's like a hundred degrees outside. We can get you some short-sleeved shirts if you need them."

Kinley had said the same thing a few weeks earlier, but I didn't want to risk anyone seeing the symbol on my arm. "I'm usually cold and I won't get sunburned this way."

"Good point." Rochelle glanced down at her arms, still red from the bad sunburn she suffered after we helped Alexander with a landscaping job the week before. "I should probably go help with lunch."

I could feel the outline of the pendant pinned between my leg and the cushion. *Ignore it. This is your chance to protect the Aumonts, to repay them for everything they've done for you.*

"I'd better clean up the table before Kinley flips her lid." Standing, I held my hand out to Rochelle and helped her to her feet. We parted ways in the dining room where I gathered up all of my homework then rushed downstairs where I dumped my books and notes on my bed. Pulling out the top drawer of my dresser, I removed the pendant from my pocket, dropped it into a sock, and shoved it to the back of the drawer.

CHAPTER 18

ROCHELLE

July 28, 2090

"What's wrong, hummingbird?" My dad sat on the open tailgate of his truck, smiling.

"I keep telling everyone I have everything under control, but I don't really know what I'm doing." Bracing my arms on the tailgate, I hoisted myself up next to him. "Kat's good at cooking, Todd's good at drawing, Kinley's good at everything, but I . . ."

"You're good at sewing. You made my favorite shirt." He held out his arms so he could proudly survey my work.

"I put the buttonholes in the wrong place. It's all lopsided."

"You mean it's not supposed to be like that?" Dad's green eyes sparkled with laughter. "I kind of like it. Thought I was making a fashion statement."

A big yellow butterfly glided in front of me, and I struggled to remember what I was talking about. "I'm trying to take care of everyone, but Kinley and Kat are always fighting and now Todd's gone."

"Don't give up, Rochelle." Dad wrapped his arm around me and pulled me closer. "If they didn't have you, they'd be far worse off." He kissed the top of my head, and I suddenly felt like everything would be okay. "You're the glue that keeps this family together, even when it's hard. That's what you're really good at."

I huddled closer to him, trying to remember why it was strange for him to be sitting on the driveway with me.

"But what about Todd? And Molly keeps asking me about your pendant . . ."

"I promise tomorrow will be better." His voice sounded softer and farther away. "You'll figure it out, Rochelle."

"Rochelle. Rochelle." I opened my eyes to Kinley sitting on the edge of the couch next to me. "Hey, how are you feeling?"

Alexander stood behind her, dressed in a suit and tie. My cousin wore a blue dress and her hair fell in loose curls to her waist. Dr. Brooks and the students in his medical training program were hosting a dinner, inviting interested doctors and educators from other communities to showcase the success of the program and hopefully spark interest for more programs like it. Kinley had written a speech and rehearsed it in front of me a hundred times.

I sat up, starting to scratch my arm before making myself stop. The day before, I had spent the morning helping Alexander with some landscaping work and ended up with poison ivy that both Keppler and Alexander had managed to avoid. "I had a dream about Dad." It still felt so real I expected him to walk into the room any minute.

Kinley smiled and brushed my hair behind my ear. "Was it a good one?"

I nodded. "You guys look nice." Back in March, when my cousin had first told me about the dinner, I had planned to go with Todd. Now it was hard to look forward to anything when I feared I'd never see him again. Part of me was thankful for the rash since it was a good excuse to stay home. I didn't feel like even leaving the couch.

"Are you sure you'll be okay here all alone?" She looked at me as if I were a little kid. "Emma said she can come over."

"I'll be fine." I'd have a few hours to cry without everyone getting all worried. "I wish I could see you give your speech though. It'll be so good."

"Thank you." She smiled but studied me as if I were her patient.

"Stop, you're going to wrinkle your shirt." Kat followed Keppler into the library. "I just got your tie right."

"I can barely breathe." He stood in front of me, wearing black slacks with a long-sleeved red button up shirt and a tie, which he tried to pry away from his neck.

Kinley stood. "Here, let me see." She adjusted his tie and refolded his collar while Kat fidgeted with her hair that fell over her bare shoulders. "There." She glanced from Keppler to Alexander. "Who would ever believe you two clean up so nice."

Alexander shrugged. "Only for special occasions. Usually, I just stand next to the prettiest girl in the room and no one notices me."

Kinley shook her head and looped her arm through his, but her smile said she appreciated the compliment. "We should probably get going. Kat, come here a second." She looked her up and down, then brushed some of her hair to the front of her shoulder and the rest behind. Kat rolled her eyes, but at least she didn't start a fight.

"Maybe I should stay here." Keppler's eyes met mine. He would welcome any excuse to change back into his usual jeans and t-shirt, but the dress clothes did look good with his new glasses and haircut.

"You look too nice to stay home." Part of me wanted to take his offer. He had been distant in the past weeks, working on the truck more and talking less.

Kat backed away from Kinley. "That's what I told him." She had been the one to pick out some of dad's old clothes for me to alter. "But he won't stop complaining."

Alexander clapped a hand over Keppler's shoulder. "Look at

the bright side. It's only a couple of hours and then you won't have to wear those clothes again until Christmas."

Kinley laughed when Keppler made a face. "Come on, Kat, let's get our shoes." They both kissed the top of my head and then disappeared into the next room.

"Sorry you're not feeling well enough to come with us." Alexander pulled a little candy bar out of his shirt pocket and handed it to me.

I pulled the blanket over the blotches coated in white cream on my arm. "Do me a favor and clap extra loud for Kinley so it sounds like I'm there."

Alexander grinned. "You've got it. I'll even cheer a little and tell her it must have been the people at the next table."

Keppler tugged at his collar. "I really wish I would have gotten poison ivy instead of you."

"Be careful what you wish for." Alexander laughed, then put a hand on Keppler's shoulder and guided him toward the door. "Take it easy, Rochelle. We'll be back by ten."

I listened as voices moved into the kitchen, the back door closed, and the house settled into silence. Fighting the impulse to scratch the skin off my leg, I carried my candy bar to the desk, placed it near the edge for motivation, and sat down in front of my history book. When I picked up my notebook, a paper slid out. The letter from Aunt Audrie.

Did it come from the same place as the letter Todd thought was from his mom? Why hadn't he come home?

When I'd talked to Molly a month after my last conversation with Todd, she had accused me of telling him about the pendant. *Rochelle, the TCI probably came for him. They're probably holding him for questioning.*

Although I denied telling him anything, Molly just shook her

head and then asked whether I'd found the pendant or remembered anything important. The conversation had ended with a
firm, *Don't tell anyone else. You have to figure this out, Rochelle.*
She was losing patience with me, but Todd had advised me to avoid
her, and I had been all summer. I didn't care about the pendant or
her dad's research, even if my dad had been involved. Molly and
I couldn't save the world unless it led us to billions of doses of
vaccine ready to go. I was optimistic, but that was impossible. I
just wanted Todd back.

Picking up the letter, I walked into the kitchen, lifted the phone
off its cradle and dialed the number written by my supposed aunt.
Maybe it was a scam like Kinley said, or maybe it was my chance to
solve the mystery around Todd's disappearance.

Holding the phone to my ear, I listened to it ring, and ring, and
ring again.

"Audrie Aumont." The voice on the other end of the phone was
authoritative and familiar in some corner of my memory.

"Hi, Aunt Audrie. This is Rochelle. I got your letter." My
excitement squashed any caution.

For a few seconds the line went silent. "Rochelle, I'm so happy
to hear your voice. Is Kinley there too? And your little sister . . .
Kat, right?"

My aunt had never even met Kat. How did she know about
her? "That's right, but it's just me."

"Well, that's okay, kiddo." I remembered her calling me that
such a long time ago. "The last time I talked to you, we were
drawing chalk pictures out on the sidewalk and you told me you
wanted to be a superhero for Halloween." There was a catch in her
voice. "How have you been?"

Had she heard about Dad, Uncle Arthur, and Grandma? Why
hadn't she come? My excitement soured. "Kind of rough, actually."

"Oh, Rochelle. I'm so sorry I haven't been there." Her voice sounded sincere. "I wanted to come, in November, but I couldn't get away from work."

"Why not?" I didn't know what my aunt did for a living, but who couldn't get a day off for her mother's funeral or to care for her nieces left parentless?

"I was investigating an important case..." Her voice trailed off. "I can't go into detail, but we're all a lot safer now that the threat has been eliminated."

"Are you a spy or something?" I blurted it the way Max would and regretted it immediately. I was supposed to be doing the interrogation, not getting caught up in the story.

"Your dad and grandma never told you about that, I guess." She laughed. "I'm not surprised. Mom was particularly worried I would give you ideas and you'd follow in my footsteps."

"She was?" I didn't have a clue my grandma and aunt had spoken since Audrie left. Dad, Grandma, and Uncle Arthur had all told us Audrie walked away from our family and never reached out again.

"Yeah, that's one of the reasons she didn't want me to visit. Your grandma never forgave me when I went against her orders and took a job with the Threat Collection Initiative, but your dad and I still talked every week."

My mouth went dry and my heart beat faster as I remembered Molly's words. The TCI was the enemy trying to steal the pendants and, therefore, the vaccine. She had implied they had something to do with my dad's death. "That's who came to search the house." My voice shook. "After Dad..."

"I wanted to come instead of a bunch of agents you didn't know." Audrie's voice faded under guilt. "I didn't like the way that was handled, but I had to follow orders."

The last thing I wanted was to reveal that I knew any more than she believed I did. "What were they looking for? My dad wasn't involved in fraud like they said?"

"Of course he wasn't, kiddo." I couldn't be sure without seeing her, but it sounded like she was trying not to cry. "He was the only good person I've ever known in my life, but we couldn't reveal our true reason for the search or it would have destroyed any advantage we believed we had at the time."

"What case?" The forcefulness in my voice startled me.

"Rochelle, this is really important." She sounded so calm, patient, like my dad. "Did your dad ever say anything to you about a necklace, or a pendant?"

I took a moment to swallow, trying to relieve my dry throat. "No."

"Are you sure?" She'd heard me pause a little too long. "I have reason to believe he had one, and my colleagues never found it in the search."

"He never mentioned a pendant. Is it something dangerous?"

"No, not by itself anyway." My aunt spoke slowly. "It could give people access to something that threatens national security though. This isn't easy to explain on the phone. Maybe we could meet in person?"

Was I being pulled into the same trap as Todd? If someone was pretending to be my aunt, she had done her research.

"Okay, but we can't meet in Maibe. Kinley can't find out I called you." It destroyed the illusion that I was an adult capable of handling things, but what else could I say?

"Maybe my mom was right. You are a little like me." She laughed. "How about you decide on the time and place for us to meet and then call me and I'll be there."

"Okay, I'll let you know."

"Perfect. Be safe, kiddo. I love you." How long had it been since I'd heard that from Kinley? Would it be better for her, for all of us, if Aunt Audrie had custody of Kat and me?

"I love you too." I lowered the phone to its cradle, feeling sick to my stomach. Calling my aunt had left me with more questions than answers, and I wasn't any closer to finding Todd.

CHAPTER 19
CHARLIE

August 7, 2090

Although thick clouds blanketed the sky, the temperature hadn't dropped below ninety. Sweat dripped from my face as I set a box of computer parts on a table in the little wooden building beside the train station. I mopped my forehead with my sleeve and surveyed the room piled with what appeared to be junk. But to Max, it was a treasure trove of pieces he would use to build the surveillance system that would monitor the train station.

Since Todd hadn't returned to fulfill his council duties, Max had talked me into helping him with the security project. So, I spent the scorching afternoon hauling old computers and electronics Alexander had helped him collect from attics and basements.

A radio murmured to life, and Max crawled out from under a counter lining one wall. "The outlets work. That's a good sign."

In national news, several cases of the fever have been reported in Austin, Texas. Train service will be halted to the city and surrounding areas beginning tonight at midnight. He leaned closer to the radio to listen to the news report. *This situation has only been exacerbated by continued flooding in the state . . .*

Max wiped sweat from his forehead with the back of his hand. "We'll have to keep an eye on the news. I bet you anything that'll be the next outbreak." He played with the dial until the news faded to a murmur. "It's just like I predicted. The fever hit the north part of the country hard last year, now it's heading south."

The news made me think of the pendant hidden in my sock drawer, ominously reminding me that a threat worse than the fever waited to be brought to life. Every night since I had put it there, I woke up in a sweat, gripped by a nightmare about Griff, sometimes grinning with all of the pendants in his hand, sometimes beating me until I revealed the location of the last one he needed. If I told Rochelle about the pendant, I would have to tell her about my connection to The Defiance. If I didn't tell her and she found out, it would come across as a betrayal. Maybe I would feel better if I had a confidant, but I knew she would want to investigate. Then again, if I didn't tell her and Griff showed up asking questions . . .

As always, every choice came with a consequence.

"Are you okay, Keppler?" Max pulled items out of the box I'd just brought in and examined them one by one. "Maybe you should drink some water."

"I'm fine." I looked around the little building that had once been some kind of concession stand. Three of the walls contained large windows with smaller sliding windows where, I supposed, people used to order and pick up their food. Dull light filtered through dirty glass, illuminating the built-in counter tops and a wooden table covered with the boxes and old computer monitors we'd unloaded from Alexander's truck. "Are you sure you know what to do with all this stuff?"

"I'm reasonably sure I can figure it out within . . . ten years." He looked at me and grinned as he pulled from one box something with a bunch of wires sticking out of it and tossed it into another box. "Just joking. With you and Alexander helping me, we'll be watching the outside world in a matter of months." He tipped his head to the wall without windows. "The hardest part will be sorting through this mess."

"The bad news is, we didn't bring a fan." Alexander hoisted a plastic tote onto the table. "The good news is, there's only one more box in the truck."

"I'll get it." Hoping to catch even the lightest breeze, I dashed out into air as still and stifling as the air inside. It couldn't be later than five o'clock, but the darkening clouds had tricked the streetlights into buzzing to life prematurely. I pulled the last box out of the truck's back seat and lugged it into the rickety little building.

Alexander and Max stood around the radio listening to what sounded like a high-pitched screech as I hoisted my box onto the table. *Line of severe storms . . . radar indicated tornadoes . . . Maibe . . . Take cover . . .*

Max gripped the radio, eyes wide with excitement. Not even the overbearing heat and thick humidity could suppress his energy. "There's a tornado coming. We should go storm chasing." He reached into his pocket and pulled out a rectangular device that I recognized from my history book as a smartphone. "It took me two years, but I finally narrowed down the global Wi-Fi code for the username ABaker. Now I can access weather radars even when I'm not at the library or close to my TV."

"No way." Alexander looked over Max's shoulder. "That thing has to be an antique."

I approached Max to see if he really had hacked someone's Wi-Fi access code. The average person didn't need an Internet connection for day-to-day life. Anyone could conduct research or read up on news reports from around the world at the library. It was, however, necessary for some people, like those working at banks, hospitals, or trying to conduct a long-distance business meeting. They had to apply for permission to receive the codes and passwords they needed for the level of use they required. Many people had the communication clearance, which meant they could use email for their job, while higher clearances provided access to medical records or bank accounts.

"What about ABaker? You can't just steal his code like that." I ignored the fact that I had done far worse during my time with The Defiance.

"He, or she, will never even know." Max held his phone up so we could all see the green and red blobs sliding across his screen. "I'm not doing anything that'll get him in trouble."

"If you get caught, you'll be the one in trouble." One of my elementary school teachers had compared accessing the Internet without authorization to robbing a bank.

"Charlie's right. You have to stop using that code." Alexander glanced from the radar to the dark sky outside. "But . . . this is an emergency."

Max raised his eyebrows at me, knowing he had won, and pointed to a little curve on the red blob headed right for the dot labeled *Maibe*. "That has to be the tornado."

"Let's check it out." Alexander picked up his walkie-talkie. "If we see anything, we can radio in for Lucy to start the siren." They both headed for the door, but I didn't move.

Max turned around. "Aren't you coming?"

I shook my head. "There isn't going to be a tornado. I bet I can get all of this stuff sorted while you guys waste time."

Max shrugged. "All right. Anything with screens goes over on that counter, anything with wires on the table, and anything else over by the window." He nodded toward the walkie-talkie on the counter. "If you have any questions, you know how to reach us."

I rolled my eyes and watched through the window as they jumped into the truck and sped away.

. . . radar indicated tornadoes . . . The radio beeped several times. *If you're in the Maibe area, find shelter immediately. The most dangerous part of the storm is two miles southwest of town moving northeast. . .*

Thunder rumbled softly outside, and I started digging through the box in front of me. I had heard storm warnings on the radio every summer of my life, but they never resulted in more than a torrential downpour, a little wind, and my sister waking me up in the middle of the night because she was scared of thunder.

I wondered if Rochelle was paying attention to the weather as I lugged some old computer screens over to the counter and lined them up along the wall. She had been less talkative recently. I figured it had something to do with her missing Todd or the constant bickering between Kat and Kinley.

Max would have probably been able to convince her to help, too, but Emma had started her teacher training and planned to spend the day at the library, so Rochelle promised Lily they would work on her dress.

"Keppler?" Max's voice crackled over the walkie-talkie. "Keppler, are you there?"

I picked it up and pushed the button. "Did you find the storm yet?"

"I'm looking at the tornado right now, it's just west of town. Do you hear the sirens yet?" Max spoke so quickly I wondered how he could breathe.

I laughed and pushed the button in again. "I don't have time for jokes."

A low whirring rose to a high-pitched wail right outside.

"No joke—"

"Do you see it?" Alexander's voice interrupted. "I lost it in the rain."

"We have to move, now . . ." Max again.

"Too late." Alexander's usually calm voice rose in panic. "In the ditch. Go. Go."

"Delgado?" My breath caught in my chest. "This isn't funny."

A gust of wind slammed against the building, and I thought it would topple right off its foundation. The radio went silent and the overhead light blinked off as a loud roaring engulfed the building. A wall of rain and leaves slammed against the window, and I dove under the table with my arms over my head.

"Delgado? Alexander?" I shouted into the walkie-talkie.

Only silence answered.

CHAPTER 20

ROCHELLE

August 7, 2090

Kat gripped my hand as I pushed the basement door open and looked into the dining room, walls and windows still intact, sunshine glittering through the rain-speckled patio doors.

"See, the house didn't blow away." I stepped onto the wooden floor, taking my sister with me.

"I never thought it did." Kat was notoriously afraid of storms, but her courage always returned once the threat passed. She walked over to the glass door and pulled it open, letting a blast of rain-cooled air swirl into the house.

Tree branches and other people's patio furniture littered the yard. It would take me an entire day to clean up, even with Keppler's help.

"No one goes outside without shoes." Kinley stood at the top of the steps, arms cradling Lily.

Kat rolled her eyes and hugged one knee to her chest, displaying her tennis shoe. "Rochelle had everything under control before you got here. If anyone was irresponsible, it was you walking home from the hospital during a tornado warning."

When it started getting dark outside I had turned on the radio, and before the weather service even issued a warning, Kat, Lily, and I had put on shoes and gathered flashlights and snacks to hang out in the basement for a while. Kinley left the hospital early to beat the storm and arrived home a few minutes before the siren sent us scrambling down the stairs.

"Forgive me for worrying about you." Kinley kept her voice steady, probably for Lily's sake. "I didn't know how bad it would get and I wanted you to be safe."

"What if Emma was walking back from the library?" Lily looked at the destruction outside, then up at Kinley with wide eyes.

"She wouldn't do that." Kinley guided Lily toward me. "Your sister would trust that you're safe here with Rochelle." She nudged Lily into my arms and gave Kat an annoyed look. "I'm going to make sure we don't have any broken windows."

"Take it easy on Kinley," I whispered to Kat after our cousin left the room. "She's just looking out for us." They had been fighting ever since Kat received a flyer in the mail advertising a culinary arts camp that would take place in Omaha in October. Of course she wanted to attend, but Kinley refused to let her take a train without an adult or to take a day off class to accompany her.

"There's Charlie." Lily stepped out onto the front patio, one hand shielding her eyes from the sun, the other pointing down the street.

I walked outside and squinted against the bright light, such a contrast to the night-like darkness less than an hour earlier.

Keppler sprinted toward us, dodging branches and debris. By the time he skidded to a stop in front of us, he barely had the breath to talk. "I told them . . . not to go . . . they won't . . . answer." He held up a walkie-talkie clutched in his left hand.

Kat looked at me, brow furrowed, trying to make sense of the situation.

"It's okay. Take a minute to catch your breath." I felt bad for him, drenched in sweat, shirt smeared with dirt, looking at us as if he hadn't seen us in years and hadn't expected to ever again.

"Charlie, weren't you working with Alexander?" Kinley's voice shattered the vacuum of almost silence. "Didn't he drive you home?"

Keppler shook his head and sank to the top step of the patio. "Max and Alexander went to— " He coughed to clear his throat. "They went storm chasing, but I lost them."

"What?" Kinley snatched the walkie-talkie he held out and pulled it close to her face. "Alexander Brewser, you'd better answer me right now." We waited for a minute, but no one replied.

"Do you think they're okay?" Lily sat down next to Keppler with her chin on her knees.

"This is Max we're talking about." Kat shrugged. "It's probably a prank."

"I have to do something." Kinley rubbed her forehead. "If they were caught outside, even in the truck . . ." She looked at the huge tree limbs down in front of the house across the street where she had once lived with her parents, and her face paled.

"Let's not panic." I looked from Keppler with his face buried in his hands, to Kinley, shoulders tense and forehead wrinkled, to Kat, concern starting to register in her eyes. "Maybe they lost their walkie-talkie, or the batteries died."

The sound of a car engine sounded down the street, and we watched as Alexander's truck parked in front of the house, unable to get past a huge tree branch in the driveway.

Max leapt out of the passenger seat and bounced up the walk. "That tornado was the most spectacular thing I've ever seen in my life." He was plastered with mud from head to toe.

Kat wrinkled her nose and took a step away from him. "What happened to you?"

"We got a little too close." Alexander trudged up the front

walk. He was just as filthy as Max and holding a stack of napkins to his forehead. "We took cover in the ditch, and the wind kicked up a lot of debris."

Keppler glared at Max. "Why didn't you answer me?"

"Sorry, the walkie-talkie stopped working when I dropped it in the water." Max shook his head. "Everything was going so well until my radar glitched just when I needed it most."

The next five minutes was a jumble of Max retelling his tornado experience, Alexander downplaying the most dangerous details, and Max showing off his antique cell phone.

"Isn't that illegal?" Kat turned her face from Max's device as if it were week-old garbage. "Remember that kid from school, Tommy? He used his dad's Wi-Fi code and got sent to reform school or something."

"She's right." Alexander took the phone from Max's hand and slid it in his pocket. "This is only going to get you in trouble."

"It's a little late for that." Kinley stood with her hands on her hips, eyes burning into Alexander. "How old are you anyway? Putting your life and theirs in danger." She gestured from Keppler to Max. "If you knew there was a storm coming, then you should have driven to a house with a basement . . ."

He met her eyes and spoke quietly. "I know, Kinley. I messed up, and it won't happen again."

"Definitely not after the conversation we're going to have."

"Hey guys. What's going on?" Emma approached, one shoulder sagging under her bag of books.

Lily scurried down the steps into her sister's arms. "Kinley walked home during a tornado warning and then Alexander and Max drove after the tornado and got stuck in it."

Emma shook her head at my cousin and Alexander and laughed. "This is why I always leave Rochelle in charge."

"I'm not the one who went looking for trouble." Kinley's voice shook and her hand was equally unsteady as she slid it under Alexander's chin and turned his head to get a better look at the wound. "Do you know what could have happened?"

Emma stepped up onto the patio, pulling Lily along with her. "But everything's okay. Our houses are still here, we're all safe, and I got my assignment sent in right before the electricity went out."

"The electricity's out?" Alexander groaned and sank to the patio with his legs folded under him.

Kinley sighed. "You can worry about that after I deal with your laceration." She turned to us. "Max, go find the hose and get cleaned up. Charlie, you too. You're both a mess. We'll have a long talk later."

Keppler sighed and walked away, shoulders slumped and head hanging. Max took a step forward. "But Kinley . . ."

"This way." I took his hand and pulled him onto the sidewalk that led past the porch to the backyard.

"I can't live my life in bubble wrap, and neither can you," he complained when the others couldn't hear us anymore. "Someone has to make Kinley understand."

"Now isn't the time." We approached Keppler, already splashing water from the hose over his face. "Kat already has her in a week-long bad mood. And if you're going to chase tornadoes, you should take a storm spotter class first so you know what you're doing." I squeezed his hand tighter, acutely aware of how easily I could lose the people I loved even after the danger of the fever had passed. Todd's absence left my heart crumbled into powder. There weren't even pieces left to put back together. If I lost someone else, even the powder would blow away.

"I promise I'll know what I'm doing next time." Max reached a hand toward the stream of water, then turned back to me. "And I'll take both of you along with me. Alexander isn't the best assistant."

"That's supposed to make me feel better after you got me in trouble?" Keppler splashed water over the back of his neck.

Max laughed and reached for the hose. "Kinley will get over it by tomorrow."

I took a few steps toward the garden packed tight with tomato plants and cucumbers, carrots, beans, potatoes, and some of the seedlings from Alexander's greenhouse that hadn't sold in the spring. The produce was already more than we could eat, and we'd canned or frozen the extra. The taller plants were a little bent and twisted from the wind, but I figured a little sun and perhaps some strategically placed support stakes would solve that.

The sun shone through the dripping leaves above me, illuminating the treehouse in a comforting gold that reminded me of old-fashioned photographs. Memories of the same color flooded my brain. Todd and I had made the treehouse our hangout spot, spending hours talking after an afternoon of swimming, watching Fourth of July fireworks with our feet swinging against the rope ladder, and even jumping into an eight-foot snowdrift until Dad told us we'd break our arms. I closed my eyes tightly. There wasn't a square inch of town that didn't remind me of Todd, and there was nothing I could do to forget he was gone.

"How could you think there wouldn't be a tornado? I showed you on the radar." Max was determined to argue with someone. I turned in time to see Keppler twist the hose so it sprayed Max right in the face.

"You shouldn't have even had access to that." Keppler watched him spit and wipe water out of his eyes. "If you had to steal it, then it wasn't yours to use."

"Says the guy who stole key codes to break into houses." With lightning reflexes, Max lunged forward and turned the hose on Keppler. "If anyone understands adventure, it should be you."

"Guys, enough." I stepped between them with my hands on my hips. "How old are you anyway?" It wasn't until the words were out of my mouth that I heard the echo of my cousin's phrasing. I bit my tongue before I blurted that they fought like kindergarteners.

"I didn't break into houses for the adventure," Keppler muttered as he sat and tried to clean his glasses with the bottom of his shirt.

Max dropped the hose, looking at me as if I'd hit him. "Rochelle, you sounded just like Kinley."

"Good." I sank next to Keppler, too distracted to think about the lawn being wet. "If I would have been more like her a few months ago, Todd would still be here." The image of him walking away for the last time played over and over in my head.

They both looked at me, confused. Sighing, I explained my last conversation with Todd, minus any information about Molly and the pendant.

"It's not your fault, Aumont." Keppler slid his water-spotted glasses back onto his face. "If seeing you didn't stop him, nothing could have."

"That is something I can agree with." Max looked down at his filthy shirt then up at me. "I would hug you, but . . ."

Before he could finish the sentence, I wrapped my arms around him, not caring that he was soaked and smelled like pond water on a hot day. Since my conversation with Aunt Audrie, I'd been trying to decide what to do. I wanted to find out more, but I didn't want to walk into a trap. "Remember that letter I got from my aunt?" I lifted my head in time to see Keppler's face pinch in disappointment.

"You called the number, didn't you? Aumont . . ."

"It was really her." I let that sink in for a minute, careful to choose my next words to explain the situation while leaving out anything about the pendant. "She said she hasn't been able to be a part of the family because she's an agent for the TCI, and she's been busy keeping the country safe from really dangerous threats."

Max's jaw dropped and his eyes grew wider and brighter with each word I said. "I've read about those TCI people." His voice was a whisper of awe. "They're practically spies. You're related to a spy."

Keppler swallowed hard, blue eyes watching us in disbelief.

"She wants to meet with me, to talk about some family stuff." I brushed my hair over my shoulder, feeling a little guilty about withholding crucial details from my friends. "But Kinley can't know, so I thought maybe I should meet her in Omaha, but I know how Kinley feels about me taking the train by myself."

"I'll go with you." Max sprang up halfway and sat back on his heels, giddy with excitement. "It'll be the greatest adventure—"

"Absolutely not." Every last speck of color drained from Keppler's face, and I didn't understand the sudden terror in his eyes. "Neither of you are going anywhere to meet someone who's probably a fraud." His hands shook, and it took him a minute to catch his breath. "Do you want to end up like Todd?"

"Keppler . . ." I reached for his hand, but he pulled it away from me. I'd never seen him so upset. "It's not the same."

"It's exactly the same." He scrambled to his feet. "Todd had a good life, everything he needed, and he threw it all away to go chasing hope that he could find someone who abandoned him in the first place." He shook his head and wiped his forehead with the back of his sleeve. "Life is hard enough without looking for more trouble. Trust me, this is as good as it gets." He swept his arm crosswise in front of him. "Just be thankful."

Max stood. "But we could—"

"No." Keppler spoke the word more firmly than even my cousin. "If either of you make plans to meet with her, I'll spill everything you just said to Kinley." His blue eyes landed on me, and they were so full of panic and guilt that I believed every word of his threat.

"Okay." I took Max's hand and stood. "I won't meet with her. I won't call her again." Keppler's reaction was a reminder that although he'd shared details of his life, there was more beneath the surface that he kept to himself. My curiosity impelled me to question him, but I knew that would only push him farther away.

"Good. Believe me, it's for the best." He turned and made his way toward the house.

Max watched him retreat until the house blocked him from view. "What was that all about?"

"He knows more about life than we do." I picked up the hose. "If he says meeting with my aunt is a bad idea, I trust him." Although I believed I really had spoken with my dad's little sister, I suspected others had been fooled in similar ways.

"So do I, but I still want to know how he knows." Max collected water in his cupped hands and splashed it over his face, and then we followed Keppler inside.

CHAPTER 21

CHARLIE

August 16, 2090

On a crisp fall day, I accompanied Griff to meet with Roger Zimmer, one of his dad's colleagues and fellow pendant owner. During the drive from Kansas City to St. Louis, he told me his mom had been diagnosed with cancer when he was young and lost her fight when he was eight. His mom's brother, Uncle Mac, had been the one who was there for him, visiting him often, helping him with homework over the phone, attending his baseball games, and sending him money after he ran away from home and didn't know where to turn. Griff looked up to his uncle the way I looked up to him.

When we arrived at the farmhouse where Zimmer lived alone— he'd never had any children, according to Griff—I waited outside so I wouldn't make the meeting awkward. Lying on the hood of the car, I watched crimson leaves flutter against a perfectly clear blue sky and tried not to think about the sinister backstory behind the pendants and what it would mean for the world if they became property of The Defiance. Nothing I said could convince Griff that using a virus to gain power was a terrible idea. He believed himself to be some kind of Robin Hood who would save lost, abandoned, and neglected kids by punishing the adults who put them in that situation.

"Hey, kid." I sat up as Griff tossed the car keys to me on his way across the gravel driveway. "Your turn to drive."

I looked down at the keys in my hand and then scrambled to the *driver's seat, feeling a sense of pride that he trusted me. "Did he give you the pendant?"*

When we were both in the car, Griff reached into his pocket and pulled out a pendant, identical to the one he'd already had except the letters across the bottom spelled out B-E-T-T-E-R.

"He was happy to give it up." Griff looked through the windshield instead of meeting my eyes. "He's sure some TCI people are after it and suspects they had something to do with my dad's death. I think the same. Those people aren't the force for good they claim to be."

I put the key in the ignition but didn't start the engine. "What do they want it for?"

Griff sighed. "Same reason we do, except they'd use it against us. It would be convenient for them if a bunch of street kids came down with a virus they couldn't survive. To them, the country looks cleaner and safer without us, but it'll be better when we're in charge." He slid the pendant into his shirt pocket and patted it. "Let's go home, kid."

I turned the key and the engine roared to life, bringing me back to the driver's seat of Auggie's truck in the Aumonts' garage. Despite having both overhead garage doors open, sweat dripped from my face and soaked my shirt.

"Hey, it's running." Max stood in the doorway of the garage, arms raised in victory. Rochelle smiled beside him but didn't say anything. We'd been distant in the week following the storm, more my fault than hers. She was preoccupied with mediating the ongoing feud between Kat and Kinley. I had the growing feeling I needed to tell her about Griff and the pendants and my life with The Defiance to keep her from unknowingly walking into danger, but the apprehension of how she would react was holding my tongue for now.

Turning off the engine, I got out of the truck and closed the door, trying to find the words to explain that I'd betrayed her by hiding the pendant, and that I only knew its meaning because of my affiliation with The Defiance.

"Are you okay?" Rochelle closed the distance between us and took my arm. "You look a little flushed. Have you been out here this whole time?"

I nodded. Rochelle and Max had been at the library for hours, following the news on the latest outbreaks of the fever. I had worked through lunch since Kat was volunteering at the home for children and Kinley was eating at the hospital.

"No wonder he doesn't look excited." Max pushed the door away from him and caught it when it hit the wall and bounced back. "He's probably halfway to heat exhaustion."

"Let's get some lemonade." Rochelle put her arm around me and guided me out of the garage toward the back door.

"Aumont, I have to tell you something." Her gentle concern even after a week of my standoffishness shattered the walls I'd built to seal off my knowledge of the pendant. She deserved the truth, even if it meant she would hate me forever.

"Okay, but first sit down here." She pulled out a kitchen chair and I collapsed into it. Max walked straight to the sink and splashed water over his arms and face.

"When your aunt asked to meet with you . . ." The air conditioning collided with my sweat-soaked shirt and I shivered. "Did she say anything about a pendant?" It was my greatest fear that she knew Rochelle had the one thing she wanted.

The glass she was holding thunked onto the tabletop, and she abruptly sat next to me. "How do you know that?"

"Because that's what the TCI wants most. They'll do anything to get their hands on those pendants." I dried my face with my sleeve to avoid Rochelle's puzzled stare.

Max poured lemonade in the glasses. "Do you work undercover

for them or something?" He laughed but looked at me expectantly, waiting for a logical explanation.

I shook my head and drank two refreshing gulps. "If I show you guys something, do you promise to let me explain before you kick me out?"

"Keppler." Rochelle smiled but her concern showed through. "How many times do we have to tell you, you're part of this family no matter what."

As much as I wanted to believe her, there was only one way to know her true reaction. Slowly, I pulled my arm out of my sleeve and lifted my shirt so they could see the symbol burned into my arm.

"That's just like the one in the paper." Max stood and leaned forward to study it more closely. "The one that means someone is in The Defiance."

Rochelle lifted her eyes from my arm to my face. "Who did that to you?"

I looked at the blue sky out the window, so I wouldn't see her expression. "The Defiance. I was one of them for a while, but it was a mistake." And then it was all pouring out of me—everything I'd been through, running away from the home for children, meeting Griff and his obsession with the pendants, attempting to stop him and the consequences. "That's why I was so beat up the night I met you guys. I tried to take a pendant from him and . . . you saw the result." I flopped back in my chair, forcing my shoulders to relax. Rochelle had looked interested and compassionate during the telling, which was a much better reaction than what I'd expected—furious and distrustful.

"Could it be possible that the Griff you know is the same Griff Molly knows?" Rochelle jumped when the refrigerator started and pressed a hand to her chest.

"What does Molly have to do with this?" My heart began to beat faster.

"Her dad was the head of the project that the pendants came out of. My dad got involved . . . There were five others: Iverson, Zimmer . . . Welch . . . Davis . . ." She was uncharacteristically inarticulate, but I could follow her train of thought.

"And Spencer. Griff's dad."

Max stared at both of us. For the first time in the six months I'd known him, he was speechless.

Rochelle squeezed her eyes shut and took a deep breath. "There's so much I have to tell you guys, but you have to promise not to tell anyone else and to be careful because it might be the reason Todd is missing." She waited until we both nodded and then recited her conversations with Molly, described her dad's part in the pendant saga, and recounted her thorough search for the pendant that didn't yield any results. "Molly told me the TCI probably lured Todd away for questioning, but they couldn't possibly know I told him anything, right?"

Despite cool air roaring through the vents, sweat beaded my forehead. I had trouble forcing air into my lungs.

"The TCI . . . The Defiance . . ." I could barely get the words out. "If Griff finds out I'm here . . . If he knows I'm alive . . ."

"He won't find out." Rochelle gently squeezed my hands in hers. "Let's be logical about this. Molly doesn't know there's any connection between you and Griff, and there is no reason for you to come up in their conversations. The Defiance has no reason to come here since Molly is already cooperating with them and her entire plan relies on me never finding out who she's working with."

Focusing on slowing my breathing, I nodded. Her words made sense, but a few minutes ago, I thought Maibe and my new family were so out of the way Griff would never find them. Now, he already had.

"So, you're telling me after everything you went through to escape all of this stuff..." Max scratched his head, trying to process all of the information that had been thrown at him. "You just ran back into all of it without even knowing. That's bad luck."

"No, it's good luck." Rochelle stood. "Now, thanks to Keppler, we know what we're dealing with."

Max watched her, eyes wide with a mix of adventure and disbelief. "So The Defiance wants the pendants, but they're not the good guys, The TCI also wants the pendants, but they're also not the good guys, and Molly wants the pendants and she's definitely not with the good guys. Who exactly can we trust?"

"No one. At least, not until we know more." Rochelle sank back into her chair. "Molly is trying to manipulate me, but I'm not sure how because I still have no proof that my dad actually had a pendant."

"I do." It took all of my effort to choke out the words. The Defiance was only the first part. Now came the betrayal.

"You've seen it?" Rochelle and Max spoke at the same time.

"I found it weeks ago in the seat of the truck . . . Aumont, I'm sorry I didn't tell you. I just—"

She scooted closer and wrapped her arms around me even though I didn't hug her back. "You don't have to apologize. After everything you've been through . . ." She leaned back and shook her head. "Your first instinct was to protect us because that's who you are. You don't belong in The Defiance, and that's why you're here now. Nothing happens by chance."

A flood of relief washed through my body, taking with it the lump in my throat, the bricks on my shoulders, and the weight on my chest. But that phrase, *nothing happens by chance,* brought it all back. That meant I couldn't run from the pendants. They had become my responsibility, my destiny, and I would never be safe until I faced the problem and solved it.

"So, Keppler has your dad's pendant. Molly, the TCI, and The Defiance all want it." Max leaned forward, arms stretched across the table in front of him. "What do we do about it?"

Rochelle's eyes narrowed and seemed to take on a fiercer shade of green. "First of all, we don't tell anyone else about anything we've just discussed. Second, I'll continue to deny knowing anything about a pendant, but the three of us will take turns having it on a weekly rotation to share the responsibility of keeping it safe. And third, I have to meet with my aunt and find out what she can add to this story."

"I'm ready to take my turn with the pendant." Before I could protest, Max jumped to his feet. "And Keppler and I will go with you to spy on the spy. We can listen in on the conversation and we'll be close by in case she tries anything."

"Kinley took me to this restaurant in Omaha. It would be the perfect place . . ." Her eyes lit up at the chance of adventure and blissful underestimation of the dangers ahead.

Max grinned. "Just don't schedule it for a couple of weeks. I have some things to get ready."

They both turned to me. After everything I'd confessed, they still wanted me around and trusted my input. And they still wanted to meet with Rochelle's aunt.

"You don't have to do this, Keppler." Her eyes were understanding, forgiving. "But this time would be different. You won't be alone and we'll save the world. Do you want in?"

I sighed and nodded slowly. "I'm in." It had always been easier to run away than face my problems, but now the worst mistake of my life had caught up. I had a family to protect and running wouldn't save them.

CHAPTER 22
ROCHELLE

September 7, 2090

“T he kitchen was a disaster, and I was on the floor crying when Uncle Arthur and your dad got home from football practice. Arthur just laughed and said Mom and Dad would never trust me to stay home alone again, but Auggie told me he forgot to put the lid on the blender lots of times, and he helped me clean everything up.” Audrie laughed as she cut a piece from the stack of pancakes on her plate. “That happened more than twenty years ago and, as far as I know, your grandma never found out about it.”

I smiled, visualizing my dad, aunt, and uncle as kids. Of course Uncle Arthur would have been annoyed by his baby sister’s irresponsibility; and my dad, the one to make it all better. It sounded like my aunt was just trying to keep up with her older brothers.

“You remind me a lot of your dad.” She brushed her shoulder-length hair behind her ear. It was cut to fall in perfect straight layers, the shortest of which rested against the collar of her green blouse worn under a black blazer. I had immediately recognized her when she walked into the restaurant due to her startling resemblance to Kinley and even my own reflection. She strode across the café with natural confidence, high-heeled boots clicking, and I felt at ease when she smiled and slid into the booth across from me without hesitation.

"That's what everyone says." I was careful to make eye contact with her as I observed Keppler and Max in my peripheral vision. They sat at a table across the room, hoods bunched up to their ears to hide the earbuds plugged into an old phone in Max's pocket, picking up the conversation through the old phone in my pocket. It turned out Max had a huge stash of old electronics in his workshop plus the fascination, genius, and patience to make them work.

"It's so good to finally meet you in person." Audrie's eyes constantly scanned the room, occasionally landing on the man at a table behind us. I figured it was a habit from her line of work. "The first summer you and your dad moved back to Maibe, I spent my entire break from college with the two of you and Kinley. We had so much fun." She sighed but smiled. "Even though your dad sent pictures, it's still sinking in that the toddler I hugged goodbye fourteen years ago is the smart, pretty young woman sitting in front of me."

"I wish you could have visited." It wasn't flattery to get the answers I wanted. In the hour we'd been at the restaurant, my aunt and I had talked about our lives and memories over blueberry pancakes. She made me feel innovative, smart, and capable in situations Kinley would have labeled me irresponsible and an embarrassment to the family. The longer I spoke with her, the more I wished she would have been there after the fever to take care of Kat and me. At least Kinley wouldn't have been so stressed.

"Me too, kiddo." She smiled and her eyes glittered the way Dad's used to. "I'm going to do a better job of being here for you from now on."

Out of the corner of my eye, I noticed Max scratch his nose, the signal he was having trouble hearing and a reminder I hadn't gotten any of the information I'd come for. Sighing, I shifted the device in my pocket. "Aunt Audrie, on the phone you said my dad was under investigation because he had a pendant. But you said he didn't do anything wrong. I don't understand."

She nodded, eyes growing sad. "About three years ago, the TCI got a tip about a potential threat, and one of the guys involved happened to be a friend of your dad's, so I asked Auggie to keep his ears open for anything suspicious."

"It was Eric Bennett, wasn't it?" I leaned forward, arms folded on the table. Anyone in Maibe would have said Eric if a friend of my dad's was brought up.

My aunt cringed and nodded. "Good guess. Eric and his research team had been commissioned to find a universal vaccine for viruses, but the anonymous source seemed to think they had actually been working on some kind of bioweapon that could amplify seasonal viruses."

"So which one was true?" Her explanation was a combination of Molly's hopeful scenario and the more disturbing details from Keppler's story.

"There was never evidence to support anything unethical." Audrie slid a piece of her pancake around on her plate like I often did when distracted at mealtime. "Auggie knew the whole team through Eric. He played cards with them, went to football games with them, and overheard plenty of information about the topic. He reported back to me that there was nothing dishonest or dangerous about the project. We sent agents to speak with each of the team members, found nothing of concern, and closed the case. From what I heard, the team ran out of funding soon after, and their potential vaccine never made it to human trials."

I observed the way her shoulders slumped. Her gestures and physical reactions were so similar to mine that reading her emotions was easier than I expected. I tried to think of what I'd say if I were hearing this information for the first time. "Okay, so the research didn't go anywhere . . . But what does that have to do with a pendant?"

"I shouldn't be surprised by your perceptiveness and persistence." Audrie glanced around the café, then leaned forward and lowered her voice. "Your dad and I talked on the phone twice a week, but it wasn't until he got sick that he confessed to being given a pendant. There are eight pendants, all held by Eric and the other five men on the project, and Auggie said that together they would provide access to the research. Apparently when they had funding again, Auggie had been the tie breaker deciding to lock it away because the world wasn't ready to use the results for good." Doubt flickered across her face.

"You didn't believe him?"

She nodded, resting her face in her hand. "Can you blame me? We never turned up a pendant in the search. When he told me that, he had been sick for months and I knew that he got . . . a little confused." Her eyes landed on my face, then quickly shifted to the traffic rushing by outside the window. "I'm sorry, kiddo. You've been through so much and I don't want to make things any harder."

Suddenly her sympathy, whether real or an interrogation strategy, felt like an insult. "You should have visited him, even if Grandma wouldn't have liked it. He was so sick, and he would have been happy to see you. We needed your help so many times in the past year."

She didn't flinch as I imagined I would have in a reverse situation. Instead, she met my eyes and held them. "I'll always regret staying away, but I'm going to protect you and your cousin and sister now."

I wanted nothing more than to shake the lingering suspicion that Audrie reached out not because she cared about us, but because she wanted something. Hopefully with time, I would trust her. "Protect us from what?"

"I'm not entirely sure." She sighed. "Several members of that research team have died under suspicious circumstances in the past year. I'm worried they're being targeted because of their work on that project, and I don't know whether Auggie would be associated with the group." Audrie reached across the table and took my hand. "I don't believe you're in any immediate danger since Auggie had already passed and wasn't actually working on the project, but I don't want to take any chances."

Was it wrong to hold back what I knew about The Defiance, what Molly had told me about her dad, and that my dad did indeed own a pendant? Could I trust Audrie? I needed more information.

"Who would want to hurt them? Do you think it's because they really do have pendants?" I didn't pull my hand away. It was comforting having an adult, instead of Kinley, looking out for me.

"Not one pendant has turned up in our searches." Audrie squeezed my hand reassuringly. "It's the Welch family's situation that keeps me up at night. We made contact with them, but hours before the meeting, Adam Welch and his wife were murdered." She looked at me like I was that toddler she remembered instead of the capable teenager she'd claimed I'd become. "Their daughter, Ava, is about your age, and as far as I know, she's still missing. I just want to be sure that you, Kinley, and Kat are all safe."

Nodding, I pulled my hand from hers to tuck my hair behind my ear. My gut was telling me there were things she was keeping from me. Despite how nice it felt to reconnect with her, I could not ignore the anxiety knotting inside me. "I guess I'm still confused about why the research is so important. If it's not dangerous and it won't save the world, why would anyone want it? Why would anyone want to hurt Eric Bennett's team, and why would anyone even believe my dad had anything to do with the project?"

Curiosity pushed me to ask questions, and I hoped she would slip up and tell me something new.

"Those are all excellent questions, kiddo, and all things I have no evidence to answer. The truth is, you probably have nothing to worry about, but I'd like to make up for lost time." Her smile returned. "I'm hoping I can visit Maibe, see the old house, spend time with all three of my nieces. I'll feel better seeing for myself that your house is secure and knowing all of you feel comfortable contacting me anytime."

"I'll talk to Kinley." I dreaded her reaction, but I needed more time with my aunt to decide whether I could trust her. She hadn't done anything wrong; I just got the feeling there was more to the story than what she was willing to reveal. "But when you actually meet Kinley, could we tell her we talked about all of this on the phone? If she knew I was here . . ." I felt myself cringe.

"I would never want to get you in trouble with your cousin." She nodded in an approving way that assured me her opinion of my behavior was far more favorable than Kinley's would have been. "I suppose I should get going or I'll miss my train back to New York." She tossed some money on the table and stood.

Scrambling to my feet, I ignored the uncanny feeling I was looking at myself through some kind of time portal to the future. "I'll call you soon."

"I'm looking forward to that." She wrapped me in a hug, and I felt the security of childhood I had known before Dad and Grandma were gone. "Don't be afraid because of what I told you, just cautious." She held me at arm's length in front of her. "I love you, kiddo. Safe travels."

"I love you too." Someday, I would be as pretty and poised as my aunt, especially with her there to guide me. "I'll call you soon."

From my booth, I watched her exit the building, walk across

the sidewalk, and get into a black car that pulled away from the curb and merged into the endless traffic.

Glancing toward Max and Keppler, I noticed the man Audrie had been watching, waiting at the register to pay, looking right at me.

Before I could think too much about it, Max slid in beside me and whispered, "That was perfect. We heard every word and she didn't suspect a thing."

"Are you okay, Aumont?" Keppler sat down across from us, his blue eyes calm and soothing after the intensity of Aunt Audrie's.

I nodded. "Yeah, just confused. Molly said the pendants lead to a vaccine, The Defiance thinks they'll be able to start the next pandemic, and Audrie doesn't think either of those things even exist. Someone is lying to us."

"Do you trust her?" Keppler scratched his eyebrow. "Your aunt?"

"I want to." My heart told me Audrie was happy to see me, that she loved me and wanted to be part of my life. She was proud of me like Kinley would never be, and she was rearranging her life to make time for us. My head told me it couldn't be a coincidence she suddenly reached out after fourteen years of no contact, and that she didn't have any plans to hurt me, but she was also keeping something from me. "But I don't think we can afford to trust anyone right now."

"Agreed." Max bounced a little beside me, only able to contain his excitement through physical movement. "What do we do next?"

"We should check the news for information about the other researchers. Maybe she's exaggerating to scare you into telling her something." Keppler shook his head doubtfully. "I know Griff's dad drowned."

"Don't start to worry. We're still in control of this . . ." Squirming in my seat, I realized I had the same problem as Max but with apprehension instead of excitement. "I have to tell Kinley I spoke with Audrie and convince her to let me set up dinner or something. Maybe then we'll understand her motives better . . ."

Keppler made a face that told me he felt the same dread, then looked at the clock above the door of the restaurant. "If we're going to get home before Kinley does, we should get to the station."

He had a point. Kinley and Kat thought we were with Alexander, and Alexander thought we were at the library doing homework. "It's odd that she asked me about the pendant in our first conversation, yet she claims my dad was delusional when he told her about it."

Max wrapped his arm around me. "We know he wasn't, and I bet she does too. We'll piece it all together, and we're one step ahead because as far as anyone knows, you don't have a pendant."

Keppler stood, looking troubled. "Let's just go."

CHAPTER 23

CHARLIE

September 16, 2090

"So, Kinley, how would you feel about me inviting Aunt Audrie over for dinner?" Rochelle bounced along next to her cousin as if simply asking permission to buy new shoes.

Kinley stopped so abruptly, Kat and I almost ran into her. "You'd better not mean the Aunt Audrie who abandoned our family." She stood with an ice cream cone halfway to her lips, eyebrows raised at Rochelle.

We were on our way home after an evening on Main Street celebrating the reopening of Maibe's only restaurant, the relocated pharmacy, and a new store that sold clothing, books, and household goods. There had been a barbeque, music, games, and even ice cream. We were all in a good mood after the rare evening out, so I understood why Rochelle chose that moment to break the news to her cousin.

"It's actually more complicated than that." The words came out so fast they jumbled together, and she took a deep breath before continuing more slowly. "She's a TCI agent, but Grandma and Dad knew, and that's why she couldn't visit, but now she wants to make sure we're safe because of the case Dad helped her with."

"Wait, what?" Kat's face scrunched in confusion.

"Ignoring the fact that you called her when I asked you not to . . ." Kinley's forehead wrinkled and her free hand rested on her hip. "I can't believe you would let some stranger, who probably isn't even our aunt, put a bunch of wild ideas in your head. Rochelle Irene Aumont, you're smarter than that."

"She really is your aunt." I had to say something to get Rochelle out of the hole she was digging. "She had all of the right answers to our questions . . ." Kinley's glare sent me back a step. "When we talked to her on the phone."

"Unbelievable." She pulled a tissue out of her pocket to dab at melting ice cream dribbling over her hand. "Do all of you ignore what I say on purpose, or do I need to get your hearing checked?"

"Do any of you think to fill me in on important details, like we're talking with our aunt who I've never met?" Kat popped the last part of her ice cream cone into her mouth and spoke around it. "I vote we invite her to dinner."

"None of us will have anything to do with her." Kinley let her eyes slide from Kat to Rochelle to me. "Life is finally getting to some kind of normal, and we're not going to derail that."

"Come on, Kinley." Kat would fight for anything her cousin opposed. Unfortunately, that wouldn't help here. "I can make a fancy dinner; she'll love it."

Kinley shook her head and started walking. "I'll think about it and get back to you."

Rochelle shrugged and looked at me as if to say, *We'll bring it up another time.*

After three days at the library with Max and Rochelle, searching for news articles containing the names of the research team I remembered from conversations with Griff and Rochelle had heard from Molly, we verified that Audrie's description of the team's demise hadn't been an exaggeration. Matt Spencer, Griff's dad, had drowned in his own backyard pool under suspicious conditions. In July, Adam Welch and his wife had been found dead at their home in Dallas. Their daughter's body had been discovered in San Antonio just last week. Brandon Iverson had been presumed murdered—plenty of blood in his apartment but no body—in San Antonio in August. Last, and most disturbing to me, there was Roger Zimmer who had been strangled on what I believed to be the same day Griff visited him about the pendant. If I had my notebooks, I'd be able to verify the date, but I was sure enough to question how Griff could be so cold he was able to choke the air out of someone and then have a normal conversation on our drive home.

Although the pendant hung around my neck this week, I tried not to think about any of it. Life was good. I was walking home with my family on a warm fall night under changing leaves and sparkling stars ...

"Didn't we close the door when we left?" Kat stood on the back step, arm stretched toward the screen door, suspiciously eyeing the inside door standing wide open and the door between the laundry room and kitchen ajar.

"I pulled both of them shut on the way out." After three lectures from Kinley about letting cold drafts in or air conditioning out, I'd learned my lesson. Dread settled in the pit of my stomach and the pendant burned into my chest. "Stay here. I'll check it out."

My search of the house didn't turn up an intruder, but the main floor and Rochelle's room were trashed. Every drawer and cupboard had been dumped, books swept off shelves, cushions tossed from chairs and couches, but we couldn't identify even one missing item. Kinley called the police.

Two officers investigated the scene, told us it was probably just some bored kids messing around, and finished with advice to keep the doors locked. By the time Kinley walked them to the door, two hours had passed, and any carefree joy from earlier in the evening had evaporated. Kat and I picked up the mess while Rochelle sat on the cushionless couch holding two halves of a drawing Todd had given her. Every one of the dozens hanging on her wall had been viciously ripped down and scattered among the items emptied from her drawers and torn out of her closet. The rest of the upstairs rooms were untouched.

"Is this what Aunt Audrie was worried about?" Kat tossed a throw pillow onto the couch and sat down next to her sister.

Rochelle looked up from the drawing and blinked watery eyes. "What?"

"Never mind." Kat slid closer, wrapped her arms around Rochelle, and laid her head on her shoulder. "I have a huge roll of tape in my room. I'll put all of them back together and hang them up again."

I wanted to say something comforting, but my head whirled with questions. Had someone from The Defiance been here? Or was it the TCI? Did Rochelle indicate to her aunt that we would all be away from the house? Did Griff know I was in Maibe?

Kinley walked in, rubbing her forehead in tiny little circles. "I'm going to call Alexander and ask him if he'll come sleep on the couch for tonight and then first thing in the morning, I'll call Emma. Her dad can put some better locks on the doors."

"We've never locked the doors in my life." Rochelle looked up for the first time. "And nothing like this ever happened."

Kinley sighed and sat down next to her cousin. Kat got up to continue straightening the mess. Kinley said, "Although I don't think this has anything to do with what Audrie told you, maybe it wouldn't hurt to let her visit and hear what she has to say. We'll call her tomorrow. All of us together." She played with Rochelle's hair, brushing it away from her face. "For now, I'm going to call Alexander. Kat, how do you feel about making some hot chocolate?"

"I'm in." Kat looked at me, still picking up books. "We can

clean up more tomorrow, Charlie. Rochelle, you can sleep in my room until we put yours back together."

Kinley smiled and rested her hand on top of Rochelle's head. "Or mine."

"Or you can both sleep in my room." Kat took a backward step toward the next room. "I'll make snacks and it'll be a sleepover. Like when we were kids."

Rochelle nodded and the sadness on her face faded for a minute. "As long as you're both there, I'm in." It was the first time in months Kat and Kinley were working together instead of fighting.

Kat darted out of the room to get started on her new mission, and Kinley wrapped her arms around Rochelle. "I know you miss him. We'll spend all day tomorrow putting those drawings back together until they're as good as new." She kissed the top of her cousin's head and stood, unable to make any other reassuring promises concerning Todd. "Charlie will stay here with you and I'll be right back."

I replaced a cushion on the couch next to Rochelle and sat down. "Maybe . . ." I looked toward the door and lowered my voice. "Maybe we should just tell your aunt about the pendant and turn it over to her. If The Defiance was here—"

"They weren't." Rochelle held up the pieces of Todd's drawing. "Molly isn't one of them yet, but she's getting impatient. She wants to hurt me, scare me, make me vulnerable enough that I'll go along with whatever she says." Over the past month, the intense girl had called, stopped by, and pulled Rochelle aside after council meetings with pleas to help her save the world or guilt trips about being too selfish and lazy to spend time looking for the pendant. "No matter what I tell her, she knows my dad had a pendant, and she knows I'm lying to her."

"You think she did this." The realization that only someone who knew Rochelle would find any significance in destroying the drawings was both a relief and disturbing. Molly was trouble. "You should stay away from her unless I'm with you. Or Delgado."

Rochelle shook her head. "I have to keep playing her game to find out what we're up against. I can handle Molly, and even if she doesn't know it, she needs my help. You told me if you had one person to offer you help, you never would have joined The Defiance. I can't let Molly fall into that trap."

I believed that about myself, but Molly seemed like a perfect candidate for The Defiance. Her vicious disregard for people's feelings and well-being reminded me of Griff. "Just be careful, and let's hurry and decide whether we can trust your aunt."

"Okay." She smoothed the crinkled drawing over her leg. "Did you check to make sure the pendant is still . . ."

Glancing toward the kitchen, I slid the pendant from beneath my shirt for Rochelle to see.

"Good idea to keep it close." She studied it as if she could find the answers we needed on its shiny surface. "It's hard to believe so many people want to get their hands on that thing. That they even believe it exists."

"You'd have no reason to believe it did if I hadn't been so persistent about working on the truck." I let it slide into hiding once again, regretting ever stumbling across it.

"Nothing happens by chance. You found it because we're supposed to finish whatever my dad started." Rochelle frowned. "What I can't understand is why Todd hasn't come home. He would be here right now if I would have begged him to stay, told Kinley, cried . . . Every time I think about it, I just should have *done* something."

I'd noticed the sadness that seeped into Rochelle's demeanor anytime she stopped moving. She used studying, prepping for council meetings, working with Alexander, and helping Kat with gardening and canning as distractions. She'd rather run herself into the ground than face such a painful loss.

"It was his mistake to leave." How he could walk away from people who still wanted him back after five months of absence puzzled me. "It's pretty rotten for him to do that to you."

"He wouldn't stay away on purpose. I have to figure this out." She spoke more to herself than to me, and I realized she had formed an association between solving the pendant problem and finding Todd.

"The pendant has nothing to do with him, Aumont." Absent-mindedly, I pulled my shirt away from my chest, afraid the shape would show through.

"It's a step toward making the world a better place." Rochelle sighed and sank into the cushions behind her. "As long as we have it, no one can use it for their selfish purposes. And if it does lead to a vaccine, we'll get it into the hands of someone who will use it for good."

I nodded. It wasn't the time to convince her that The Defiance would do anything it took to get their hands on that pendant.

CHAPTER 24

ROCHELLE

September 20, 2090

"I understand it's expensive, but if Maibe invests in this update to the electrical grid now . . ." Neil paused dramatically to look at each face lining the conference table, stopping at Molly. "We'll avoid those annoying outages in the short term and a complete blackout in the long term."

Between scribbled notes, I glanced up at Molly's sour expression. When I left the house, Keppler and Max were covered in grease to their elbows trying to figure out what was causing the truck's latest refusal to start. Although he had never missed a council meeting, Keppler felt he was making good progress on the truck, so I volunteered to fill in as notetaker just this one time. He probably wouldn't let me do it again after not being able to read my handwriting.

"I understand the benefits, Neil. I'm not stupid." Molly brushed her bangs out of her eyes. "My question is, as it was before you broke into that ten-minute answer, where is the money for that kind of project?"

"Molly, Molly, Molly." Neil grinned and shook his head slowly back and forth. "That's a problem for the next meeting. I'm not going to waste my time looking into funding until I know I have approval for the project." He threw his arm around me and glanced at my notes. "I know my best buddy Rochelle is following my logic."

Rolling her eyes, Molly leaned back in her chair. "Brown-nosing is not an acceptable way to get your plan voted through."

I dropped my pen and shook the cramp out of my hand. "Neil does have a good plan, and he'll have to find a solution to the budgeting problem if he wants to carry it out. For now, let's just vote on the plan."

Alexander held up one hand in front of him. "All in favor of updating our electrical infrastructure."

Four hands shot into the air. Molly folded her arms.

"There we have it." Alexander smiled, looking far more relaxed in his position as facilitator of our meetings than he had been five months earlier. "Neil and I will take a look at our infrastructure funding and available grants, then report at the next meeting." He closed his binder. "Before we adjourn for the week, I have big news. A month ago, I alluded to setting up a summit to bring together Nebraska's mayors or leaders. I've been in contact with enough of them to know there's plenty of interest, so I've decided we'll host the summit here in Maibe in November."

Murmurs of surprise went around the table. "Really?" Kiara leaned forward with her arms on the table. "I have a million ideas!"

Alexander nodded. "I want all of you to attend, of course. We'll start making plans at our next meeting. I'm proud of the leaders you're all becoming, and I'll see you next week."

"Rochelle." Molly squeezed my arm as the room broke into the usual concluding chatter. "Since you don't have a ride, let's walk together and talk."

I had spent months trying to avoid Molly as Todd had advised, but she was persistent. Her impatience with me had become annoyance, but breaking into my house was crossing the line in a big way. She could scare me, make me feel guilty, and say awful things about me, but Kinley and Kat didn't deserve to be involved in a problem I was responsible to solve.

"Sure, I want to talk about a few things."

She narrowed her eyes at my falsely cheery tone and continued packing her notes into the little bag she slung over her shoulder. I waved at Alexander as I followed Molly through the building and onto the sidewalk. A cool breeze and hazy blue evening sky contrasted the stuffy warmth of the conference room.

"I heard someone broke into your house during the grand opening bash." She swept her bangs to the side and waited expectantly for my response.

"And you want me to believe it was the TCI looking for my dad's pendant?" I couldn't hide the annoyance in my voice.

"Who else would it be?" She stepped in front of me. "I warned you they'd show up again, and now you don't even know whether they found your pendant."

"If I haven't found it yet, how would *they*?" I sidestepped her and started across the street. "Anyway, I've recently been informed my aunt is a TCI agent, and I doubt she would walk back into my life just to trash my house a week later." I watched her face contort into a strange emotion, nose scrunched in confusion, eyes wide with panic and loss. How much did she know about the investigation into her dad's research team? Knowing how much she admired him, I couldn't bring myself to even imply something negative about him.

"Your aunt? You didn't tell her what I told you—"

"No, Molly. I don't tell anyone about the pendant or world-saving research because I don't believe it. I don't believe my dad was involved in it." I couldn't hide my frustration. I could tell she knew more than she was telling me.

"Why? Because you want to pretend he didn't prevent the development of a vaccine that would have saved thousands of lives? He messed up big time, and this is your one chance to redeem him."

I stopped so abruptly that Molly had to turn around and retrace her steps. "If he made that decision, he had a good reason. What are you not telling me?"

"I'm sorry. I shouldn't have said that." She shifted her bag to the other shoulder as she sidestepped my question. "It's just, Griff wants all of the pendants together by the end of this year and if we don't hurry . . ."

Molly's downcast eyes and slightly slumped shoulders didn't tell me what would happen, whether she really felt bad about her comments concerning my dad, or if she was just trying to avoid my questions.

"What do you know about this Griff guy? Why do you trust everything he tells you?" Did she even suspect what Keppler already knew?

"I've known him since we were kids. Of all the families we went camping or skiing with, the Spencers were my favorite because I liked talking to Griff." She glanced up and down the sidewalk then squeezed my arm and propelled me forward. "It's none of your business, but he's the leader of The Defiance, and before you say anything, you should know he plans to ensure that kids without anyone to look out for them get the vaccine first, and he's making sure they have shelter and food even now. The Defiance isn't the evil organization the papers make it out to be. They're not doing anything so different from what you and your family did for Charlie."

"You're forgetting the part about The Defiance derailing trains and violently taking over cities." The papers, radio, and TV traded off focusing on the fever and The Defiance, which was destroying anything that stood in their way as they took over more territory. Travel was no longer advised in the area extending from the middle of Kansas to Kansas City to St. Louis and south into Oklahoma and Missouri.

"They've been forced to make that choice, Rochelle." She slowed down and let go of my arm. "Don't you understand what's happening to most kids our age? We're not old enough to be on our own, but we don't have parents to fight for us. The world is collapsing, and if we don't fight our way to the top, we'll be buried under it all." Her eyes were fierce, but her face showed fear.

"That's not true. We have Kinley and Alexander to look out for us—"

"As if they know what they're doing." She shook her head. "Do you think Kinley's little math lessons are going to get you into college over a kid with real parents finding them the best educational opportunities? Do you think you'll be able to compete with these kids you're opening a school for? We're lost, Rochelle, destined to be tossed to the street and forgotten."

"How can you say that? We're on the town council. We're helping to bring Maibe back to life—"

"It's not enough." The setting sun caught half her face, leaving the rest shadowed by the awning of the building that used to be a bakery. "When we were first elected I thought we would be able to . . . well, I thought we would be less worried about schools and paving streets and more focused on finding a way to side with people who can ensure our safety."

Comprehending what she meant, I swallowed hard. "You mean, invite The Defiance to walk in and take over?"

Gripping my shoulders, Molly shook me. "Wake up, Rochelle. It's only a matter of time before they take the whole country. Everyone's too busy with their own problems to stop them. You have to choose a side, and choosing The Defiance is the only option."

"But, you haven't . . ." I touched my arm halfway between my shoulder and elbow, the location of Keppler's brand. As The Defiance expanded their territory, Nebraska papers had started printing photos of the brand and warning readers to be on the lookout for the symbol that would reveal whether a suspicious runaway was really with The Defiance. They were to be reported to local authorities immediately.

"Not yet." The doubt in her eyes brought me hope. "I'm waiting for you to find your pendant so we can give them to Griff together. Then the three of us will be equal partners in all decisions going forward."

My mouth went dry. So this was the plan she had been holding back, hoping I would cooperate and everything would fall into place. "I can't just leave. What about Kat and Kinley?"

"You don't need them, Rochelle. Kat isn't even your real sister and Kinley just wants to control your life. Why can't you understand they're standing in your way? Just like Todd. He's gone, and look at everything you've accomplished on the council without him here."

Struggling to form any words, I took a deep breath and willed myself not to let one tear slip in front of Molly. "How can you even ... I can't ... I won't let anyone hurt them."

"Try to think about it this way." Molly spun around to face me. Around us were worn, out-of-business storefronts. "If this is what matters to you, if you want to protect this pathetic little town and the people in it, fine. You can make all the calls involving Maibe. This is an opportunity to protect them."

"And what happens to the rest of the world?" I walked to the bench in front of the boarded-up bakery and sat down. "Please, Molly, because I care about you, I'm asking you to think about this. You won't have a future with The Defiance, but without them you can do whatever you want."

She slumped beside me. "How? My parents are dead. My sister doesn't care that I'm alive. And I haven't even finished high school."

"You're my friend. That makes you part of my family, and I'll help you. When you're ready, we'll figure out who should really have that pendant." I took her hands. "And you're always welcome at my house for dinner, to study, or just to hang out."

"It's not really the same." She stared down at my hands, gripping hers as if she were about to fall off a cliff and only I could prevent her from slipping over the edge. "Kinley and Kat never liked me much. Maibe just doesn't feel like home to me."

"I can help you. Just give me a chance." Whether the pendants represented a vaccine or a virus no longer mattered to me. I had let Todd make a terrible mistake, and I couldn't let Molly do the same.

Her eyes teared up. "You don't understand. I've already..."

"We'll figure it out." I pulled her into a hug. "The Defiance won't be your family. Don't let them fool you."

She nodded and brushed her hair over her shoulder. Before I could say another word, a horn honked and my dad's truck pulled up to the curb. Molly and I watched as the passenger window rolled down and Max stuck his head out.

"We're going to the diner for dinner." He glanced at the passenger seat and laughed. "Keppler's paying."

A muffled comment came from the driver's seat and Max laughed again. I had planned to walk home with Molly, but this felt like the perfect opportunity to make her part of my family. "Are you hungry? You should come with us."

She looked from the truck to me and a veil of disappointment fell over her face. "No, that's all right. But I'm glad we talked." As she stood, any doubt cleared from her eyes and a smile spread over her face. Something about her expression gave me an awful sinking feeling.

"Are you sure, because—"

"Absolutely," she interrupted as she adjusted the bag on her shoulder. "Have fun with your friends, Rochelle."

"Okay." I took a backward step away from her, not sure what else I could say. "I'll see you soon." I jogged over to the truck where Max waited with the door open so I could slide to the middle of the bench seat. "Does Kinley know we won't be home for dinner?"

"Kinley and Kat are the reason we're eating out." Keppler glanced over his shoulder as a single car passed us on its way down Main Street. "They're fighting *again*."

Max scooted in beside me. "Keppler was too chicken to go in the house and ask Kinley's permission to go out for dinner, but I took care of it and that's why he's paying."

Ignoring Keppler's annoyed glare, I glanced through the back window at Molly walking into the shadows left by the sun sinking behind buildings across the street. Any sense of relief I felt during our conversation faded with each passing second.

Keppler turned to follow my gaze. "What was that all about? Did she break into the house?"

"She didn't admit to it." I handed him his notebook. "I'll tell you what she said over dinner." As much as I wanted to believe my words had convinced her to stop communicating with The Defiance, part of me already understood we'd chosen different sides.

CHAPTER 25
CHARLIE

October 1, 2090

"I know he's the one who took it, Griff. I saw him leave your room an hour ago." Shane, one of Griff's top confidants, stood just inside my Defiance room pointing an accusing finger. He had been working with Griff throughout the fall on missions to track down pendants in Texas, but as far as I knew, they had come up empty-handed. He had also been out to replace me as Griff's righthand man.

I sat on my bed, still lost in the story I had been writing. When voices approached my door, I shoved the notebook under my pillow. The hero in the story had been on an undercover mission that turned bad, and I had a feeling that as much as I didn't want it to, my real life was about to imitate the story in my head. I had taken one of Griff's pendants. It was for his own good. He had become so obsessed he forgot to eat, went days without sleep, and didn't think twice about harming anyone in his way.

Now, that meant me.

Standing, I faced Griff, eyes narrowed and scrutinizing, any familiar camaraderie gone. Through the last half of 2089, The Defiance had become well-known and feared for their connection to theft, extortion, and murder. None of it was something I wanted to be a part of, but there was no way out. The last guy who decided to walk away didn't even make it through the door alive. All I had going for me was the favor of our leader.

"What's wrong?" I stood and tried to sound confused. "What happened?"

"One of the pendants is . . . missing." Griff shoved his hands in his pockets but didn't take his eyes off me. "It was there a few hours ago. Did you tell anyone about it?"

"Of course not." I slapped my hand against my chest so hard it made a hollow thunk. "Why would I?"

"Because you're a traitor." Shane took two steps toward me. "Probably being paid to steal the pendants."

I felt my hands curl into fists at my sides. Shane's jealousy had gone too far. "Go ahead and search my room. I have nothing to hide."

"There you go." Griff sighed. "Do you really think he'd let you search if he had it?"

Shane shrugged. "He probably figured you'd say that. We all know the pendant equals power, and not even Charlie can resist that." He lunged forward, shoving me hard enough I stumbled back a few steps. "I'll bet it's here."

Without hesitation, he dumped the drawers of the old dresser containing the little clothing I owned, then slid it forward to check behind. My muscles tensed as he walked toward the bed, and I forced myself to look away so I wouldn't draw his attention to my pillow, the unfortunate hiding place for everything I didn't want found. Shane held my pillow in one hand and reached for the notebook with his other.

"Looks like someone's a writer." He let it flop open with one hand and held it up for Griff to see.

I lunged forward, jostling the pillow as I ripped the notebook from his hand.

We all froze as a soft metallic clink echoed against the floor.

"What did I tell ya?" Shane tossed the pillow aside, picked up the pendant by its chain, and handed it to Griff. "Your supposed brother is a liar and a traitor."

"Griff?" I looked up at the disbelief turning to anger on his face. "You can't believe him. He's setting me up." I choked out my last attempt to save myself. "We're brothers . . ."

"I should have known better." His eyes narrowed as he took a step away and stuffed the pendant into his pocket. "Family is a dangerous thing. They're the people who know all of your secrets, which makes it easy for them to turn on you."

My chest hurt and everything seemed to happen in slow motion.

"Come on, Charlie." Shane rolled his eyes. "Be a man and take responsibility for your actions."

Griff looked from me to Shane then back again. He reached for my throat and pulled me toward him, squeezing so hard I couldn't get an ounce of air in. "Admit what you've done."

Just as darkness began to close in at the corners of my eyes, he let go. I stumbled and fell, coughing and gasping for air. "I didn't . . ."

Shane kicked me hard in the ribs. "What should I do with him, boss?"

"Take him to the basement," Griff barked. "We'll deal with him when we have time."

Gripping my arm, Shane pulled me along the hallway and down flights of stairs to a big wooden door. When he opened it, cold, musty darkness rose up to meet me.

"You should have been more careful, Charlie." He squeezed my arm hard. "In this world it's everyone for himself. Families are extinct." He shoved me forward, laughing as he closed the door.

Laughter drifted through the library into Rochelle's sewing room where I sat at the little table with my notebook balanced on the edge next to her sewing machine. Audrie Aumont had arrived early in the afternoon. We had finished dinner hours earlier, and still she remained in the dining room with Rochelle and Kat, looking through photo albums and telling stories about her life.

I looked down at the two sentences of my council column but

couldn't concentrate. The only enjoyable part of dinner had been the food. Kat had begrudgingly listened to Kinley, and instead of making some fancy meal with a long French name went with the more traditional roast beef, mashed potatoes, garden vegetables, and peach crisp for dessert.

Everything else about the family meal had been awkward. Kat was so ecstatic to meet her aunt for the first time, she couldn't stop talking. Kinley, less than thrilled, gave short replies only when she was expected to speak. Rochelle, as usual, did everything in her power to keep the conversation civil and inclusive. Although she had provided me opportunities to talk about my writing and fixing up the truck, I wasn't able to help much because Audrie either interrupted me or studied me so suspiciously I forgot what I was saying. No one else seemed to notice, but my paranoia assured me she somehow knew I wore the pendant.

Resting my forehead in one hand, I tugged at my shirt collar with the other. I had already taken off my tie but didn't want to change completely without Kinley's permission. She wanted to make a good impression, so we were all dressed up and the house was spotless.

"All right, everyone, it's getting pretty late." Kinley's voice sounded like it came from right outside the library. She'd been "doing dishes" for the last three hours, and I suspected she wanted to avoid Audrie without being too far from her cousins. "I'm sure Aunt Audrie has an early morning tomorrow."

"Come on, Kinley. Can't she just stay the night and leave in the morning?" Kat sounded like a child begging for permission to have a friend over.

"Kinley's right." Rochelle's voice broke in before an argument could erupt. "Aunt Audrie has important work to do." I was sure she'd embellished the endless stories of missions she'd run to save the world.

To her credit, she had told Kinley and Kat the same information about the pendant and Auggie's involvement as she
had told Rochelle at the restaurant. Still, I couldn't shake
the impression she was a practiced liar. As much as I wanted to
hand her the pendant before it led to the downfall of anyone else I
cared about, I had already failed to stop Griff and I wasn't about to
let this one end up in the wrong hands.

"Actually, I'd like a minute with Kinley." Audrie's voice was
self-assured and calm. "Why don't you two find your shoes and
we'll walk out to the car together."

Chairs scraped across the floor, footsteps padded into the
library, and the French doors clicked shut. I froze, knowing I
should make my presence known, but not wanting to appear as if I
had been eavesdropping, so I remained still and quiet.

"Kinley, I'm proud of you for stepping up and taking care of
your cousins, but I imagine it must be pretty . . . overwhelming
keeping up with two, or should I say three, teenagers." Audrie's
voice changed from smooth to condescending.

"It's nothing I can't handle." Kinley answered brusquely, and I
didn't blame her.

"I just mean I could help out." Audrie's voice had that sweet
tone that I didn't believe reflected her real personality. "Rochelle
and Kat could live with me, where they can attend a real school,
and I'll bring them back here to visit in the summer."

"I can assure you they're getting a more rigorous education
than I did in high school."

"I'm not saying you're doing anything wrong." She sighed as
if to imply Kinley was overreacting. "They're just missing out on
so much. Kat really wants to go to that culinary arts camp and
Rochelle has such an adventurous spirit . . ."

"They're my responsibility and I know what's best for them."

"Do you? It doesn't seem ideal for you to put their lives on hold while you follow your dreams." Audrie's voice was quietly innocent, her implications hanging in the air. Her next words knocked the breath from me. "And it wasn't very responsible of you to let a boy you found on the street move in and wander around the house freely."

"Charlie has been nothing but respectful, polite, and helpful since he's moved in here." Kinley started off too loud and adjusted her voice. "Maybe if you would have actually let him talk during dinner..."

"I heard enough from him. He's hiding something. He was far too jittery, too careful about his words."

"Probably because you made him uncomfortable." The exasperation in Kinley's voice was clear. "Do you have any other problems with my parenting?"

In a snap, Audrie's tone changed from sweet to challenging. "From what I hear, you never tell the girls you love them. Is that a tough love trick you learned from your dad?"

"You don't get to stand here and criticize my dad. He was here. You just abandoned all of us for fourteen years—and don't tell me Grandma kept you away and don't say your job wouldn't allow you to visit." This time Kinley didn't even try to lower her voice. "If I can become a doctor while I'm taking care of my family, you could have visited for Christmas."

Audrie laughed. "Tell me how that's going a year from now. I'd feel better if Rochelle and Kat were safe with me, but you are their guardian, I suppose."

"Call them if you like. Visit them when you have time. But they stay here with me." Kinley's words sounded far calmer and more controlled than mine would have if confronted in the same way.

"You'll change your mind. If, on the off chance, you come across a pendant like I described, contact me immediately. I'll check in once a week, but I'm always available by phone."

"If Uncle Auggie had something like that, we would know. It's late. You should get going."

There were no further goodbyes, just one set of footsteps clicking to the door. Another set of footsteps padded toward the sewing room, and Kinley peeked inside.

"Oh, Charlie." She jumped back a step and held a hand over her chest. "I figured Rochelle just forgot to turn off the light in here."

I stood, scooping up my notebook. "Sorry, I was just working on some writing. I didn't mean to listen in."

Kinley turned and took a few steps into the library. "You couldn't help it." She turned back to me. "Everything she said is out of line. We're so happy to have you here." In the next room she sank onto the window seat, face a little pale, forehead wrinkled in thought.

Stuffing my hands in my pockets, I nodded. "You should forget what she said too. It's not true."

"I hope you're right." Kinley pressed her hands over her face then let them drop to her lap. "Let's not tell Rochelle and Kat about that conversation. I don't know how I'll ever convince them to stay if they find out they have an invitation to live with Audrie."

"I won't tell them, but they would never leave." Tugging at my collar, I tried to come up with proof as voices approached from the kitchen.

The door pushed open and Rochelle walked in. "Hey guys. Aunt Audrie wanted me to tell you both goodbye for her. She said she had a lot of fun visiting."

"Good to hear." Kinley's voice contained no enthusiasm.

Rochelle looked at me with questioning eyebrows, but I only shrugged in response. "Are you getting a headache? You know, if you would have waited I would have helped you clean up the kitchen."

"I'm fine." Kinley forced a smile. "Where's Kat?"

"She went upstairs to change."

Kinley nodded. "Rochelle, your dad never said anything to you about that pendant Audrie keeps bringing up . . ."

Rochelle shook her head. "He only gave me that bracelet with the hummingbird charm."

"Like mine with the sunflower and Kat's with the canary." She rubbed her forehead in the small circles indicative of a headache. "For claiming there's no evidence it exists, she sure brought it up a lot. I'm starting to feel like that's the only reason she came."

Rochelle helped Kinley to her feet. "We'll worry about it to-morrow. You should get to bed so you're ready for class in the morning."

"You're right." Kinley took a few steps forward, then turned back to us. "Rochelle, do you feel like you're missing out? I mean, if you could choose a different guardian . . ."

"I would choose you every time." Rochelle pulled her cousin into a tight hug. "No one else would take such good care of me."

Kinley squeezed Rochelle tight. "Don't stay up too late." She kissed the top of her head. "I'll see you in the morning. Tomorrow will be better, right?"

"Every time." Rochelle watched until Kinley left the room, then turned to me. "What was that all about?"

I shrugged and sat on the window seat. "I think she's worried you like Audrie better."

"Ridiculous." She sat down next to me and smoothed her dress over her legs. "Now that you've met my aunt face to face, what's your impression of her?"

It was more than just the feeling that Audrie didn't like me or the way she'd treated Kinley. Something felt off about her. "I think she knows more about the pendant than she claims." *In this world it's everyone for himself. Families are extinct.* Shane's words echoed in my head. "I know it's not what you want to hear, but I don't believe she wants to be part of your family. Kinley's right, her motives seem more selfish."

"There's a chance she was just a little uncomfortable because she's getting to know us." Rochelle ran her fingers through her hair to fluff it in front the way Audrie did. "Do you think I'll be like her when I'm older?"

Thinking of the exchange I'd heard minutes earlier, I shook my head. "You'll never be like her, and that's a good thing."

Rochelle sighed and her shoulders slumped. "So we still don't know if we can trust her with the pendant and we definitely can't trust Molly. Now what?"

I rested my elbows on my knees, knowing she was disappointed by my answers so far. "We'll just keep it hidden. Problem solved."

"Unless they really did develop a vaccine."

"If it led to anything good, they would have told someone. The vaccine would be in development right now." I shook my head. "It doesn't make any sense, Aumont."

Rochelle nodded. "I wish I could just tell Kinley everything. She always knows what to do. She always helped me fix everything. But now she has so much to worry about. I'm afraid if I give her one more thing, she'll have a nervous breakdown."

"We'll figure it out. Try not to worry." I wished we could drive to the middle of nowhere and bury the pendant in a field where it wouldn't be found for hundreds of years. Leaving it anywhere, though, felt too risky, and I couldn't sleep unless I felt it against my chest, reassuring me Griff would never complete his collection.

"I don't know what I'd do without you." Rochelle smiled and stood. "I'm sorry Audrie was so rude. You seem more like my brother than she does my aunt."

The word "brother" made me shiver. If families were really extinct, had I set myself up for the same fate I'd faced with The Defiance?

"Good night, Keppler." She walked halfway across the room then turned around, green eyes glittering. "We should make Kinley's favorite breakfast tomorrow and all be there to eat with her to cheer her up. I'll tell Kat."

"I'm in."

Rochelle grinned. "See you in the kitchen at six o'clock."

The difference between aunt and niece was clear. They had the same green eyes, same brown hair, and same thin frame, but Rochelle cared more about other people than she did about herself. That one quality made her different than Audrie or anyone else I had ever met in my life. It made her incorruptible and because of that, I trusted her, over anyone else, to make the right decision concerning the pendant.

CHAPTER 26

ROCHELLE

October 19, 2090

I pushed the heavy church door open and stepped into a wall of rain. It had been three o'clock when I told Keppler I was running to the post office for the mail. I couldn't tell how much time I had spent at church, but it hadn't been raining when I went in. Flipping the hood of my jacket over my head, I tucked the electric bill, our only mail, into my pocket and started jogging the four blocks toward home. Between no word from Todd in six months, confusion about Aunt Audrie, worry about Molly, and uncertainty about the pendant, I had no shortage of prayers.

Rain splattered my face, blurring the familiar neighborhood around me. As promised, Audrie had called every Sunday evening to talk to us, Kat and I for an hour each and Kinley for five minutes. Despite what Keppler had said, chatting with my aunt still made me feel grown-up and loved at the same time. Molly, on the other hand, wouldn't answer her phone and stopped sitting next to me at council meetings. Kat and Kinley, in a renewed dispute about the culinary arts camp, had stopped talking to each other completely and relied on Keppler or me to communicate messages between them. I had begun a desperate search for any notes about the pendant my dad may have left behind. I believed more and more every day he must have left me a clue, advice, instructions. I just didn't know where to look.

Reaching my house, I stopped on the front patio to catch my

breath before darting to the back door. Inside the relative warmth of the laundry room, I hung my dripping jacket and kicked off my shoes.

The door to the kitchen pulled open before my hand found the doorknob and Kinley stood in front of me, hair falling around her face where it had come loose from her braid, still wearing her scrubs from the hospital, face tight with worry and drained of color. "Rochelle Irene Aumont, where have you been? Is Kat with you?"

I handed her the slightly damp electric bill. "Post office then church for a little bit. Kat should have come home before you." My sister had left in the morning to volunteer at the home for children but promised she would be back by late afternoon.

"Well, she didn't." Kinley's voice cracked as she stepped aside to let me into the kitchen where Keppler sat at the table, hand subconsciously tapping the glass surface. "She never went to the home for children, she isn't at the Tatems', and Alexander is out looking for her right now."

"That can't be right." I glanced around the room, gloomy and cold without my sister. "Maybe she's visiting one of her friends." My head raced through scenarios to explain her failure to return home. I wouldn't put it past Kat to stop by the library or a friend's house and come home a little late to get back at Kinley for their latest argument. On the other hand, I felt the same twinge of panic I'd felt the night Todd walked away. I couldn't handle losing her too.

"I've called everyone I can think of." My cousin's words were little gasps of air as if she were crying without tears. "Something terrible must have happened. I should have taken better care of her."

"I'll call Max, maybe he's seen her." I took a step toward the phone.

"I already talked to him when we were looking for you."
Keppler stood. "Maybe I should go drive around—"

"No." Kinley blocked the door. "Kat is already missing. No one
is leaving this house until . . ."

Taking her shaky hand, I guided her back to the center of the
kitchen. "It's okay. We'll find her. Let's just go upstairs and change.
I'm sure by the time we get back down here, Kat will be home with
a funny story to explain everything."

Kinley just nodded and didn't resist my nudging her toward
the next room.

Keppler took off his glasses and rubbed his face. "I'll stay right
here in case someone calls."

Giving him a thumbs up, I walked my cousin upstairs, left her
in her room, and continued down the hall where I exchanged my
rain-soaked clothes for a sweatshirt and jeans. The more I thought
about my sister, the more I noticed the hollow feeling in the pit
of my stomach, yet I couldn't bring myself to believe someone in
Maibe would hurt her. There had to be a logical explanation.

Combing my fingers through my hair, I walked back to Kinley's
room and found her sitting on the bed. She hadn't changed her
clothes.

"I had a bad feeling this morning. This whole week." She looked
past me down to the window over the middle landing of the stairs.
"October is a bad month. It was last year, and it always will be."

A year earlier, I had been lying on the Tatems' couch, too weak
from the fever to do anything else. Kinley had come home the
minute trains were allowed out of Omaha, which happened to be
the same day she was released from the hospital. When Emma
had ushered her into the house, I barely recognized her. She was
too thin, face shadowed by lack of sleep, hair greasy and tangled.
It wasn't until Emma talked her into taking a shower and braided
her hair that I believed she was really my cousin.

"I should have been here instead of at school." Kinley shook her head, hand pressed to her forehead. "I let myself believe you were safer here. That I could help people . . . but I was wrong."

She had never talked about her experience with the fever other than to say she couldn't leave the city because of the quarantine and got sick while helping at the hospital.

"That's not true." I patted her hand. "You couldn't be in two places at once, and I know you did everything you could."

"It wasn't enough, Rochelle." She turned to me, tears glistening in her eyes. "The hospitals were overwhelmed before we even saw it coming, and I wanted to be brave. I never imagined . . ." For the first time since Kinley told us Grandma was gone, tears slipped down her cheeks. "I wasn't a doctor. I was only three years into my program. All I could do was hold their hands. I didn't even have time to be afraid I'd get sick . . ."

I shivered, imagining Kinley, cold and afraid in a lonely hospital bed. Kat and I had been lucky to be with the Tatems where we were loved, coaxed to eat, and reassured everything would be okay.

Tears welled in my eyes as I took her hands. "You didn't do anything wrong."

"Yes, I did. I should have been *here*." Her voice was resolute, even through the sobs. "When my parents stopped answering the phone . . . when I talked to you and found out you were taking care of Grandma and Kat all alone . . . I knew I messed up, and I was afraid if I lived everyone would be gone." She buried her face in her hands.

Wrapping my arms around her, I rocked her gently back and forth as if she were a child instead of my confident, self-reliant cousin. "It's okay. You're safe. I'm right here." I whispered the phrases over and over as I thought about Kinley's shaky voice on the phone a year earlier. *Everything will be okay, Rochelle. Just keep Grandma and Kat hydrated. Do your best to keep their fevers down. I'll be home as soon as there's a train.* I had told her I was fine, even though I felt feverish and dizzy, because I didn't want her to worry.

"Rochelle, we have to find Kat." Her voice was no stronger than a whimper. "I can't lose either of you. You're all I have."

"I'm right here and she'll be home soon." I tried to sound reassuring as I dried my cousin's tears with a pile of tissues, found her a t-shirt and sweatpants to change into, and walked her downstairs.

"I'll get you a glass of water and come right back." I wrapped a blanket around her shoulders, hugged her one more time, and left her sitting on the couch.

In the kitchen, Keppler paced from the door to the stove, stopping to glance out the window every time he passed it. "She's never done anything like this, Aumont." He didn't stop to look at me. "If she never went to the home for children, where has she been all day?"

"Take a deep breath. Kinley already has the panicking covered." I walked to the cupboard and pulled out a glass, imagining scenarios of Kat running into someone on her way to the home for children and volunteering to help them make a fancy family meal. "She must have said something to one of us . . ."

"I've been back over every conversation and I can't think of anything." He stopped and stared out at the rain, not letting up. "You don't think your aunt would kidnap her . . . or Molly?"

I stopped with my hand halfway to the faucet. "What do you mean? Why would they?"

Keppler ran his hand across his forehead, resorting to the nervous habit of brushing phantom hair out of his eyes. "Because that's what their kind of people do." He kept his voice low, for

Kinley's sake I figured, but I couldn't miss the agitation. "I've been trying to tell you, that pendant changes people. It makes them dangerous, and they'll do anything to get it."

"Kat has nothing to do with that." I lowered the glass to the counter as my hand shook.

"They all know you care more about her than yourself, and it's the perfect way to get what they want."

The accusation in his voice pushed me back a step and my eyes caught the refrigerator door, covered in lists and reminders held in place by magnets. With one hand I nudged Keppler aside, too relieved by how wrong he was to care about pointing it out. With the other, I plucked the culinary arts camp flyer from beneath a magnet shaped like a butterfly and found the date:

October 19, 2090
1:00 p.m. – 3:00 p.m.

"She went to the camp in Omaha." I handed him the flyer and filled the glass with water. "She'll probably be calling for a ride from the train station any minute. Stay close to the phone, and I'll break the news to Kinley."

CHAPTER 27

CHARLIE

October 19, 2090

I held the flyer in front of me, elbows on the edge of the kitchen sink, exhausted from building terrible scenarios about Kat's fate and guilty for putting my fears onto Rochelle. The soft murmur of conversation in the next room indicated Rochelle had succeeded in calming Kinley for the moment.

A gust of wind pounded rain against the window, and I glanced up in time to see Kat on the front walk, arm up to shield her face from the deluge. Energized by relief, I rushed into the laundry room and pulled the door open just as she reached the back step.

"Are you okay?" I pulled her inside, studying the hair plastered to her forehead and black makeup smudged from her eyes to her chin. "We've been looking for you for an hour."

"No, I'm not okay." She ripped her arms out of her sopping jacket and threw it on the floor. "I spent a bunch of money on a train ticket to Omaha, got lost trying to find my camp, missed my train and had to take a later one, then walked home in the rain."

"Katia Rose Aumont, what were you thinking?" Kinley's voice was too weak to convey any anger, but it carried into the laundry room.

"I don't need one of your lectures." Kat pushed past me as she stormed into the kitchen. "If you really cared, you would have taken me to that camp. You don't even want us. You just want the freedom you had before we were your responsibility—"

Kat froze when she saw Kinley sobbing. She stared at her cousin as if seeing her cry was the equivalent of a blizzard in July.

Rochelle looked between sister and cousin, then draped one arm around Kinley's shoulders. "We're having a family meeting. Right now. Keppler, go to the library with Kat. We'll be there in a minute."

Nodding, I led the way to the next room. Kat, soaked and shivering, picked up a blanket and wrapped it around herself before sitting on the couch. I slumped into one of the armchairs, feeling as I had when my parents fought: that any glimmers of good were caught in a slow downward spiral of destruction. A family could only fracture so far before shattering beyond repair.

"You figured out where I was." She nodded toward the flyer still clutched in my hand, but her eyes remained on the doorway.

"Rochelle did. About ten minutes ago." I rubbed my eyes, trying to erase the image of Kat locked up in a dingy basement waiting to be traded for the pendant. "Kinley was frantic. Why didn't you tell me where you were going? I would have gone with you."

She rubbed her cheek but the smudges didn't wipe away. "I was afraid you would tell her and ruin everything."

"I wouldn't have." My anger melted as I watched her shivering and trying not to cry. "I would have gone with you to keep you safe."

"Kinley just needs a minute to catch her breath." Rochelle crossed the room and collapsed next to her sister, pulling her into her arms. "I'm so glad you're home." She dropped her voice to a whisper. "If you ever plan anything like that again, promise you'll talk to me first."

"Don't worry." She huddled closer to her sister. "I've learned my lesson. I'm never leaving this house again."

"Don't say that." Kinley walked in, eyes puffy and voice a little raspy. "Next time I'll take you."

"You're not mad?" Kat looked like a confused child wrapped in her blanket.

"Not at you." Kinley wiped her cheek with the back of her hand and sat down on the coffee table so she was knee to knee with her cousin. "I'm sorry if I've ever done anything to make you feel like I don't want you. Nothing could be further from the truth."

She took a deep breath and played with the fraying end of her braid. "You're all more important to me than anything else." She swallowed hard and looked up at her cousins. "I moved back here because I want to be with you guys . . . I'm supposed to be." Wrapping her arms around herself, she looked down at her socks. "I watched so many people lose their battle with the fever, even a few of my classmates. I'll never forgive myself for not being here when you needed me, but I got a second chance to get it right this time around. I know I'm not getting everything right, but I'm trying to do what's best for you." Her voice faded as new tears filled her eyes.

If any one Aumont would dismiss the mantra *nothing happens by chance*, it would be Kinley, but even she used it to make sense of her life. It was her reason for taking on more responsibility than any nineteen-year-old would want. It was her justification to put an unfair amount of pressure on herself. It was the same sacrifice I had made for my sister, and I felt an uncomfortable empathy aching in my chest.

"You're here now, and you're doing a good job." Rochelle stretched her free arm toward her cousin, who slid in beside her so the three of them were huddled together, sharing one couch cushion.

"I'm sorry about what I said." Kat's voice was muffled against Rochelle's shoulder. "I just don't like you making all of my decisions. I'm not a little kid."

Kinley reached for Kat's hand and squeezed it. "I know, and

I'm sorry too." She closed her eyes. "I love all of you so much. It's just scary to say it because it feels like I've lost everyone I've said it to."

"It's okay." Rochelle's gentle, soothing tone helped to alleviate my feelings of dread. "We love you too." Her head slid to the side until it rested against her cousin's.

Kinley opened her eyes halfway and glanced in my direction before turning back to her cousins. "Speaking of making your own decisions . . . Audrie said you could live with her and go to a real school. I told her no, but that's not fair to either of you." She spoke so quickly her words blended together.

"She did?" Kat's eyes lit up with excitement but dulled just as quickly when she saw the look on her cousin's face. "Audrie's fun to talk to, but I'd rather stay here with you guys." Kat smiled at me. "If I wasn't here to cook for you, how would I know you're eating? I'd be worried all the time."

"Very funny." A weak smile wavered on Kinley's lips. "Rochelle?"

"Are you kidding? I'm not going anywhere." She raised her eyebrows in my direction. "Keppler?"

I sat forward in my chair, trying to figure out how we went from crying and yelling to laughing and hugging in a matter of minutes. That never happened with my original family and definitely not The Defiance. "I guarantee Audrie's invitation didn't extend to me."

"See. Keppler's staying too." She reached her hand in my direction. "Get over here. This is an important family meeting, and you're missing it."

Still shaken from the events of the day, I felt reluctant to be pulled any deeper into a family I could lose at any minute. They didn't deserve the trouble I had brought to Maibe. Rochelle wouldn't have even believed Molly's stories about her dad if I hadn't been there to work on the truck. Or would she have eventually looked there? Would she have been in a more dangerous situation without my warning about The Defiance? Could it be true that nothing happens by chance?

"Come on, Charlie." Kat held her hand out to me.

I felt myself smile, and my feet carried me to the couch where I was enveloped by three hugs at the same time. Despite Kat's clammy hair against my chin, I didn't squirm away. Instead, I let gratitude that I'd found a family that wanted me overpower any uncertainty.

Kinley sat forward on her cushion, color finally returning to her cheeks. "I have an idea. In a few weeks, I have tests in Omaha again." She ran a hand over her hair to smooth down all of the loose ends. "Kat, do you want to come with me? We might be able to find another cooking camp you can go to."

"Really? You mean it?" Kat dove over Rochelle to tackle her cousin. "And you'll take me there so I don't get lost?"

"I'll drop you off and pick you up for every session." She laughed and took Kat's face between her hands. "And we'll have a little talk about wearing makeup in the rain. You're a complete mess." Sighing, she looked from Rochelle to me. "Would you two be all right here for a week if I have Emma and Alexander check in on you?"

Rochelle flung one arm around me. "We have everything under control. Keppler makes amazing peanut butter and jelly sandwiches and I'm pretty good at laundry." She laughed and shrugged. "What more could we need?"

Kinley stood, shaking her head but grinning. "We'll go over a few things before then, but that can wait. For now . . ." She held out her hands to Kat. "You need to get cleaned up so we can make some dinner, and I suppose I should call everyone and let them know they can stop worrying."

In a rare moment of compliance with her cousin, Kat took Kinley's hands. "Can we eat at some fancy restaurants, you know, so I can get ideas for mine someday?"

Kinley wrapped her arms around Kat and made a face at us. "Maybe one or two. I don't want to spend your whole college fund. Go upstairs, and I'll be there to talk in a minute." She sighed, watching Kat obediently walk away, then turned back to us. "Charlie, do you still remember how to make macaroni and cheese like Kat taught you?"

"Like it was yesterday. I can get started right now." Hoping having something to do would steady me, I forced myself to my feet. I hadn't felt so shaken, so mentally exhausted, since I was seven and saw my sister sink underwater in a neighbor's pool. After that I convinced my mom to enroll Isabelle in preschool so I could keep her close to me all day.

Rochelle bounced off the couch. "I'll help him. I'm getting better at cooking."

"I put clothes in the dryer an hour ago, Miss I-Love-Laundry." Kinley pulled Rochelle closer and kissed her forehead. "Fold it and stay away from the stove. I'll be back in a minute."

"You start oatmeal on fire one time and no one trusts you anymore." Rochelle rolled her eyes dramatically, then laughed and shook her head as Kinley left the room.

"From Kat's stories, that happened more than once."

"I was ten. And she's exaggerating." She squeezed one eye shut and cringed. "A little."

Laughing eased the tension in my shoulders and weight on my chest. "Aumont, I'm sorry about the way I spoke to you earlier. I was just worried."

She shrugged. "Compared to Kinley when she's worried, or my second grade teacher when Max got us in trouble, you were the picture of calm." Her smile faded. "I'm sorry I didn't come right home. I just thought maybe today would be the day . . ."

She brushed her hair behind her ears, just as I imagined her brushing away the disappointment of Todd not writing. "All of that stuff you said earlier . . . I don't want you to be worried all the time. Most of the things that happen aren't related to the pendant."

Rain slammed into the window, and I jumped. "We can't just plan that everything will work out okay. That never happens, Aumont. We have to be prepared for the worst."

"And we are. Remember we're dealing with Molly and Audrie, not The Defiance." She started walking toward the kitchen, and I followed. "I can handle both of them. Audrie is family and Molly doesn't even talk to me anymore. Our plan is working."

How could I make her understand that, affiliated with The Defiance or not, all people were on some level selfish and power hungry. She was the exception, a twinkling light of hope in a world of darkness. "Before I got home, Kinley told me stories about when you were a kid. She said if she let you out of her sight for a second you were falling out of trees, or crashing your bike, or being attacked by a swarm of wasps."

Rochelle pushed the door into the laundry room and disappeared. Her voice floated out. "She exaggerates . . . a little. What does that have to do with anything?"

I glanced behind me, but Kat and Kinley were still out of earshot upstairs. "That's the kind of approach you still use with everything. You know, run at it full speed, and then realize you're in trouble when it's too late." I rubbed my eyes. "It happened with running for the council, helping Max with the thistles, coming back here to help me when you were supposed to be in Omaha with Kinley . . ."

"Okay. I get it." She appeared with a full laundry basket in hand and hoisted it onto the table. "This time is different because I have a strategy. I know my dad must have left some kind of message or explanation behind for me, and I'm going to search every last inch of this house until I find it. Then we'll have all of the information we're missing, and we'll know exactly what to do with the pendant."

Every possibility she viewed as a ladder rung carrying us to a solution, I interpreted as quicksand pulling us in ankle-deep, knee-deep, waist-deep. Our heads might still be free, but we were too far in to ever escape on our own. I didn't believe her dad had the answer, but I was too tired to argue.

"Are you okay, Keppler?" Her green eyes, hopeful and bright, studied me.

"It's been a long day. Aren't you tired?" No matter how late I stayed up or how early I got up in the morning, I could always find her in the library working on homework, council plans, or just reading a book. "Do you even sleep anymore?"

"Only when I'm tired." She pulled a towel from the basket and folded it in half. "With everything going on, I have no time to waste."

"Whatever you say, Aumont." I turned to the window, beaded with rain, framing an already-darkening sky. My sister had relied on me for everything from finding a way to buy food to comforting her during a thunderstorm. But I had failed to provide the stability and reassurance she needed to trust that every decision I made was to protect her. Perhaps the reason I wound up in Maibe was to help Rochelle navigate the pendant situation and use my knowledge of The Defiance to keep the Aumonts off their radar. It was a chance to redeem myself and, more importantly, to protect my new family.

CHAPTER 28
ROCHELLE

November 3, 2090

"Rochelle?" Alexander's voice sounded concerned. His hand rested gently on my shoulder. "We're in your driveway. Are you feeling any better?"

I opened my eyes, lifted my head away from the headrest of the passenger seat, and nodded even though it wasn't true. My throat had been a little scratchy during the previous two days, but that morning I felt the first chills signaling a fever. Still, I felt an obligation to report to the auditorium and help the other council members set up for Alexander's Leaders of Nebraska Conference that evening. If Kinley had been home, I never would have made it out of the house, but she was in Omaha with Kat and I didn't mention any of my symptoms to Keppler or Alexander when he picked me up after lunch.

Molly leaned forward from the back seat. "I'm sure she just needs to lie down and get rehydrated. Then she'll be ready to come right back for the conference." She had insisted on riding home with me after I got a little dizzy hanging strings of lights. We had worked together all afternoon, and she had actually called me the night before to ask if we could get ready together at my house.

Alexander pressed his hand to my forehead. "I don't know about that. She feels kind of warm and it's pretty cold in here." The heater hadn't warmed the cab more than a few degrees against the biting wind outside. "I think it would be best for you to stay home and rest in case you're coming down with something."

Picturing the old basketball court transformed into an elegant banquet hall complete with blue table coverings and silver centerpieces, I felt the sinking sensation of defeat through my body. "But I promised to greet the other mayors and help . . ."

"I know, but you look miserable." His hand felt warm and comforting even through my coat. "I'd rather be safe than see you get really sick again. When Kinley gets home tonight, she can check you out and decide if you need to see Dr. Brooks."

A dull ache radiated across my forehead, and although I didn't want to admit it, sleep sounded more appealing than anything else. I had avoided telling Kinley about my sore throat when she called to check in because I wanted her to focus on bonding with Kat instead of worrying about me. But, suddenly, I wanted her home to reassure me I wasn't getting another severe illness that would keep me in bed for months. I couldn't deal with that again.

"I'll come by and check on you before I head to the conference." Alexander interrupted my thoughts before I could worry myself into tears.

I forced a smile. "Don't worry about me, I'm feeling a little better and Keppler can update you." He was attending with the official press pass Alexander had given him so he could write a report for the paper. He was so excited about it, he asked my advice on what to wear, which wasn't my area of expertise, so we called Kat. "You're already busy enough."

"Come on, Rochelle." Molly pushed her door open, letting in a rush of cold air. "Let's get you inside where it's warm. Don't worry, Alexander, I won't leave until she's resting comfortably." She sounded just like the old friend I feared I'd lost, and I was so relieved to have her back I slid out of the truck without a second thought.

I waved to Alexander and let Molly link one arm through mine as she hoisted her duffel bag over her shoulder with the other. Together we hurried up the front walk, fighting the howling wind fringed with the first snowflakes of the season. Shivering so intensely my teeth chattered, I was relieved to sink into a chair in my warm kitchen.

"You just take it easy and I'll make us some tea." Molly picked up the kettle and turned on the sink. "It'll help your throat and get some fluids in you."

Swallowing against the scratchy sandpaper feeling, I shook my head. "You don't have to do that. There isn't much time for you to get ready and I don't want you to be late . . ."

"I'll have plenty of time, Rochelle." She turned on the burner with a click. "You're my friend and I'm here for you. It's pretty rotten that even though you take care of everyone, I'm the only one taking care of you when you're sick." We had been making small talk all afternoon, almost like old times, so I wasn't expecting the attack on my family.

"Kinley and Kat will be home soon, and Keppler mentioned something about stopping by the library, but he'll have to get ready soon so he should be home any minute." I folded my arms on the table and buried my face in them.

The chair next to me scraped across the floor and Molly patted my shoulder. "Do you remember that Halloween when we both had strep throat so we stayed here and watched movies while everyone else was trick-or-treating?"

That was the same Halloween Kat and Kinley stayed in my room and took turns reading me scary stories until I fell asleep. The next day, Todd came over and gave me half of the candy he had collected the night before. I tilted my head to the side and nodded.

"What's wrong?" Molly rested her chin in her hand. "You look sad."

"I was just thinking about Todd . . ."

"Oh, Rochelle." She rolled her eyes and stood. "People leave, and in this case it's for the best. When you learn to tell the difference between who actually cares about you and who's just using you, you'll be so much happier."

"He didn't leave on purpose." I couldn't find the energy to lift my head.

"Of course he did. It was his choice, just like Kat and Kinley decided to take a vacation and leave you here." The tea kettle let out a shrill whistle and Molly crossed the room to take care of it. "You'll wear yourself out trying to hold onto all of these people who don't care about you as much as you care about them."

I shivered but remained silent as I listened to Molly rummage through her bag behind my chair then return to the counter again. I'd known her long enough to understand once she got an idea in her head, no amount of arguing would change it.

"Think about it this way. If you, Kat, and Kinley were on a sinking raft and only two of you could fit on the rescue boat, which one of you would be left behind?"

"I would make them leave me."

"What if I was there too?" Molly looked at me, eyebrows raised, expression hurt even before I could reply.

Knowing I couldn't give her the answer she wanted, I hid my face in my arms again. "I couldn't choose. I couldn't let any of you drown."

She didn't say any more. In a cocoon of darkness, I listened to her pour water and a cup clunk against the tabletop in front of me.

"Sometimes you have to make a choice or you lose everybody." Her voice was close, back in her seat next to me. "One day you'll learn not to let people manipulate you. You have to choose a family that will give you a future, not one that will suck the life out of you."

Slowly, I lifted my head to Molly brushing her blonde hair aside and watched wafting steam rise from two cups of tea. "What do you mean?"

She pulled her cup closer. "You'll understand in time. We're sixteen, so it's inevitable we'll be making important decisions soon. I just wish things could have worked out differently." She sighed and nodded toward my cup. "Drink your tea. It'll make you feel better."

Lifting the cup to my lips, I let a little of the warm liquid slide down my throat. Was Molly referring to her plans to join The Defiance again? My head was too foggy to put the pieces together.

She smiled, gripping her cup between her hands. "I've been thinking about what you said last time we talked, and I've decided to get away for a while. Visit my sister for a few weeks."

Despite my misery, a calming relief rose through my body with a warmth that slowed my shivering. "That's great. She's going to be so happy to see you."

"I hope so." A veil of disappointment shadowed her face again.

We sipped our tea in silence until the basement door creaked open and footsteps padded toward us. I turned in time to see Keppler appear in the doorway wearing black slacks with the blue shirt and checkered tie Kat had picked out over the phone. His hair, a little damp, was slicked to the side.

"I never would have guessed *you* can actually look civilized." Molly smirked and crossed one leg over her opposite knee. "You should really lose the glasses though."

"Why are you here?" His face wrinkled into a scowl and then softened when his eyes landed on me. "Aumont, are you okay?"

"She almost passed out earlier." Molly stood and helped me out of the winter coat I hadn't bothered to remove. "I'm here to take care of her since her *supposed family* doesn't care."

Keppler ignored her and pulled out the chair on the other side of me. "You should have called. I've been home all day." He tilted his head as if seeing me from a different angle would provide the answers he needed. "Do you want me to call Emma? Kinley and Kat won't be home for a few hours yet."

"If they even make it home before the blizzard." Molly stood over us.

A sharp ache pounded inside my head, but I forced a smile. "I'll be okay until they get here." Kinley and Kat had to come home. I needed them.

"Come on, Rochelle." Molly reached for my arm. "We should get you to the couch where you'll be more comfortable."

"I'll take care of her." Keppler stood and gripped my elbow. "I'm guessing you're not dressed for the conference yet and I'll have to give you a ride, so get ready."

"Fine." Molly let go of my arm and reached for her bag. "But I'm not leaving until I see that she's resting comfortably. I know what's best for her."

Relieved that I didn't end up in the middle of a tug-of-war, I stood a little shakily as a strange rushing sound roared between my ears. Molly made her way toward the bathroom and Keppler guided me into the library.

"Maybe you shouldn't be here by yourself. I could just drop Molly off and come back home." He eased me to the couch cushions. "Or make her walk like she deserves."

"I'm fine." He had been looking forward to reporting on the conference for the past month—the first time one of his articles would potentially have a bigger audience. I would be okay for a few hours. "I just need a little sleep."

Keppler took all of the pillows from one side of the couch and piled them together. "This is a perfect example of why you need to take better care of yourself." He had been gently pushing me to get more sleep and stop skipping meals. Since Kinley had been away, he accompanied me any time I left the house unless I was with Alexander, Emma, or Max. The pendant had him paranoid.

"You're right." I fell back against the pillows and closed my eyes. If I could just fall asleep, Kinley would be there beside me when I opened my eyes.

"Are you sure you don't want me to call someone?" He draped the blanket from the back of the couch over me. "Emma or Delgado?"

"They're too busy to babysit me. Quit worrying."

"Okay." He sighed and sat down on the coffee table, elbows on his knees. "But you have to promise you'll stay right here and rest. Don't decide you're feeling better and pass out doing the laundry."

"Keppler, I'm just going to sleep." With my eyes closed, the crashing roar between my ears and nausea were tolerable. "Just promise you'll bring Kinley and Kat home."

"Of course." His hand brushed my forehead in a rare tender moment that almost broke me down into asking him to stay. "I'll sit with you until Molly's ready to go."

I slipped into sleep and didn't open my eyes until a loud crash ripped me out of a dream before I could reach Todd's hand. Feeling disoriented, I pulled myself into a sitting position, squinting into a room blurred beyond recognition. The light coming from the kitchen made my head feel like it would explode. The house shook with another crash that came from upstairs, and my stomach clenched. Someone was in the house, tearing it apart. I needed to call for help and then throw up.

Too dizzy to stand, I slid to the floor and crawled to the kitchen, pulled myself up to the counter, knocked the phone off its cradle and dialed the first number that came to mind.

The shrill ringing of an unanswered phone ached in my head as heavy steps pounded down the stairs.

CHAPTER 29

CHARLIE

November 3, 2090

I squinted through the windshield as I navigated dark streets invaded by swirling snow. Between Kinley passing to the next level of her program, Kat's culinary camp experience, and my excitement from using my first press pass, we had no shortage of excited discussion.

"I'm looking forward to a cold, snowy weekend to catch up on sleep." Kinley tucked a strand of hair under her hat as I turned onto our street. "And I can't wait to see Rochelle. She'd better be resting. I've told her a million times she needs to get enough sleep to keep her immune system up."

Kat and I made quick eye contact, both knowing Kinley's bad habits were the same as Rochelle's. I had informed them about Rochelle feeling under the weather at the train station. She had been sound asleep when Molly and I left the house, and we agreed she looked comfortable and would probably sleep for hours. After that we argued about the weather, my driving, and my choice of a parking place.

"There's someone running around the house." Kat leaned over Kinley to press her face to the glass. "He's knocking on the windows."

Feeling a sense of panic, I swung the truck into the driveway and shifted to park. "I'll check it out. Stay here." Without waiting for an answer, I pushed the door open and hurried toward the silhouette jumping up to slap a hand against the kitchen window despite the gusty wind and pelting snow. "Hey, who's there?"

The shadowy figure turned and hurried toward me, becoming the familiar lanky figure of Max. Kat and Kinley, ignoring my instructions, were right behind me.

"It's just me." Max panted as if he'd run ten miles. "Rochelle called, at least the caller ID said Aumont, but she wouldn't say anything, so I ran over here, and now she isn't answering the door."

My throat went dry and my chest tightened before he could finish explaining. Pushing him aside, I rushed to the door, shoved my key into the lock, and pushed my way inside. Other than the phone, off its hook, buzzing on the counter, everything looked exactly as I had left it, but in the library I only found pillows and blankets where Rochelle should have been.

"Aumont?" I ran back to the kitchen where the others had gathered trying to make sense of the situation. "She's not on the couch." Then louder, "Aumont, where are you?"

"Who's there?" Rochelle's voice was weak with exhaustion and muffled through the closed bathroom door.

"It's all of us and Max." Kinley rushed to the door and jiggled the knob, but it didn't budge.

"Prove it's really you." Rochelle's voice came through as a whimper.

Kinley looked at us, forehead wrinkled with worry. "Rochelle Irene Aumont, open this door."

It unlocked with a pop and slid inward slowly until Rochelle's face, ashen and beaded with sweat, appeared. "Kinley. We have to get out of here." She stumbled forward into her cousin's arms. "There was someone . . . in here tearing the house apart . . . he came down . . . the stairs . . . and I could hear him throwing things around . . . getting closer to the door . . ."

"Who was here?" Kinley held onto her cousin, swaying to find her balance. I grabbed her arm to steady her. "Rochelle, what's going on?"

"There was a man in the house when I woke up." Her breathing sounded rough and strained, making her voice shake. "I was afraid he'd hurt you, and I didn't know what to do . . ." She broke into sobs.

"Here." Max pulled out two chairs and helped them sit down. Rochelle wrapped her arms around Kinley so tight I didn't know how she could breathe. "Keppler and I will find him and take him down." Max darted into the next room.

Kat caught my arm as I tried to follow and held me in place, speaking quietly. "The doors were still locked. Does it look like someone's been searching?"

Glancing around the room, I realized Rochelle's panicked story didn't match up with the tidy kitchen I stood in. I knew the concerned confusion on Kat's face mirrored my own expression.

"You're safe. It was just a bad dream." Kinley hugged Rochelle with one arm and tried to brush matted hair off her face with the other. "You are burning up though."

"She was just a little warm earlier." I couldn't take my eyes off Rochelle, clothes soaked with sweat, shaking in her cousin's arms, freckles the only evidence of color on her face.

Rochelle watched me through frightened, frantic eyes that didn't seem to recognize me. "We can't stay here, Kinley, please . . ." I didn't understand how her condition could deteriorate so completely in a few hours.

Kat lunged forward, gripped her sister's shoulders, and shook her. "Snap out of it, Rochelle. There's no one here. Max couldn't even get in because the doors were locked. Look around, everything is where we left it."

"Katia Rose Aumont, that's enough." Kinley lifted a protective arm in front of Rochelle, who huddled closer to her. "Just give her a minute to catch her breath . . ."

"You have to do something." Fighting tears, Kat took a backward step. "This is exactly what happened to Dad. Someone should have been here . . ." She turned and smacked my arm with the back of her hand. "How could you have left her alone?"

Before I could answer, she pushed me aside and stormed out of the room.

"The ghost is clear." Max slid into the kitchen on his socks. "But Kat seems a little upset." He looked at me, deflated by Kat's accusation, then swiveled his head to Rochelle, shaking in Kinley's arms. "What did I say? Ghosts are clear, right, Rochelle?"

She blinked back tears and nodded, but her chest rose and fell too rapidly.

"You're okay." Kinley's voice remained rhythmic and soothing. "Just focus on breathing." She held two fingers against her cousin's wrist and looked at the clock. "Deep breaths. I won't let anyone hurt you." She glanced at me, then Max. "Can you get me a glass of water, please?"

Rochelle's breathing slowed, and she drank some of the water Max offered her. "It seemed so real, but . . ." She looked around the room, rubbing her forehead. "I don't feel so well. Kinley, I have so much to do. I can't be sick like last year." She tried to stand, but her knees buckled and she crashed back into Kinley's arms.

"Easy, you're still a little shaky." She sighed and eased Rochelle back in her chair. "I'm going to take good care of you, and you'll feel better in no time. How about you tell me exactly what happened, from the beginning."

Max pushed the glass into her hand, and she cringed as she swallowed another mouthful of water. "When I woke up, my head and stomach hurt and my heart was beating so fast . . . Everything looked blurry and I thought I could hear someone upstairs, so I crawled to the phone, but I had to get to the bathroom to throw up . . ." She watched us through wide green eyes. "Guys, what's wrong with me?"

"Nothing's wrong with you." Max knelt next to her. "You probably just heard the wind while you were still sleepy and it all mixed together. Like one time, when I was ten, I had this dream I was exploring a waterfall in the rainforest, but I was really just sleepwalking outside in a thunderstorm and my dad had to get me back inside. It was so neat."

We all looked at Max, and for a minute no one said anything.

Finally, a smile spread over Rochelle's face. "You've never told me that before. Did you ever sleepwalk again?"

"Only a few times, but nothing so exciting." He squeezed her shoulder. "Maybe I'll learn how to sleep call, and you guys can run an experiment."

Rochelle laughed and hugged him. "Thank you for coming. I should have let Keppler call you in the first place, but I didn't think I was this sick."

Kinley shook her head. "You just got a little dehydrated and disoriented. A sore throat and fever sounds pretty typical of what's going around right now."

"We should still take her to the doctor." Kat slipped into the room carrying a thermometer and a washcloth. "Just in case."

"I'm sorry I scared you." Rochelle sat up a little straighter. "I'm feeling better now. I have everything under control."

Kat held up the thermometer. "You know the drill. Under your tongue."

Rochelle cooperated with her sister placing the thermometer and pressing the cold washcloth against her forehead.

"Her pulse is back to normal and her color is getting better by the minute." Kinley squeezed Kat's hand. The thermometer beeped, and she glanced at the screen. "One hundred point eight.

We'll go see Dr. Brooks first thing tomorrow morning, but I think she just needs a few days of rest."

"And maybe a bath." Rochelle picked her damp shirt away from her shoulder with two fingers. "I don't even sweat this much working outside in the summer."

"I can arrange that." Kat jumped to her feet. "I'll even spend the night in your room, just in case you need something."

Nodding, Rochelle swallowed the rest of her water. Kinley and Kat helped her to her feet, but she looked steady enough that she didn't need her sister's arm around her to walk through the house and disappear up the stairs.

Kinley picked up the thermometer and abandoned washcloth. "I'm going to help Rochelle get settled, then I'll make us some hot chocolate." She hugged me with one arm. "Charlie, I want to hear all about that leader's conference and the article you're going to write." I knew she was trying to make up for Kat's comments, but I didn't feel any better as I watched her walk away. They had been counting on me to look out for Rochelle and I had failed miserably.

"I've known Rochelle since kindergarten and I've only seen her cry twice." Max sank into a chair. "Like when she scraped half her elbow off riding her bike down the hill too fast."

Tugging at my tie until it came loose, I tossed it on the table and kicked the chair in front of me. "After everything that's happened and everything I know, I still left her here alone." I kicked the chair again, this time so hard it toppled over.

"Hey, take it easy." Max jumped up and righted the chair. "You're going to send Rochelle into another panic attack."

"Whatever." Unable to calm down, I walked over to the sink, kicked the cupboard underneath, and looked out at the wall of snow falling horizontally with the wind. How could I have been so selfish? When Isabelle had a fever, I never left her side for more than a few minutes. I always had the nagging fear that her illness would worsen to something requiring a doctor and medicine that my dad would call an unnecessary expense or a scam.

Feeling miserable, I rubbed my hands over my face, trying to calm down. "This is why I don't deserve a family. I can never get it right." My hand slapped the counter so hard it hurt.

"Come on, *hermano*, don't be so hard on yourself." Kat had informed me that *hermano* meant brother, but I had too many real problems to confront him about it. "She needed Kinley and Kat. They're the only ones who could have calmed her down. Neither of us could fill in for them, and it's not like they were here either."

"It's just . . ." A wall of snow made it impossible to see anything more than a few feet from the window. "She's been through so much and now she has to deal with this pendant. It's too much for her. She's not sleeping."

"You have to give her a little more credit than that." He rubbed a hand through his hair, still wet from running across town in the snow. "She's a lot tougher than she looks. I'm sure she's just having a bad day."

My eyes landed on the two teacups from earlier, washed and drying on the mat beside the sink. Was Molly that much of a neat freak that she would take the time to wash them instead of leaving them in the sink?

"Unless . . ." I shook my head. "She said she felt the worst right before she threw up. You saw her go from frantic to normal right before our eyes."

Max leaned back against the table, eyebrows sliding together. "Yeah, she was having a panic attack, and Kinley—"

"No, it all happened too quick. When I left, she said it was just a sore throat and her forehead felt a little warm. Molly made her tea while I was in the shower." I picked up the cups and studied them, trying to find a residue in one that didn't exist in the other.

"You think Molly tried to poison her?" Max bounced to his

feet and stood at my elbow, observing the cups over my shoulder. "I guess, theoretically, she could have given her something that raised her heart rate, made her imagine things, and Rochelle got it out of her system when she threw up. But why? What would she get out of it?"

Molly wanted the pendant and she had connections to The Defiance. Rochelle's dad died after months of a mysterious illness that caused hallucinations. He was good friends with Molly's dad, who was a pharmacist and medical researcher. The pieces were all there, but not the motives to make them fit together.

Frustrated, I set the cups back onto the mat. "She's a rotten person." I patted my pockets until I found the truck keys. "She doesn't need a reason. When I find her—"

"Hold on. Hold on." Max gripped my shoulder and pulled out a chair he shoved me into. "I'll be the first one to acknowledge that Molly is evil, but if she wants the pendant, killing Rochelle won't help her get it, and if you go accuse her of anything, you're going to verify that we actually have it and blow our cover."

"Maybe she didn't want to kill her. At least not yet." I leaned back in the chair and loosened the collar of my shirt so I could take a full breath. "Delgado, think about the way Rochelle's dad died. He was involved in this pendant stuff. He trusted Molly's dad like Rochelle trusts Molly. What are the chances history repeats itself?"

Max sat down across from me, scratching his head as he contemplated my theory. "That's really sinister, but you could be on to something." A gust of wind crashed against the house and we both jumped. "How exactly do we break that news to Rochelle, let alone Kat and Kinley?"

I shook my head. "Gently. She's in too deep for us to keep it from her, but Kat and Kinley are better off not knowing." Standing,

I walked to the door and turned the deadbolt. "None of them deserve this."

Max fisted his hands. "Don't worry. We won't let Molly get near any of them, especially Rochelle. And if any of those Defiance thugs come around here, we'll take them down."

"It won't be that easy." I sank into my chair and watched confusion play over his face. I couldn't make him or Rochelle understand that the little we knew put us ten miles behind the others in the race for the pendants. We were running through a blizzard with our arms out in front of us, but without joining a side, we had no other choice.

Letting Rochelle deal with Molly was no longer an option. I had to take matters into my own hands. I would have to give up everything, but if my plan worked, the Aumonts would be free, and I was willing to make that trade.

CHAPTER 30
ROCHELLE

November 6, 2090

My dad sat on the couch in the library, eyes closed, face shiny with sweat and contorted in pain. Grandma and Arthur were getting my uncle's car ready so Dad could ride comfortably to Omaha while Kat and Kinley packed a bag so he would have everything he needed while at the hospital. I stood frozen, unable to leave his side.

"Don't look so worried, hummingbird." He opened his eyes and managed to smile. "I'll be at the hospital for a week or two and the doctors will figure out how to get me back to normal, and then I'll be home. Just like last month."

"Two weeks is a long time." Fiddling with the hummingbird charm on the bracelet he had given me days earlier, I sank next to him. This time felt different than the other bad days during his four months of illness. The fear I would never see him again squeezed my heart like an overgrown vine.

Dad wrapped his arms around me and kissed the top of my head. "I know, but just remember everything I've taught you and it'll be like I'm right here with you."

Nodding, I huddled so close to him that I could feel his chest rise and fall with every ragged breath. "I love you."

"I love you too." His cheek rested against the top of my head. "You and Kat and Kinley are more important to me than anything else in this world."

"Okay, Uncle Auggie, I think we packed everything you'll need to feel right at home." Kinley had his bag over her shoulder and held Kat's hand. "We even remembered the snowman socks Rochelle gave you for Christmas and the picture of all of us together when we went camping last summer."

"Thank you, sunflower and my little canary." He extended his free arm. "One more group hug before I get in the car." Kat and Kinley piled onto the couch, and he held us tight. "I'm so proud of all of you. Take care of each other while I'm away." For a minute we were frozen like that and life was perfect. I had everything I could possibly ever want.

"Please don't leave." I had been the one to say it, but suddenly I sat on the window seat observing myself on the couch, and she couldn't hear me. I watched Grandma and Arthur come for Dad, saw tears run down my own face the minute he was out of sight.

Kinley pulled me into her arms. "It's okay, Rochelle."

"It's okay, Rochelle." A cold hand touched my face. "It's only a dream."

My eyes shot open and the familiar library came into focus, along with Emma, sitting on the edge of the couch, hand resting gently on my forehead.

"You were crying in your sleep." She brushed a tear from my cheek. "Is your throat hurting again? I can get you something."

Sitting up, I shook my head. It seemed too exhausting to explain that my nightmare had been a replay of real events and I had only woken into the reality in which Dad would never come home. I swallowed, expecting the scratchy feeling to have returned, but my throat felt normal. When Kinley took me to the doctor, he assured me I would be feeling much better within the week. I'd spent the weekend resting, watching movies with Kat and Kinley, sometimes playing board games that Keppler joined with some prompting.

Although I no longer felt sick, I couldn't shake the panic I'd felt being alone and helpless. I glanced down at the photo album open on the blanket in front of me. In one picture, Todd and I were ten years old, sitting on the porch swing, arms around each other. In the second we were seventh graders, Todd in his football uniform and me in my volleyball uniform.

Emma sighed and pulled me into a hug. "I know you miss him, sweetie."

"He's supposed to be here right now." Looking at the pictures made me feel something like homesickness, so I gently closed the photo album. "He promised he'd be back in a week . . ." Tears rushed to my eyes. How many more people would break that promise before I stopped believing them?

"We'll see him again." She slid the photo album onto the coffee table and brushed a tear from her own cheek. "I still believe it'll be here rather than heaven, but it's not up to us." Emma blinked a few times and rubbed her eye with the back of her hand. "It's hard for me to accept sometimes, but we have to remember there's a plan in place bigger than we can understand, a bigger picture that we don't have the perspective to see in its entirety."

"And none of it happens by chance." I let my head rest on her shoulder, feeling the warm comfort of her familiar calm optimism.

"Exactly." She played with my hair, gently sliding it away from my face. "I bet when Todd gets home, I won't even see him for the first month because he'll want to spend all his time with you. He's not staying away on purpose, and I know he's doing everything in his power to get home."

Loud laughter drifted in from the kitchen and Emma smiled. "Kat is teaching Lily how to make some dishes she learned from camp. I'll be here with you for the rest of the day. Just in case you need anything."

"Good. I've missed talking to you." Emma had always been a

confidant for me, but we hadn't talked much about Todd because I knew his absence made her sad. She was also busy with her classes, but she was much more comforting than Kinley.

"I've missed talking to you too. And the good news is, I'm all caught up on my assignments until I get the new ones tomorrow."

The back door slammed followed by a loud, indecipherable conversation. Keppler walked into the room, shoulders slumped forward and cheeks flushed from the frigid air outside.

"What's wrong with you today?" Kat followed, wearing a flour-splotched apron over her clothes. "I just asked where you were."

"Why? Are you keeping tabs on me now?" He shoved his hands into his pockets. Conversation between Kat and Keppler had been tense since she accused him of abandoning me when I was sick, even though I assured both of them that wasn't the case.

"That's not what I meant." Kat threw her arms in the air. "You know what, never mind. Emma, can you come to the kitchen for a minute? I need your help with something."

"I'll be right there." She stood and walked over to Keppler as Kat turned on her heel and strode out of the room. "Are you feeling okay?" She pressed her hand to his forehead, and he didn't even pull away.

"I'm fine." His monotone voice and head bent forward didn't support his statement.

"Sit down for now and we'll talk when I get back." She squeezed his shoulder.

As she left the room, I swung my legs off the couch and sat up to make room. "Are you sure you're feeling okay? You look like you're about to cry."

"I don't cry." He trudged over and sat down beside me. "Then again, maybe that's all that's left to do."

"Is it because Kat is giving you a hard time? She made up with

Kinley, so she has to fight with someone else." Smiling, I sank back into the couch.

Keppler tossed his glasses on the cushion beside him, rested his elbows on his knees and covered his face with his hands. "I went to talk to Molly this morning, but she wasn't home." He shook his head. "I planned to give her the pendant and let her turn me into The Defiance in exchange for leaving you out of everything." He didn't look up.

I sat there, stunned, for a good minute. Then I said slowly, "She's in Minnesota visiting her sister." I wasn't sure how to feel about the rest of what he told me, but he looked too upset for me to be angry. "She even called me on Saturday morning to ask how I was feeling and invited me to go with her."

He didn't move, but his shoulders trembled. "How did I miss that? Don't ever go anywhere with her."

"I won't." I leaned forward, trying to see his face, but he turned away. "But don't worry. I think now that she's reconnecting with her family, she'll give up on joining The Defiance and hopefully stop caring about the pendants."

"You believe all of that?" Keppler turned to me, blue eyes incredulous.

I nodded. "She's just feeling kind of lost. You know, looking for a place to belong. Hopefully everything goes well with her sister, and of course we'll be her family too—"

"If feeling left out is enough to excuse her behavior, I should be the dictator of my own country by now," Keppler interrupted as he slid his glasses back on. "If she talked to Griff once, she'll be in The Defiance eventually. There's no walking away from him, Aumont. Not alive, anyway." He shook his head, voice so despondent that I felt his despair.

Keppler leaned back next to me so we sat shoulder to shoulder.

"I didn't want to tell you while you were sick, but Delgado and I have been investigating the possibility that Molly put something in your tea and it caused hallucinations."

I nodded. The information should have been shocking, but I'd considered the same impossible theory. Kat had been right when she said my symptoms were exactly like those in the early stages of our dad's illness. I could either believe Kinley, that it was the result of a fever and dehydration, worry that I had inherited some rare genetic condition, or worst of all, conclude that my dad's best friend had slowly poisoned him and Molly knew far more than she was telling me.

I took a breath to remind myself Kinley was usually right. "Killing me or even making me sick isn't going to help her get my pendant." I stretched the blanket so it would cover Keppler also.

"Maybe she's just trying to scare you, or . . . I don't know." He pressed one hand to the top of his head. "She'll do whatever it takes to get what she wants, and now she's changing her strategy. We don't have a clue what we're up against."

"But we will." Dad's words repeated in my head so clearly I almost believed he was in the room. "If I just remember what my dad taught me, I'll know what to do." Maybe that in itself was some kind of clue. He must have known he might not make it home.

"What could he have possibly taught you that'll get you out of this mess?" He sounded tired, and I realized he had probably been awake all night, considering how to deal with the pendant all by himself.

Glancing at the closed photo album on the table, I smiled. "He taught me that tomorrow will be better if we learn from today."

Keppler looked at me, face scrunched in confusion.

"We have to take a step back and try to see the bigger picture, so we can figure out how all of the pieces fit together. You know Griff, I know Molly, and I'm getting to know my aunt better every time I talk to her. We'll figure out their motives so we can predict their next moves. Just like we do with fictional characters during Emma's literature class."

Keppler shook his head. "I overheard Kat talking to Audrie on the phone yesterday. If she didn't like me before, she hates me now."

"Give me a week and I'll make them both see reason. You're the one who spent all week telling me to get more sleep and making me eat lunch." I leaned closer to Keppler. "Now, I have to give you the same advice. You need to get some sleep."

"I know, but I'm afraid for you. Afraid I won't be able to protect you from them." He rested a hand on his chest. "And this pendant gets heavier every day."

"How about I take it off your hands for a while? It's almost Max's turn anyway." It really wasn't, but Keppler had been the one making excuses to take longer turns with the pendant, and I needed him to hand it over for his own sanity.

"It's my responsibility. It has been ever since Griff told me about it." He tilted his head back and closed his eyes. "I guess our fates are tied together in the big picture."

"Which is why you should let me carry the weight for a while." I held out my hand. "Nothing bad is going to happen to me just because I'm wearing it."

He reluctantly slid the pendant over his head and dropped it into my hand. "Just promise you'll be careful."

"I have everything under control." Glancing around, I slipped the chain over my head and tucked the pendant beneath my shirt. "Did you write your article yet? About the leader's conference?"

"Between helping Delgado try to prove Molly poisoned you and imagining Griff murdering me, I've been a little distracted." He rubbed the side of his face without opening his eyes.

"You'll never see him again. I won't let it happen." After

everything he'd been through to escape, I couldn't push him back into that life, not even if it would save mine. "This afternoon, I'll help you with your article. It'll take our minds off our problems."

"They want to choose one person to act as a kind of temporary governor until they can set up an election. I think Alexander wants the position, but it's hard to believe any one of them will be in charge for long. According to the papers, The Defiance will take Texas by Christmas. For all we know, we're next."

"Then again, they're going in the opposite direction." In the last year of his life, my dad regularly told me to hope for the best. "Maybe there's nothing in Nebraska they want."

Keppler squeezed his eyes shut. "Yeah. Except you, me, and the pendant."

CHAPTER 31

CHARLIE

November 18, 2090

"I don't understand why they're all putting so much energy into finding this." Max sat on the couch next to Rochelle, examining the pendant in his palm. He tilted it up and then back. "Anyone with access to a 3D printer could make one of these. We could make our own and collect them all a lot faster."

"Don't say that." I stood, looking down at pages of notes sprawled over the desk. It was a compilation of everything we knew about the people who wanted the pendants and everything we'd learned about the pendants themselves. "The only thing preventing an illness worse than the fever is that pendant. You have to have the originals."

"Take a breath, *hermano*. It's just an observation." Max dumped the pendant into Rochelle's hand. "Tag. Your turn."

"Quit calling me your brother." *We'll take care of each other . . . like brothers.* Griff's words bulldozed through my memory. I pressed a hand to the top of my head. "You're not. You never will be."

Max's smile vanished and he sat up straighter. "I'm sorry. Someone woke up on the wrong side of the bed."

I didn't have time to worry about hurting his feelings. Molly could return from her trip any day, and I knew that when she did, she would have a brand-new plan. But every time we met to review what we knew and form our own plan, Max and Rochelle spent too much time chatting and joking around, never taking the threat seriously.

"Let's just go back to the pendant for a minute." Rochelle, as she always did with Kat and Kinley, tried to break the tension. "They all have words on them. That must be important. Maybe that's why they aren't so easy to duplicate." She held it up in front of her, dangling by its long chain so it glinted in the light. "What does *pessimus* mean?"

"Worst." Max swallowed and glanced at me out of the corner of his eye like he expected to be scolded. "You know, like the Latin phrase, *spero optimus instruo pro pessimus*."

Rochelle lifted an eyebrow. "Since when do you speak Latin?"

"No one speaks Latin, Rochelle, it's a dead language." He pretended to brush dust off his sleeve. "I read it sometimes—"

"What does it mean?" My voice sounded far more agitated than I intended, but I had to make my friends feel the same urgency in getting the pendant out of our lives. After all, their lives depended on it.

Max shrugged. "'Hope for the best, prepare for the worst.' Not bad advice, I suppose. Maybe the rest of the phrase is written on the others?"

I took my glasses off, sank into the desk chair and rubbed my eyes. "Griff's pendant had something Latin on it, but the one he got from that Zimmer guy said *better*."

Rochelle's shoulders sank. "Molly's said *tomorrow*. Like, 'tomorrow will be better.' My dad really was as deep in all this stuff as Molly said."

"But for the right reasons." He patted her shoulder. "And we're going to finish what he started. Once we figure out exactly what that is. But we're definitely on to something now. Keppler, write all of that down before we forget."

I shook my head at my worthless notes. Everything just

circled back on itself to a dead end. "None of that helps us." With one hand, I swept the papers off the desk. "This is getting us nowhere."

Rochelle stood as if to lecture me, but the phone rang in the next room. "That's probably Kinley. We need a break anyway." She disappeared into the dining room.

Max sauntered over to the desk where I sat slumped in my chair and started gathering up the papers one at a time. "Don't worry so much." He paused as if rethinking his next words. "Just remember, most of the things we waste time worrying about never actually happen."

"In my life, they always happen." I stood, feeling like I needed to move, pace the room. "You're so naive about how this world works. You wouldn't survive a day on your own."

He dropped the stack of papers on the desk and took a step away from me. "Is that why I'm not good enough to be your brother? You think I'll expect you to bail me out of trouble all the time?"

It had less to do with him and everything to do with my fear that any chance I had at a real family was slipping through my fingers. The rift with Kat was just the beginning. "I think you have to start taking life seriously. It's not one big joke, and you're not doing any of us a favor by acting like it is." I shoved my hands into my pockets. I hadn't even been with the Aumonts for a year and it was already crumbling.

Max looked at me, eyes narrowed, face twisted in irritation. "In that case, I'll go home. Call me if you decide I'm worthy enough to be useful, and tell Rochelle I'll talk to her tomorrow at church." He didn't wait for me to reply, just picked up his coat off the coffee table and left.

"Whatever," I muttered. The back door slammed, and the murmur of Rochelle's voice drifted into the room. Picking up the stack of notes, I straightened them and shoved them into the middle drawer that we kept locked.

"I need you to drive me somewhere." Rochelle stood in the doorway, face drained of color, clutching a piece of paper in her hand. She didn't even seem to notice Max had left.

"What's wrong?"

"I'll explain on the way. We have to hurry."

Tendrils of worry crept through my chest. Kat was at the home for children and Kinley was at the Tatems'. Had something happened to one of them? The urgency in Rochelle's voice convinced me to grab my coat and the keys, get into the truck, and back out of the driveway.

"Where am I driving?" I crept down the block. "Are Kinley and Kat okay? Should I be worried?"

"Follow Main Street to the golf course and take a left. They're both okay. I'll tell you when to turn again after that." She looked out her window so I couldn't see her face. Her stiff shoulders and rigid posture indicated I shouldn't ask any more questions.

We drove in silence for another mile before Rochelle told me to turn onto a gravel road. I did as she instructed, but when I glanced over at her, I could see her shaking. It was cold in the truck, but she was bundled up in her coat and hat.

"Aumont, what's going on? If you don't tell me where we're going, I'm turning around." A cloud of dust followed us, but we were alone and heading for the middle of nowhere.

"Promise not to panic?" She waited, but I didn't respond. "That was Molly on the phone. She has Todd with her and we're going to bring him home." Rochelle said it so matter-of-factly she could have been giving a weather report.

"It's a trick." I stepped on the brakes. "What exactly did she say?"

"No, Keppler, keep going." She looked at me hard until I sped up again. "He's hurt really bad and he needs a doctor. When she put him on the phone, he said my name, but his voice sounded really weak." Rochelle glanced through the windshield. "Turn left here."

I slammed on the brakes and skidded onto a minimum maintenance road. "We should have called the police. We should have told someone where we were going."

"No," Rochelle blurted. "She said just the two of us or she'll drive away and I'll never see him again." After a brief pause, she turned to me. "Have you been paying attention? Will you know how to get back home?"

My breath caught in my chest. "Why would you ask that? You'll be here, giving me directions."

"I'll leave my paper here just in case so you can follow it backwards. I know I promised to never go anywhere with Molly, but Keppler . . ." Shaking her head, she looked out at empty fields, already harvested for the year. "It's a trade. You can't take Todd to the hospital unless I stay with her."

"No way." My foot shifted to the brakes again.

"Don't slow down." She gripped my arm. "Please."

Fighting every instinct in my body, I returned to a normal speed. "You have to think this through, Aumont, with your head, not your heart."

"Either way, I won't let Todd die." She took a sharp breath in. "Please, Keppler. I need your help and I promise, I will never ask you for anything else ever again."

She misunderstood. I didn't care that she was asking for help. I would help her with anything she wanted. But if I helped her with this, would I ever see her again? I was caught in an impossible dilemma. I didn't want to lose Rochelle, and I couldn't let Todd die. "I'll take you there, but I'm not leaving without you."

"Turn here." Rochelle slid forward, pointing through the windshield.

Up ahead, a small red dot grew into a freshly painted pickup as we approached. Molly waited near the back bumper accompanied by two boys about our age. My heart sank through the floorboards when I noticed a gun hanging from each of their belts.

We wouldn't be negotiating.

CHAPTER 32

CHARLIE

November 18, 2090

"'ll handle this; we just have to stay calm." Rochelle stared through the windshield as I parked twenty feet back from the other truck. "I have everything under control."

She took a breath, pushed her door open, and stepped onto the gravel road. I watched her approach the three teenagers standing in front of a backdrop of clouds tinged pink by the rapidly sinking sun, Molly in her winter coat, the two boys in heavy flannel shirts. Although I didn't recognize their faces, the domineering way they stood convinced me they were with The Defiance. They might recognize me, but I was more worried about Rochelle. I jogged to catch up with her, unsure of what I would do to fight them all off but determined to protect her.

"Rochelle, I was starting to worry you might not come." Molly stepped forward, waving the other two away. They retreated to the front of the truck. "He's right in there."

Molly stepped aside, and in the truck bed lay a boy so filthy he was unrecognizable. Rochelle put one foot on the back bumper and hoisted herself up. Molly's two allies took a step forward, but she held out a hand to ward them off. As I climbed over the tailgate, Rochelle knelt down next to the boy, dressed in tattered clothes that hung from his thin body, hair matted with blood and dirt.

She didn't appear to feel the same uncertainty toward his identity as she gently took his hand between both of hers. Two eyelids slid half open to reveal familiar hazel eyes. Despite his malaise, a weak smile appeared on Todd's face.

"Shelley?" His voice was nothing more than a whisper. "Am I really awake?"

Rochelle let out a breath and nodded. Tears filled her eyes, but she smiled, and for a minute, she didn't seem to see the rest of us. "I'm going to get you home and everything will be okay."

Todd tried to lift his other hand, but it only hovered a few inches above his chest before falling back into place. "I've been..." He coughed and the pain spread over his entire face. "I'm sorry... I'm so late."

Rochelle touched her hand to his face, gently, as if he would crumble to dust if she wasn't careful. "It's okay. I'm not mad. I'm just so happy to see you." She turned to Molly with Todd's hand still gripped in hers. "What happened to him?"

Molly leaned forward, resting her elbows on the ledge of the truck. "He's been in a Defiance work camp. Earlier in the week he took a nasty fall during a building project."

Rochelle turned to me, but I could only shrug. The Defiance wasn't forcing people into work camps a year ago, but a hundred things could have changed since I'd run. "How long did you know he was there?" She looked down at Todd with tenderness then back to Molly for an answer.

"We'll have plenty of time to talk about that. Right now, Todd needs a hospital." Molly put a hand on Rochelle's arm. "I'm sure Charlie can get him home while we have a little meeting."

"She's not going anywhere with you." I stepped in front of Molly, hiding Rochelle from her view, towering over her from my perch in the truck bed.

She raised her eyebrows, blue eyes laughing at me. "Stay out of this. She knows the deal."

"Can I have just a minute to talk to Keppler?" Rochelle's voice was calm while my heart beat so fast I thought it would burst out of my chest and bounce away.

"I have plenty of time. Todd, not so much." Molly shrugged and turned toward her companions.

I squatted beside Rochelle. "Aumont, you can't do this. What am I supposed to tell Kinley and Kat when I show up without you?" Of all the questionable decisions I'd made in my life, leaving Rochelle behind would be the most unforgivable.

"Tell them . . ." She blinked away tears and took a deep breath. "Tell them this was my choice and I know what I'm doing." Todd groaned and she squeezed his hand. "Tell them I'll be home as soon as I can, but they shouldn't worry if it takes a while." She looked back up at me. "Keppler, I'm sorry, I know it's not the ideal situation—"

"Not the ideal situation?" I interrupted. "This is the nightmare scenario." It was worse than my greatest fear from only hours earlier. I thought we would deal with Molly in Maibe, not in the middle of nowhere, not when she had the one person Rochelle couldn't live without.

"I have everything under control." Rochelle laid her hand on Todd's forehead. "I know how to deal with Molly. I'll be okay."

I looked over the cab at Molly and the other two guys, talking and laughing. They were in complete control, and they knew it. "How can you say that? You remember what happened last time you were alone with her?"

"None of that matters," Rochelle whispered. "Todd is hurt. He's burning up and he needs a doctor right now. I'm healthy enough to handle whatever she has planned." Her eyes were green discs, shadowed by the same rare fear from when she was sick, yet pleading for me to let her walk into the unknown. I realized in all of the time I'd known her, she'd never asked me for anything in return for her kindness. She had taken a risk to help me months ago and I owed her, but sending her with Molly felt like the kind of revenge I would take on an enemy instead of repaying a friend I didn't deserve.

"But Aumont..." My voice shook and I had to take a few breaths to get it under control. "I don't know where they're taking you ..."

Rochelle wrapped her arms around me so tight I couldn't squirm away. "Todd saved my life last year. He's my best friend and this is the only way I can help him. I promise everything will be okay."

Before I could agree to anything, she stood. "I'll go with you, but first I want to get Todd settled in our truck."

Molly came toward us, motioning for the other two to stay back. "Go right ahead. Just don't try anything."

In the daze of a nightmare I couldn't wake up from, Rochelle and I each took one of Todd's arms and lifted him as gently as possible. He tried to help us, but he was too weak to walk, and every movement resulted in an agonized groan. We eventually got him in the cab, where he slouched against the passenger door.

Rochelle tucked her coat around him, slid her stocking cap onto his head, and kissed his mud-crusted forehead. "You're going home. Just hang in there."

"Don't go with her, Rochelle." He coughed and clutched his ribs. "I can stay instead."

"Don't worry, I'll be on my way home right behind you." She squeezed his hand, whispered something close to his ear, then backed her way out of the driver's side of the truck and turned to me. "Take care of him, Keppler."

I nodded. "Take care of yourself." It took every ounce of my willpower not to take her arm, shove her into the truck, and take our chances at outrunning Molly's gang, but reason told me none of us would make it out alive. Instead, I focused on the details: red truck, mud-covered license plates, poised to head north ...

"I'll be okay." Rochelle stepped back and Molly's two companions stood on either side of her, glaring at me.

With no other choice, I looked one last time at the only truly good person I'd ever met in my life. Then I got in the truck and started the engine.

"We can't leave her here." Todd's voice was a shaky whimper. "We have to do something."

"I know how you feel." He looked pathetic, shivering, only able to hold his head up by leaning against the window. "I'll come back for her."

I knew they would be long gone and I wouldn't be able to track them. I knew Rochelle would never trade Todd's life for hers, and Molly knew it too. Shifting the truck into gear, I slowly pulled away from the scene, watching Rochelle shrink out of sight in the rearview mirror until she vanished behind a cloud of dust.

"Can you see them anymore?" Todd tried to sit up a little.

"No." The horizon, only distinguishable from the night sky by a fading stripe of pink, was about to vanish into the darkness.

"Rochelle told me . . . you'll need this." The way he struggled to catch his breath made me press my foot down on the gas pedal. "She said they can't hurt her without it . . ."

Todd opened his hand to reveal the pendant. In the chaos of the past hour, I'd forgotten Max had left it with Rochelle. Its shiny surface taunted me, threatening to destroy every person, every family it touched.

CHAPTER 33
ROCHELLE

November 18, 2090

"Sit down right over there, Rochelle." Molly gestured to two chairs in front of a flickering fire place in an abandoned building within a ghost town. Although I felt I should be looking for a way to escape, I was drawn to the warmth of the fire.

We'd driven around on gravel roads for almost an hour, first heading north and then circling back south until we pulled into an abandoned little town I recognized as Gilbert. I had ridden there with my dad once to get a part for the truck. It had nearly been a ghost town then as residents moved to bigger cities. Most importantly, it was only twenty miles from Maibe.

We parked the truck behind a grain elevator along the railroad tracks. I walked next to Molly, closely followed by Alec and Amry, her apparent bodyguards, three blocks up the sidewalk to the first block of buildings.

As I sat down, I noticed Alec hang the truck keys on a hook by the door. Amry stood in the doorway, watching me.

Molly waved them away. "I can take it from here."

They left the room as she pulled the second chair closer and sat down directly in front of me. "Now we can talk without any distractions."

Something about the way she said it made me shiver despite the warmth from the fireplace. Behind her was a window that, if cleaned, would look out to the street. A desk stood in the middle of a black-and-white-tiled floor. A few more cushioned chairs interspersed by fake plants lined one wall, all covered in a thick layer of dust. It was a little run-down with a few missing ceiling tiles and a musty smell, but still a perfectly good shelter from the elements.

"Not a bad place, right?" She leaned back in her chair. "This town has everything we need to be comfortable for a week. If our conversation goes well, I'll show you our apartment."

"Apartment?" I rubbed my hands together trying to warm them. "How long have you been here?"

"Long enough to find ten new recruits. Kids in rural areas are just as bad off as kids in the cities, but far less likely to know they have options."

"Recruits?" My head jumped to conclusions my heart wouldn't let me believe. "For what?"

"Don't get upset." Molly took off her coat and slid her arms out of her cardigan. She wore a sleeveless blouse and turned sideways so I could see the letter D branded into her skin just below her shoulder. "It's still healing. I was only in Kansas City for initiation last week."

"I thought you were visiting your sister." My voice was a wisp of air leaving my throat.

She nodded. "For a couple of days. Then we had a big fight during which she wished I was never born." The pain of rejection played over her face, but only for a few seconds. "I had to make a choice about the kind of family I wanted. You'll understand soon, once I explain. The Defiance isn't as awful as the papers want people to believe."

My chest ached as I watched Keppler's fears playing out in front of me. "Molly, why did you bring me here?"

"Because you need me to show you that there's something better out there for you." She took my hands. "Your dad was part of the pendant project, and you're destined to be a part of saving those who deserve to be saved. All you have to do is join my new family."

"They're not your family." I stared in disbelief at the girl who had held my hand on the first day of kindergarten because she was nervous, the girl I'd shared my cookies with when she was having a bad day, the girl who had been my partner for every project in elementary school.

"If they're not, then who is?" She shoved my hands away. "Not my sister who doesn't even want to live in the same state as me. Not all of those people in Maibe who have probably already forgotten about me." She sank back down into her chair. "I have to confess, I haven't been completely honest with you, but everything I've done has been for your own good."

"What does that mean?" I wasn't sure I wanted to hear the answer, but perhaps it would help with Keppler's investigation.

"Just promise to hear me out, all the way to the end."

I nodded and settled back in my chair, all the time watching the door from my peripheral vision.

"Last October, when my dad told me about the research and his pendant, I thought it was just his delirium or maybe even mine. When I recovered, you still weren't well, and I got a call from my old friend Griff. He verified everything my dad had said and told me his plan to use the research to help the world." She stopped, and some emotion I couldn't identify flickered over her face. Something dark. Then it was gone, and she was talking again. "My dad had given me a combination, but it was different from the one to the safe in the basement, and the pendant he mentioned wasn't in the house. Then one day in February, when I was talking to Griff, he asked if Dad ever kept anything valuable at the pharmacy."

How did Molly know the pharmacy was on fire? I'd posed that question to Max and then dismissed it. "You started the fire?"

"Accidentally." True regret shadowed her face. "When I finally found the courage to check the safe, I realized I didn't have batteries for my flashlight, so I grabbed a candle instead. I found the pendant and a notebook my dad left before the candle tipped and things got out of hand."

"You tried to pin the blame on Keppler."

She shrugged. "He was a believable suspect. In hindsight, I never really had to worry about shifting the suspicion because no one asked me one question. That's when I realized people aren't nearly as smart as I give them credit for."

My heart beat so fast my chest felt like it would explode, and a lump I couldn't swallow away sat in my throat. "You promised to tell me how you found Todd."

"It was all part of the plan. I never intended for anything so terrible to happen to him." Molly folded her legs under her and smiled at my stunned reaction. Her lack of remorse at almost killing my best friend was terrifying. "It started innocently enough. When I first talked to him, I meant to find out if you knew anything about your dad's pendant. Then I realized how much he gets in the way of you reaching your full potential. Cautious Todd would never approve of you taking a few risks to change the world. He would keep you anchored to Maibe for the rest of your life. So I wrote him a letter from his mom, made sure his ticket coincided with a planned Defiance train raid, and instructed them to take him to one of the new work camps. I always intended to bring him home once you were on board with my plan, but that all took longer than I expected. When I saw all of his drawings enshrined on your wall, I knew you wouldn't let go of the people in your life so easily."

"You broke into my house," I said, voice flat. "I knew it was you."

"You weren't heeding my warnings to be careful. Anyone— the TCI, even your aunt—could have walked in and stolen your pendant anytime they wanted. Think how much more secure Kat and Kinley are now that you put some real locks on that house. You should thank me."

"I already told you, I don't have a pendant." I could still feel Todd's cold hand in mine as I pressed it against his palm. He had to be safe at the hospital by now—warm, clean, and recovering.

"Just because you don't have it with you doesn't mean you don't know where it is." Molly sighed and leaned forward. "You were so close with your dad. There's no way he could have kept this all a secret from you. Especially when he was dying. You'll change your mind. Maybe not today, but soon. Griff and I have already decided you're an integral part of our team. The three of us will change the world forever."

"So, you work for him then?" I knew the question would annoy her and hopefully make her think about her choices.

"I work *with* him. We're partners. He wants me to help him recruit more girls for next week's initiation, and of course I promised to bring you and your pendant into our family."

I couldn't believe what I was hearing. "Molly, this is . . ."

"All a shock to you, I'm sure." She took my hands in hers. "I can understand if you're a little nervous, but the three of us will be equal partners. I have so many ideas for The Defiance. I think we need uniforms. You can probably make something really nice. How do you feel about a gray jacket with a black D on the shoulder? Not too showy, but still recognizable, right?"

The realization that Molly wouldn't just let me walk away if I refused slowly sank its claws into my heart. Still, I couldn't give up on my childhood friend. I couldn't let her make a mistake she would regret for the rest of her life. "We don't have to do this. We can go home. You can move into my house like Keppler, and then you'll have a real family."

She shook her head. "Poor Rochelle. I told you a long time ago that trusting Charlie was a mistake, although I didn't know exactly why. But at my initiation, Griff told the story about a Charlie Keppler, who he treated like a brother and who ultimately betrayed him. He tells everyone Charlie's dead, but I'm sure he'd love to get his hands on that traitor. Make an example of him."

My breath caught in my chest and my entire body went cold. "I'm sure it's a coincidence. Common name—"

"No, the one you know, the one who always wears long sleeves, would have the same symbol as mine if we checked." A smile formed on Molly's lips. "But we don't have to say a word about it. He can live out his life peacefully in Maibe, but I have to know you're on my side."

"If I find the pendant, I'll call you and it's all yours." I leaned back into my chair, trying to escape Molly's scrutinizing eyes. "I don't want any part of the rest. You don't need me."

Her smile vanished. "I don't want to hurt you, but I will make you cooperate by any means necessary. My plan only works if there are three of us. If Griff and I disagree on the next step, I need a tiebreaker who always takes my side. So, you can work with me and be comfortable, or we can do this the hard way."

I stood and backed away from her. "I'm not working with you, or Griff, or The Defiance. I'm going home."

She stood, shaking her head. "You'll change your mind once you've slept on it." Molly snapped her fingers loudly. "Amry. Alec."

The two guards appeared in the doorway.

"Rochelle needs some time to think about my offer. Take her to the kennel." Molly sighed and pulled her cardigan on. "I hate doing this to you, but hopefully by tomorrow you'll come to your senses."

The two boys didn't hesitate. They appeared about my age, but each was almost a foot taller and a hundred pounds heavier. With one holding onto each of my arms, they dragged me into the cold November air.

We continued across the road and into a single-story building, through the reception area, and toward the back room. The space was filled with dog kennels, just like Uncle Arthur's old clinic. In front of one, they pushed my head down and shoved. I landed on my knees and elbows, turning just in time to see them secure a padlock over the chain-link gate.

CHAPTER 34

CHARLIE

November 18, 2090

"She told me to get Todd to the hospital . . . she wouldn't leave without him . . . They had a red truck . . ." Sweat beaded across my forehead as my tongue stumbled over an explanation of Rochelle's absence and Todd's unexpected homecoming while Alexander, Kinley, and Kat listened in silence. Although I wanted to get in the truck and drive until Maibe, Nebraska, was so far behind me I could forget it ever existed, I knew it wouldn't be that easy. Kinley and Kat deserved better after all they had done for me, and the stubborn hope in Rochelle's eyes would haunt me until I brought her home.

We all stood in the unbearably hot break room off the hospital's waiting room, Alexander with his hands in his pockets, face drawn with concern; Kinley rubbing her forehead, color fading from her face; and Kat clenching her hands in front of her, glaring at me. I pressed my hands to the top of my head, trying to focus on the facts, to remind myself to breathe so I wouldn't collapse into the panic of realizing every scenario I had worried about was a fairy tale compared to this new reality.

"You knew Molly has been harassing Rochelle for months?" Kinley took a big step toward me. "You knew she was in over her head, that she needed help, that other people knew about the pendant Audrie mentioned . . . And you're just telling me now?"

I had done the one thing Rochelle refused to consider and told them everything about the past nine months, only excluding my affiliation with The Defiance and the fact that we'd actually found the pendant.

Taking a step back, I nodded, but I couldn't take my eyes off Kat, staring at me as if I'd killed her puppy.

Alexander slid his hands under Kinley's elbows before she collapsed. "We should all sit down for a minute—"

"No, we have to do something before they take her too far away." She spun on her heel to face Alexander, shouting so loudly I was sure the Tatems could hear her in the waiting room. "You're always going on about all the things you're doing as mayor. Well, I want Rochelle home now!" Her voice broke, and hope drained from her eyes with a burst of tears.

"The police are out looking for her, and they're informing all of the departments in the state." He enfolded Kinley in his arms. "They're ramping up security at the train stations." He gave me a sympathetic nod and gently rocked Kinley back and forth as she sobbed into his shoulder. Even Alexander knew I had failed the only test that mattered. Hadn't I survived my past so I could take care of the Aumonts, warn Rochelle about the pendant, protect my family?

"How could you have left her there?" Kat lunged forward so unexpectedly, I stumbled back another step. "What's wrong with you?"

It was the question I had been asking myself for the past three hours, but looking into Kat's fierce blue eyes, all I could do was clutch the pendant no one knew was in my pocket. "I'm sorry."

"That's it? We shouldn't even be standing here talking about this. You never should have left without Rochelle in the first place." She shoved me aside and continued to the door. "I need some air."

Staring down at my shoes, all I could do was breathe in and out, listening to the ticking clock and Kinley's sniffling.

"I never liked her hanging around Molly." Her words came out a little garbled. "She was always rotten and mean. The complete opposite of Rochelle."

Looking as miserable as I felt, Alexander nodded. "Rochelle is smart, and she can handle herself with Molly." He kissed Kinley's forehead. "I'm going out to check on the search, but I'm sure she'll be home in time for breakfast. That red truck can only get so far."

Kinley wiped her tears and nodded. "I have to go find Kat. Can you sit with Emma for just a minute until I get back?" When I'd arrived with Todd, a nurse wheeled him through a heavy door, and three hours had passed without an update. The waiting was making me so anxious, I couldn't imagine how his family felt.

I pulled out my keys. "I'm going out to find Rochelle right now, and I won't be home until I do."

"Absolutely not." Kinley swiped the truck keys out of my hand and shoved them into her pocket. "Go to the waiting room and sit down." Her eyes narrowed when I didn't move. "Now."

She hadn't raised her voice at me since the night of the forum when I'd fought with Todd. That day felt like years ago instead of months, that mistake so small in comparison to the unforgivable blunder of losing Rochelle. Unable to muster the strength to argue with Kinley, I trudged to the waiting room where Emma, Lily, and their dad huddled together near the reception desk awaiting news.

I chose a chair in the corner and sank into it, pulling off my glasses and burying my face in my hands. When I'd talked to the police, I'd left out everything about the pendant, the TCI, and anything pertaining to Rochelle's dad or vaccine research. What would they do about it anyway? What they needed to investigate was a kidnapping case so they could bring Rochelle home.

She should be the one sitting with Emma, waiting for news about Todd. If I had been thinking clearly, I would have admitted to being The Defiance's most-wanted defector, removed their

302 Tomorrow Will Be Better

attention from Rochelle, and traded myself for both of them. Had I really forgotten or had I been too afraid?

My heart pounded in my chest, and my breathing came in quick gasps that seemed to lodge in my throat. I needed to talk to someone who knew all of my secrets, but after the argument I had with Max, I doubted he'd be any more sympathetic to my situation than the others. Why hadn't I been the one to walk out? Rochelle would have been safer with him.

"Charlie, are you all right?" Lily's soft voice rose right next to me.

I forced a deep breath and opened my eyes. She sat in the chair beside me, legs folded under her, brown eyes glistening with old tears. Nodding, I slid my glasses back on. "I'm fine. Are you all right?"

She shook her head. "I'm scared for Todd. Dad and Emma are talking to the doctors right now, but they wouldn't let me come." She squirmed backward so she could lean back in her seat just like me. "That's a bad sign, right? What if, you know . . ."

Forgetting about my own misery, I sat up straighter. "If he's made it this far, he'll pull through." Just like all of the times I had lied to Isabelle so she wouldn't be afraid, I couldn't let Lily believe, for even a minute, her brother would die. "Todd is pretty tough."

"I guess." She shrugged. "I wish Rochelle was here. She'd know what to do." It wasn't a jab at me, simply Lily missing the person she usually turned to for support.

Still my stomach twisted, and I focused on my breathing to ward off a wave of nausea. "Don't worry. I'm going to find her. I won't rest . . . I won't even eat until I bring her home."

Lily glanced up at Alexander and Emma approaching us, then took my hand in both of hers. "None of this is your fault," she whispered. "Rochelle would have never left Todd behind no matter what you did. Just like Todd was more afraid of losing her than he was of the fever."

I felt myself smile a little, surprised that a twelve-year-old had been the most generous in her judgment of my actions. My dilemma, though, wasn't whether Rochelle made the right decision, but why I had been too cowardly to intervene for a better outcome.

Emma sank next to her sister and pulled her into her arms. "You and I are going to go home for some hot chocolate, and then we'll get some sleep so we can sit with Todd tomorrow."

"But I want to see him right now." Lily pulled away from her sister.

"He's asleep right now, sweetie." Emma closed her eyes for a few seconds then opened them. "Dad will stay with him tonight, and we'll work out a schedule so he's never alone."

Lily just nodded and melted into her sister's arms again.

Feeling helpless, I looked up at Alexander standing in front of us with his hands in his pockets, then turned slowly to Emma. "He's going to be okay?"

She managed to smile. "Thanks to you." She reached over and squeezed my arm. "He's stable right now. They took care of his partially collapsed lung, and they're treating his infection. They'll know more about how he's responding to the treatment by morning." She cringed. "The broken ribs and fractured arm will heal in time."

I could only nod. It was clear from Emma's voice that it was too soon to predict whether Todd would pull through.

Alexander clapped my shoulder. "Charlie, do you want to ride out with me to find out how the search is progressing? It would be good to have another set of eyes to spot anything suspicious."

Molly would be smart enough to get off the road, probably lay low at an abandoned farm until the search let up. I could run it by Alexander on the way. Anything sounded better than sitting around, waiting, trapped with my own thoughts. Where else would I go, anyway? Would Kinley and Kat even let me come home? Could I even cope with being in that house without Rochelle there?

"Alexander, can I stay with you for a few days?"

"Are you sure?" His face crumpled with worry as he glanced over his shoulder at Kinley and Kat approaching. "I mean, of course you can, but we should probably run it by Kinley first."

"Run what by me?" Her hand shook as she lifted it to rub her forehead. "What happened now?"

"Nothing. We were just talking about Charlie maybe staying with me for a few days." He pressed his hand over the back of his neck.

Kinley blinked away new tears and took a deep breath. "Sure. If that's what you both want."

I studied my shoelaces so I wouldn't have to meet her eyes. Part of me had hoped she'd protest, make me come home, prove I was still part of the family. Locking me in my room, making me do all of the chores, grounding me for the rest of my life, even hitting me would have been better than just letting me go. Kat didn't argue, just squeezed her cousin's hand.

"Emma, tell Kinley what the doctors said about Todd." Lily sat up, brown eyes flitting from face to face. "She'll know if he's going to be okay."

"Of course he's going to be okay." Kinley sat down next to them, pulling Kat with her.

As they clustered together for comfort, I scrambled for the door. Outside, I fell back against the wall, slid to the ground, and pulled my knees up to my chin, wheezing and coughing to catch my breath as if I'd run five miles uphill. By failing to protect Rochelle, I'd lost all of them. A family could only fracture so far without someone to hold it together, and without Rochelle, we had shattered in minutes.

Pulling the pendant from my pocket, I held it up in front of me then tossed it down the sidewalk. It bounced once, landing in the glow of the streetlight, a glinting reminder I could never escape. Whether that little black wedge or one of the others, it would be there, ruining my every opportunity at having a family, corrupting and taking away the people I cared about.

Leaning my head back against the wall, I stared up at the dark sky, thick clouds blotting out the moon, stars, and any hope I'd allowed myself to feel during my time in Maibe. Forcing myself to my feet, I scooped the pendant off the pavement and slipped it around my neck where it hung even heavier than before. I would bring Rochelle home if it was the last thing I did. If I survived, I'd move onto the lonely life, devoid of a family, I was destined for. A life on the run, with only the pendant as a companion, always staying one step ahead of The Defiance.

CHAPTER 35

ROCHELLE

November 22, 2090

My numb fingers fumbled with the rope securing my hands to the chair in front of the fireplace as I waited for my meeting with Molly. As much as I dreaded sitting through her attempts to manipulate me into cooperating and joining The Defiance, it was my only break from being locked in the freezing cold kennel. Once in the morning and once in the afternoon, one of the two boys came to my prison and dragged me across the street to the building Molly used as an office, tied my raw wrists, and left without a word.

If I could get my hands free before Molly returned from an afternoon of recruiting, I could sneak out and walk home in time for breakfast. My stomach growled as I imagined Kat making pancakes or omelets. Rations currently consisted of a slice of bread and a bottle of water tossed into my cage every morning. If only I had the food from all of those dinners when Kinley told me to eat whatever I was sliding around my plate.

Trying to gather my muddled thoughts, I glanced around the room, noticing once again the truck keys hanging on the wall by the door. If I could get to the vehicle parked behind the grain bins, I would be home in twenty minutes. Despite the warmth of the fire, my fingers felt swollen and clumsy from hours in the cold, so I couldn't even tell the difference between the rope and my arm.

The click of Molly's boots behind me announced her arrival.

"Have you finally come to your senses?" I could hear the smile in her voice. "You should understand by now that joining The Defiance is your only choice." She stepped in front of me, holding a sandwich in her hand. "I hope you don't mind, but I'm running late. Didn't get lunch yet."

I ignored her taunt. She wanted to take away every comfort until I broke down and cooperated with her, but I wouldn't give in. "I haven't changed my mind. I'm waiting for you to come to your senses. The Defiance isn't your family."

After four days it had become clear to me that I couldn't reason with her, was in no position to save her, and wouldn't be going home unless I found a way to escape. But I kept up the charade of trying to convince her. It couldn't hurt.

She put her sandwich on the desk amid some office supplies and slipped her arms out of her coat. "Very funny. You know, this is the most we've talked in years and it's only because you're tied up. You would choose your cousin, your sister, even Charlie and Max over me every time."

She brushed her blonde hair behind her ears and sank into her chair. "The truth is, I don't need a family. I just need an opportunity." She hadn't been shy about updating me on her twenty new recruits who would soon travel with her to Kansas City. Another twenty lost kids who believed they had no better alternatives than The Defiance.

"I didn't say I'd choose them over you. I said I care about all of you." Despite the pain in my fingers, I worked at the rope.

"Don't lie to me. We're being honest with each other. Remember?" She shook her head, then looked me up and down with a sneer. "Speaking of . . . Rochelle, you're disgusting." She slid her chair a few feet back. "Give me your word that you'll cooperate with Griff and me, that you'll help us collect the pendants and find the research. In return you can have a warm bath. I'll even find you some clean clothes that'll be warmer than the ones you're wearing."

I shifted in my mud-stained sweater and jeans. As nice as a hot bath sounded, hygiene was low on my priorities. "I'm fine. I don't need your help."

"You should know our train arrives this evening. I'll be busy making preparations for our journey, so I need to know now whether you're coming as a prisoner or a friend. I'd much rather have you presentable so you don't embarrass me when I introduce you to Griff."

I forced a laugh. "As if a train is just going to stop in the middle of nowhere and pick us up."

"You should have seen how cooperative the conductor was when Griff and I met with him. It's amazing what this symbol can accomplish." She tenderly touched the skin around her healing burn. "We gave him free passage to haul goods in and out of Texas since we have to keep our supply chain strong for the takeover. Anyway, he doesn't have any passengers coming this far north, so there's plenty of room for all of us."

Blinking back tears, I took a deep breath to cope with the fact that if she got me on that train, I wouldn't be going home for a long time. "I don't have the pendant. I'm no good to you. Just let me go and I won't tell anyone about any of this." My thawing fingers scrabbled at the knot securing my wrists.

"You'll be far more useful to us than you realize." She sat back in her chair, studying me. "You don't want to go home anyway. Todd is probably dead, your family knows you chose him over them, and you're about to be the one responsible for plunging their lives into chaos." She smiled and shrugged. "Plus, I'm sure Kinley's already ecstatic to have one less anchor holding her down."

My breath hitched a little with the illogical fear she could be right.

Molly stood. "A family only cares about you when you're useful to them, not when you're disrupting their lives. That's why hundreds of kids our age and younger are abandoned and left to fend for themselves every day. Maybe you've had it cushy so far, but if families really exist, how can you explain all the rest?"

Tunneling my fingers under the loosening rope, I focused on breathing so I wouldn't cry. "The world's in a bad place right now, but it'll get better."

"Yeah, in time for kids ten years younger than us to get a real education, and then they'll roll right over us." She leaned in closer to me. "We're the forgotten generation, Rochelle. This world doesn't want us, and unless we fight for our place, we won't have one at all."

"That isn't true." I tried to come up with an argument, but what future did I really have? Was living with Kinley and mending people's clothes for the rest of my life enough? It didn't matter; I had to distract her long enough to untie myself. "Tell me the truth about the research. Is it really for a vaccine, or is it actually some kind of virus intensifier?"

She sighed and collapsed into her chair. "Both. If there's any truth in this world, it's that something world changing and life improving never comes without a price. In this case, the research gives us access to something equally as dark as the good it can do for the world. But don't worry, all Griff and I want is to protect the kids everyone else has forgotten. Imagine what would have happened to you if you had been living on the streets with no one to take care of you when you came down with the fever. The three of us can protect the most vulnerable in our society from that fate."

I believed the first part, but the rest seemed part of a memorized script.

"Don't look at me like that, Rochelle. We both know even

though you don't have your dad's pendant on you, you know where it is." Her arms folded tightly over her chest. "It might take time, but you'll change your mind and tell me all about it. You wouldn't want to carry on his mistake and deprive the world of a better tomorrow. It's our social responsibility to fix this."

Taking a breath, I met Molly's cold blue eyes. She knew how to manipulate people, and she knew far more about my dad's role in the project than I did. "When you made us tea, the other night..." My chest burned and tears stung my eyes. "Is that how my dad died?"

"Don't be ridiculous, Rochelle. I just wanted to ensure your family wouldn't be so quick to believe you if you started blabbing about the pendant. I don't know what happened to your dad, but I wouldn't put anything past the TCI."

I shook my head, knowing she would never admit the horrible truth we both understood. "They're not the ones who poisoned or kidnapped me." My wrists wriggled back and forth, finding ever-expanding space.

Molly walked over to the window and looked out. "It's your choice to be tied up right now. Maybe you don't care about your own comfort, but unless you cooperate with me, I will make life difficult for the people you love until I'm the only friend you have left. Then you'll have no choice unless you want to walk through life completely alone."

I squirmed, and one hand slid free from the rope still looped through the spokes of my chair. "Stay away from them."

She turned around, hands clutched behind her back. "I'm asking you one last time to cooperate. Meet Griff in Kansas City, help me recruit for The Defiance, and work with us to fix this broken world." She took a few steps toward me. "Last chance, Rochelle. Are you in or not?"

My dad had died to keep the virus locked away, but I didn't

need to understand how it happened to know joining Molly would disappoint him. Shaking my head, I wriggled my other wrist free, lunged for the door, and stumbled.

By the time I regained my balance Molly had crossed the room, blocking my exit.

"You can't run from this, Rochelle." She came toward me with such a menacing smile that I slowly backed away until the desk stopped me. "Neither of us can. These pendants are our destiny."

I couldn't argue with that. My dad's choices had become my responsibility. "It's my destiny to keep it away from people like you."

"I'm sorry you feel that way." She reached around me and picked up a paperweight, like a giant marble, from her desk. "Alec and Amry are asking why I'm not being more forceful with you, and I know they'll lose all respect for me if I let you just walk out of here."

My heart beat faster, but I ignored it as I sidestepped along the desk. If I could just find the strength to run, I'd be through the door and down the street before she could walk across the room in her high-heeled boots.

Her eyes narrowed, daring me to make a move.

Desperate to see my family again, to hold Todd's hand, I leaped for the door. My hand clutched the knob as a hand clenched my hair and yanked hard. The paperweight slammed into the left side of my face.

I tumbled backwards, elbows and head knocking against the hard tile. My scalp ached, and my left eye watered so I couldn't see through it.

Molly stood over me, still holding the weight in her hand. "I'm not playing these games anymore. Are we on the same side or not?"

I swallowed and tried to blink the tears away. "No."

The toe of her boot tapped against the floor right in front of my face. "That's too bad, Rochelle. Now I'm going to have to hurt the people you love until you change your mind. Should I start with Kinley, or should I tell Griff all about his old friend Charlie?"

The throbbing around my eye assured me she wasn't bluffing. "This has nothing to do with them."

She leaned down so she could see my face. "It has everything to do with them. They're your weakness and the only way I can persuade you to do what I want."

Speckles of color danced across my vision, forcing me to close my eyes and rest my head on the floor.

"We'll have plenty of time to talk it over with Griff." Molly's heels clicked across the floor and the door groaned open. "Amry, get her out of here."

"You've got it." Heavy footsteps pounded into the room, and a big hand gripped my arm too tight, hauling my stiff body upright.

A cruel smile spread over Molly's face. "When the train gets here, check the freight cars for stowaways and choose one we can use for prisoner transportation." She shifted the paperweight from one hand to the other. "Rochelle isn't ready to be one of us yet."

At that moment, I knew Keppler had been right. I was in over my head, I couldn't escape, and I would never see my family again. It took all of my willpower not to cry as Amry shoved me toward my prison.

CHAPTER 36
ROCHELLE

November 22, 2090

The ice-cold concrete floor only amplified my shivering. I pulled my knees to my chest where I lay in the corner of my cell, chin bleeding where it had met the floor when Amry shoved me into the kennel. When I dozed, I dreamed of Kinley sitting on the edge of my bed, holding an ice pack to my eye, Kat bringing me a bowl of tomato soup, Todd sketching any scene I described. The mirages never lasted long, vanishing when I woke up crying only to drift again.

"Please, don't do this. My friend needs a doctor." A female voice echoed through the building. "Let me go."

"Put her with the other girl," Amry's familiar, gruff voice ordered. "Put the boys in one of the other kennels."

"*This* is your prison?" The boy's voice was a frustrated laugh. "This is a dump compared to the last place I was locked up."

"You'll only be here a few hours." Amry laughed. "I'm sure you'll love the next place."

Two chain-link doors squealed open and clicked shut. It hurt too much to move, so I remained in the corner with my eyes closed against the throbbing in my head.

"Aaron?" the female voice asked.

"I'm okay." A different boy's voice sounded weak and strained.

"Well, here we are again." The first boy sighed. "This is what happens every time we stow away on a train."

The girl laughed. "That's not true, Nick. This is the first time it's happened to me."

"Me too," Aaron answered.

"Ha-ha. Very funny, guys." Nick sounded too calm for someone who had just been taken prisoner. They all did. "Let's just get out of here before we end up wherever they're going."

"Agreed. I bet they'll be too busy with the train to notice us sneaking out. We'll keep close to the buildings just in case." The female voice formed her plan as easily as I could recite my address. "I'm sure Maibe has to be just down the road."

At the mention of my home, I sat up against a wave of dizziness. "You're going to Maibe?" The dim light only allowed me to see the silhouette of one person in my kennel and two more in the one next door.

The girl scrambled backward, crashing into the fencing that separated our kennel from the other. "Whoa, who's there?"

I squeezed my eyes shut and rested my head against the wall behind me. "I'm Rochelle."

"Wait! There's no way," Nick's voice exclaimed. "*The* Rochelle? As in, Rochelle Aumont?"

"Quiet, Nick," the girl warned.

I wanted to move closer, but my muscles cried out in pain. "That's me. Do I know you?" I wasn't sure whether to be alarmed or relieved.

"Well, you don't know *me*," Nick answered. "But I kind of know you."

"Nick." The girl hit the fence behind her with a loud clang. "Be quiet." She stood and took a few steps toward me. "Rochelle, it's Lareina." She approached slowly as if I were an injured animal that might jump up and bite her. "I lived in Maibe for a year when we were kids. It was a long time ago. You might not remember ..."

I felt a smile spread over my face, felt my bruised cheek throb anew. "Lareina, I remember you. Did they finally send you home?" My head lolled back against the wall behind me, and I realized I was viewing everything through one eye.

Lareina knelt down right in front of me. "Something like that. I can explain the details later." In the dim prison, I could make out some of her features—a pretty face, much more grown up than the last time I'd seen her, outlined by short, dark hair.

Her hand reached toward my face but didn't touch it. "What did they do to you? Why are you here?"

I leaned forward a little and groaned. "Does it look really bad?"

"You're going to be okay. We're all getting out of here." She took my hand, helped me over to the other side of the kennel, and introduced me to her friends.

"Is it just me, or is it a bad sign that the person we've been looking for is locked up with us?" Nick scratched his head.

Her eyes narrowed. "Can you shut up for just five minutes?"

"Give him a break on this one, Lareina." Aaron leaned toward her, groaning a little. "I was kind of thinking the same thing." For the first time, I really looked at him, leaning heavily into the fence, head lolled to the side. His half-open eyes watched me out of a pale face, expression twisted into a grimace of pain he tried to disguise when speaking. His leg, stretched out in front of him, was wrapped from ankle to knee in a blood-stained bandage.

Lareina put a hand on my shoulder. "I need everyone to stay calm." She gave Nick a look, then turned back to me. "Rochelle, how did you get to this place? Is there something wrong with Maibe?" Her voice remained even, but her eyes grew wider with every question.

"No, Maibe is fine . . . for now." My three cell mates breathed a sigh of relief, and my thoughts scrambled in a million directions to explain a situation years in the making. "Molly Bennett." I was surprised by the anger in my voice. "She's trying to take me with all of her Defiance recruits. Our dads worked on a project together . . ." I shook my head. There was too much to say. "But I had to come or Todd would die." Tears welled in my eyes as my words jumbled into incoherent mush.

Nick looked horrified. "Those people out there are in The Defiance?"

Lareina took my hands in hers. "Deep breaths." She turned to Nick. "They're just recruits. They're years away from being the trained soldiers we saw in Dallas." She turned back to me. "We're going to get out of here, but we have to focus on one detail at a time. First, how did they bring you here?"

I closed my eyes and took a deep breath. There was something reassuring in her voice that helped me focus. "In a truck." My eyes shot open and I sat up straighter. "The keys are in the building across the street."

"Good. Can you take me there?"

"Yes." I slumped back against the fence. "But there's no way out of here. I've checked a hundred times."

"There's always a way out." Smiling, she unzipped her jacket and worked her fingers into a hole in the lining, pulling out a string of interlinked paperclips.

Nick rested his forehead against his hand and slowly shook his head. "You took those off the desk in the hotel lobby, didn't you?"

Lareina worked to slide one off the chain. "After that incident with Galloway, I'm never going anywhere without a paperclip again."

"Yeah, I know, a paperclip saved both of our lives. But couldn't you have just taken two or three?" Lareina raised her eyebrows at Nick, and he sighed. "You know what . . . never mind."

She grinned at him, then shifted herself over until she knelt under the lock. "How far are we from Maibe, Rochelle?" She worked her hand through one of the diamond shapes in the fence.

"About twenty miles." I watched, a little doubtful she could open the lock that had trapped me for days with something as simple as a paperclip. Nick and Aaron waited patiently.

Working her other hand through the fence, she gripped the padlock in one hand and the paperclip in the other. "I can get us out of here and I can get the keys, but I've never driven before."

"So, we are stealing the truck." Nick sighed. "I like that better than stowing away on another train, and The Defiance probably already stole it from somewhere else . . ."

"Got it." The padlock pulled apart in Lareina's hands, and she pushed the gate open with a groaning creak that caused us all to freeze in place. "Can you drive or not, Nick?"

"Yes, I can drive." Nick sat up a little taller. "I even had an official driver's license once."

Lareina reached for my arm. "Come on, Rochelle." She helped me out of the kennel and knelt down to pop the padlock, trapping her friends. "You're absolutely sure you know how to drive, because you also told me you knew how to forage for food."

Aaron couldn't stifle a weak laugh. "If you don't trust Nick, I know how to drive."

"Thanks a lot." Nick sat shoulder to shoulder with his friend, and I started to feel the seriousness of the situation they were trying to joke their way through.

The padlock clicked and Lareina pulled the second kennel door open. She crawled in, propped herself up beside Aaron, and gently touched his forehead. "Can you make it a few more miles?"

"Definitely." He lifted his head forward. "We're almost home."

Lareina took a breath and rubbed the sleeve of her jacket across one side of his face, then the other. "Could you take a look at Rochelle and let me know if she's well enough to come with me?" She took my hands and pulled me up close to Aaron. "He's going to be a doctor. He studies all the time."

I smiled. "My cousin is going to be a doctor. She's in a training program."

Aaron's eyes opened all the way. "In Maibe?"

I nodded.

For a second, Aaron forgot his injuries and a wide grin lit his face. "I'm so glad I let you guys drag me to Nebraska." He turned back to me and held one hand behind my head while he examined my face. "I wish we had some ice to bring down the swelling. Did you hit your head, Rochelle?"

I nodded again.

"Did you lose consciousness?" He looked more closely at my eyes. "Do you feel nauseated?"

"No, I think I was awake the whole time and I don't feel sick. My head hurts though."

Aaron nodded. "She might have a concussion. She can help you, but don't let her do anything too strenuous."

"What happened to your leg?" My imagination wouldn't stop making up a hundred different scenarios for how he could have been injured.

Nick cringed. "He got caught in a trap. We haven't had an easy trip." He slipped out of his coat and handed it to me. "Here, you need it more than I do."

"Thank you." I quickly slid my arms into its warm embrace. "The truck is parked down the road by the grain bins."

Lareina looked at each of us. "Nick, I want you to get Aaron to the truck and be ready to drive us home. We'll meet you guys there."

Everyone agreed, but I didn't move.

"Rochelle, what's wrong?" Lareina already had one of Aaron's arms around her shoulder.

Now I'll have to hurt the people you love. Molly's words tortured my thoughts as I weighed my options. I couldn't stay, but if I ran, what would happen to my family? Were they safer if they never saw me again? I glanced up at the puzzled looks of the three allies I never expected to meet. *Nothing happens by chance.* I had to go home, warn everyone, fix everything I'd set into motion. Shaking my head, I forced a smile. "Let's go home."

Nick helped me to my feet, then worked with Lareina to pull Aaron up. I led the way through the dark building to the door that looked out to an unlit street, quiet and empty of people.

"They're all gathered in a big building a few blocks that way." She nodded in the opposite direction of the railroad tracks. "It's probably too cold out here for those wimps." She looked up and down the street one more time. "Let's go."

We watched Nick and Aaron stumble together toward the grain bins just down the tracks from where the train sat waiting. Lareina took my hand, and we darted across the street and plastered ourselves against the building Molly used as an office. The night was cold and breezy with racing clouds that occasionally released little bursts of moonlight. I couldn't see any firelight in the windows, so I said a silent prayer that no one would be inside and slowly pushed the door open. Instead of walking in, I reached my arm through the partially open door and felt along the wall until my hand met cool metal.

"Got 'em." I gripped the keys and held them up in victory.

"Good," she whispered. "Now, let's get to the truck."

I slid the keys into my pocket as we walked down the sidewalk. Lareina kept one hand on my arm, and I was glad because I felt a little unsteady.

"Hey, who's down there?" It was a female voice I had never heard before. "Stop right there."

"Follow my lead," Lareina whispered as she pulled both of my arms behind my back and held them firmly.

We turned to see a girl dressed in jeans and a gray jacket

rushing toward us. Her dark hair was pulled back from her face, and the gun strapped over her shoulder nodded slightly toward us with each movement she made.

"What are you doing down here? Why do you have the prisoner out?" She sounded far more intimidating than she looked.

Lareina pulled me back with such force that it hurt and glanced over her shoulder toward the railroad tracks. "The boss told me to dunk her in the creek a couple of times." She laughed. "You know, make her more presentable before we board the train."

The girl narrowed her eyes at us suspiciously. "When did she tell you that?"

I took a sharp breath partly due to the pain and partly fear I would never make it home. This time, I prayed that Lareina knew what she was doing.

"Right before those stowaways showed up." Her voice lowered to a snarl. "Are you questioning me?"

"No." The girl took a step back, but her scowl didn't vanish. "I just don't think—"

"Look." Lareina thrust me forward but didn't let go of my arm. "Do you want to sit next to her all the way to Kansas City?"

The girl cringed and took two steps away from me. "No."

"Then let me follow my orders." Lareina pulled me back rough enough that a stabbing pain shot through my shoulder. "You follow yours."

"Fine. Go." The girl's eyebrows slid together. "But I'm going to check with the boss."

"Fine. With. Me." Lareina emphasized every word. She turned me around and shoved me forward but kept a firm grip on my wrist. When we crossed the first street, she let up a little. "Are you okay? I didn't hurt you?" She whispered so softly I could barely hear her.

"I'm fine," I muttered. "How did you know that would work?"

Glancing behind us, she propelled me faster. "I've had a lot of practice, and that's why I have a bad feeling about this time. We should hurry."

When we turned the corner, she took my hand and we ran toward the grain bins, skidding to a stop at the truck. She pulled the door open to Nick and Aaron already sitting inside as I dug in my pocket and pulled out the keys.

"Hey, who's down there?" The gruff voice I had become familiar with shouted from maybe a block away. "Come out right now and I won't hurt you."

"Great." Lareina tossed the keys to Nick and pulled me into the truck next to her. "Get us out of here."

I pulled the door shut as Nick turned the key. The truck sputtered and then died. He tried again with the same result. A loud bang echoed outside, and something exploded against the side of the truck.

"Nick, we have to go." Lareina put an arm around me and pushed my head forward. "Everybody stay down. Nick?"

"I'm trying." He turned the key again and again, but the truck choked out every time.

We had to get away. If they caught us, Aaron would die. I would never see Kinley or Kat or Todd or Keppler ever again. The rest of my life would be Molly's threats and ropes binding my wrists and paperweights to my face. I huddled close to Lareina, prayed that Nick would get the truck to start, and prepared for the worst.

ABOUT THE AUTHOR

Vanessa Lafleur is a high school English teacher and coach of various school activities. She lives in Nebraska where she enjoys spending summer days outside and winter days writing. Vanessa loves discussing literature with her students and helping them discover their writing talents. When she isn't teaching she spends her time reading, writing, surprising her students with homemade treats, and counting down the days to the next speech season.

Tomorrow Will Be Better is the second book in the *Hope for the Best series*.

Find out more about Vanessa at www.vanessaLafleur.com and follow her on Facebook @vanessaLafleurauthor and Instagram@ vLafleurauthor.